Susan Ee has eaten mezze in the old city of Jerusalem, surfed the warm waters of Costa Rica, and played her short film at a major festival. She has a life-long love of science fiction, fantasy and horror, especially if there's a touch of romance. She used to be a lawyer but loves being a writer because it allows her souped-up imagination to bust out and go feral.

Visit Susan's website at www.susanee.com, find her books on Facebook at facebook.com/AngelfallOfficial and follow Susan on Twitter @Susan_Ee

By Susan Ee

Angelfall
World After

WORLD AFTER

SUSAN EE

HODDER &
STOUGHTON

Originally published in the United States by Amazon Publishing, 2013.
This edition made possible under a license arrangement
originating with Amazon Publishing.

First published in Great Britain in 2013 by Hodder & Stoughton
An Hachette UK company

5

A CIP catalogue record for this title is available from the British Library

Paperback ISBN 978 1 444 77853 3
eBook ISBN 978 1 444 77854 0

Typeset by Hewer Text UK Ltd, Edinburgh
Printed and bound by CPI Group (UK) Ltd, Croydon, CR0 4YY

Hodder & Stoughton Ltd
338 Euston Road
London NW1 3BH

Hodder & Stoughton policy is to use papers that are natural, renewable
and recyclable products and made from wood grown in sustainable forests.
The logging and manufacturing processes are expected to conform to the
environmental regulations of the country of origin.
www.hodder.co.uk

Dedicated to the early readers of Angelfall.
Thanks for falling first.

1

Everyone thinks I'm dead.

I lie with my head on my mother's lap in the open bed of a large truck. The dawn light etches the grief lines on my mom's face while the rumble of the engines vibrates through my limp body. We're part of the Resistance caravan. Half a dozen military trucks, vans and SUVs weave through dead cars away from San Francisco. On the horizon behind us, the angels' aerie still smolders in flames after the Resistance strike.

Newspapers cover shop windows along the road, making a corridor of reminders of the Great Attack. I don't need to read the papers to know what they say. Everyone was plastered to the news during the early days when reporters were still reporting.

PARIS IN FLAMES, NEW YORK FLOODED,
MOSCOW DESTROYED

WHO SHOT GABRIEL, THE MESSENGER OF
GOD?

ANGELS TOO AGILE FOR MISSILES

NATIONAL LEADERS SCATTERED AND LOST

THE END OF DAYS

We drive by three bald people wrapped in gray sheets. They're taping up the stained and crumpled fliers of one of the apocalypse cults. Between the street gangs, the cults and the Resistance, I wonder how long it will be before everyone is part of one group or another. Even the end of the world can't keep us from wanting to belong, I guess.

The cult members pause on the sidewalk to watch us pass in our crowded truck.

As a family, we must look tiny – just a scared mom, a dark-haired teenager and a seven-year-old girl sitting in a truck bed full of armed men. At any other time, we would have been sheep in the company of wolves. But now, we have what people might call 'presence'.

Some of the men in our caravan wear camouflage and hold rifles. Some man machine guns still aimed at the sky. Some are fresh off the streets with homemade gang tattoos made of self-inflicted burns that mark their kills.

Yet these men huddle away from us to keep a safe distance.

My mom continues to rock back and forth as she has for the last hour since we left the exploding aerie, chanting in her own version of speaking in tongues. Her voice rises and falls as if she's having a fierce argument with God. Or maybe the devil.

A tear drops off her chin and lands on my forehead, and I know her heart is breaking. It's breaking for me, her seventeen-year-old daughter, whose job was to look out for the family.

As far as she knows, I'm just a lifeless body brought to her by the devil. She'll probably never be able to blot out the image of me lying limp in Raffe's arms with his demon wings backlit by flames.

I wonder what she'd think if someone told her that Raffe was actually an angel who's been tricked into having demon wings. Would that be any stranger than being told that I'm not actually dead but just stung into a weird paralysis by a scorpion-angel monster? She'd probably think that person was as crazy as she is.

My baby sister sits at my feet seemingly frozen. Her eyes stare blankly and her back is perfectly straight despite the weaving of the truck. It's as if Paige has shut herself off.

The tough men in the truck keep stealing glances at her like little boys peeking over their blankets. She looks like a bruised, stitched-up doll from a nightmare. I hate to think about what might have happened to her to make her like this. A part of me wishes I knew more but a part of me is glad I don't.

I take a big breath. I'll have to get up sooner or later. I don't have a choice but to face the world. I'm fully thawed now. I doubt if I could fight or anything, but as far as I can tell, I should be able to move.

I sit up.

I guess if I'd really thought things through, I would have been prepared for the screams.

Chief among the screamers is my mother. Her muscles stiffen in sheer terror, her eyes impossibly wide.

'It's okay,' I say. 'It's all right.' My words are slurred, but I'm grateful I don't sound like a zombie.

It would be funny except for a sobering thought that pops into my head: we now live in a world where someone like me could be killed for being a freak.

I put my hands out in a calming gesture. I say something to try to reassure them, but it gets lost in the screams. Panic in a small area like a truck bed is contagious, apparently.

The other refugees crush against each other as they press toward the rear of the truck. Some of them look prepared to jump out of the moving vehicle.

A soldier with greasy pimples aims his rifle at me, gripping it like he's about to make his first, horrifying kill.

I totally underestimated the level of primal fear swirling around us. They've lost everything: their families, their security, their God.

And now, a reanimated corpse is reaching for them.

'I am okay,' I say slowly with as much clarity as I can. I hold the soldier's gaze, intent on convincing him there's nothing supernatural going on. 'I'm alive.'

There's a moment when I'm not sure if they'll relax or toss me out of the truck with a blaze of gunfire. I still have Raffe's sword strapped to my back, mostly hidden under my jacket. That gives me some comfort, even though it obviously can't stop bullets.

'Come on.' I keep my voice gentle and my movements very slow. 'I was just knocked out. That's all.'

'You were dead,' says the pale soldier, who doesn't look a day older than me.

Someone bangs on the truck's roof.

We all jump, and I'm lucky the soldier doesn't accidentally pull his trigger.

The rear window slides open and Dee's head sticks through. He'd look stern except that it's hard to take him too seriously with his red hair and little-boy freckles. 'Hey! Back off from the dead girl. She's Resistance property.'

'Yeah,' says his twin brother Dum from inside the cab. 'We need her for autopsies and stuff. You think girls killed by demon princes are easy to find?' As usual, I can't tell the twins apart, so I randomly assign Dee for one and Dum for the other.

'No killing the dead girl,' says Dee. 'I'm talking to you, Soldier.' He points to the guy with the rifle and glares at him. You'd think that looking like a set of strung-out Ronald McDonalds with nicknames like Tweedledee and Tweedledum would strip them of all authority. But somehow, these guys seem to have a talent for going from joking to deadly in a heartbeat.

At least, I hope they're joking about the autopsy.

The truck stops in a parking lot. That takes the attention off me as we all look around.

The adobe-style building in front of us is familiar. It's not my school but it is a school that I've seen lots of times. It's Palo Alto's high school, affectionately known as Paly High.

Half a dozen trucks and SUVs stop in the parking lot. The soldier still keeps an eye on me, but he lowers his rifle to a 45-degree angle.

A lot of people stare at us as the rest of the small caravan stops in the parking lot. They all saw me in the arms of the demon-winged creature that was actually Raffe, and they all thought I was dead. I feel self-conscious so I sit down on the bench beside my sister.

One of the men reaches to touch my arm. Maybe he wants to see if I'm warm like the living or cold like the dead.

My sister's face changes instantly from a blank slate to a growling animal as she snaps at the man. Her razor-grafted teeth flash as she moves, emphasizing the threat.

As soon as the man backs off, she goes back to her blank expression and doll-like stance.

The man stares, looking back and forth between us for clues to questions I can't answer. Everyone in the parking lot saw what just happened, and they all stare at us too.

Welcome to the freak show.

2

Paige and I are used to being stared at. I would just ignore it while Paige always smiled at the gawkers from her wheelchair. They almost always smiled back. Paige's charm was hard to resist.

Once upon a time.

Our mother starts speaking in tongues again. This time she's looking at me while she chants, as if she's praying to me. The guttural almost-words coming from her throat dominate the hushed noises of the crowd. Leave it to Mom to add a serious dose of creepiness even in the smoky light of day.

'All right, let's move out,' says Obi in a strong voice. He's at least six feet tall, with broad shoulders and a muscular body, but it's his commanding presence and confidence that set him apart as the leader of the Resistance. Everyone watches and listens as he walks by the various trucks and SUVs, looking like a real military commander in a war zone. 'Clear the trucks and head into the building. Stay out of the open sky as much as possible.'

That breaks the mood and people start hopping off the trucks. The people in our truck push and shove each other in their rush to get away from us.

'Drivers,' calls Obi. 'When the trucks are cleared, spread out your vehicles and park them within easy reach. Hide them among the dead traffic or somewhere that's hard to see from above.' He walks through the river of refugees and soldiers, giving purpose and direction to people who would otherwise be lost.

'I don't want any signs that this area is occupied. Nothing is to be cleared or dumped within a one-mile radius.' Obi pauses when he sees Dee and Dum standing side by side, staring at us.

'Gentlemen,' says Obi. Dee and Dum break out of their trance and look over at Obi. 'Please show the new recruits where to go and what to do.'

'Right,' says Dee, giving Obi a little-boy salute with a little-boy smile.

'Newbies!' calls Dum. 'Anyone who doesn't know what they're supposed to do, follow us.'

'Step right up, folks,' says Dee.

I guess that's us. I get up stiffly and reach automatically for my sister, but I stop before I touch her as if a part of me believes she's a dangerous animal. 'Come on, Paige.'

I'm not sure what I'll do if she doesn't move. But she gets up and follows me. I don't know if I'll ever get used to seeing her stand on her own legs.

Mom follows too. She doesn't stop chanting, though. If anything, it's louder and more fervent than before.

We all step into the flow of newcomers following the twins.

Dum walks backwards, talking to us. 'We're going back to high school where our survival instincts are at their finest.'

'If you get the urge to graffiti the walls or beat up your old math teacher,' says Dee, 'do it where the birds can't see you.'

We walk by the main adobe building. From the street, the school looks deceptively small. Behind the main building, though, there's a whole campus of modern buildings connected by covered walkways.

'If any of you are injured, take a seat in this fine classroom.' Dee opens up the nearest door and peeks in. It's a classroom with a life-sized skeleton hanging on a stand. 'Bones will keep you company while you wait for the doctor.'

'And if any of you are doctors,' says Dum, 'your patients are waiting for you.'

'Is this all of us?' I ask. 'We're the only survivors?'

Dee looks over at Dum. 'Are zombie girls allowed to talk?'

'If they're cute and willing to do zombie-girl mud fights.'

'Duuude. Right on.'

'That's a disgusting image.' I give them a sideways look but I'm secretly glad they're not freaked out about me coming back from the dead.

'It's not like we'd pick the decayed ones, Penryn. Just ones like you, fresh from the dead.'

'Only, with ripped clothes and stuff.'

'And hungry for breeeeasts.'

'He means brains.'

'That's exactly what I meant.'

'Could you please answer the question?' asks a guy wearing glasses that are completely free of cracks. He doesn't look like he's in a joking mood.

'Right,' says Dee getting all serious. 'This is our rendezvous point. The others will meet us here.'

We keep walking in the weak sunshine, and the guy with the glasses ends up in the back of the group.

Dum leans over to Dee and whispers loud enough for me to hear, 'How much you want to bet that that guy will be the first in line to bet on the zombie-girl fight?'

They exchange grins and wiggle their eyebrows at each other.

October winds seep through my blouse and I can't help looking up at the overcast sky for a particular angel with bat-shaped wings and a corny sense of humor. I swipe my foot at the overgrown grass and make myself look away.

The class windows are full of posters and notices about college entrance requirements. Another window displays shelves of student art. Clay, wood and papier mâché figurines of all colors and styles cover every inch of shelf space. Some of them are so good that it makes me sad that these kids won't be making art again for a long, long time.

As we move through the school, the twins are careful to stay behind my family. I fall back, thinking it's not a bad idea to have Paige in front where I can keep an eye on her. She walks stiffly as if she's still not used to her legs. I'm not used to seeing her like this either, and I can't stop staring at the crude stitches all over her body that make her look like a voodoo doll.

'So that's your sister?' asks Dee in a quiet voice.

'Yeah.'

'The one you risked your life for?'

'Yeah.'

The twins nod politely in that automatic way that people do when they don't want to say something insulting.

'Your family any better?' I ask.

Dee and Dum look at each other, assessing.

'Nah,' says Dee.

'Not really,' says Dum at the same time.

Our new home is a history class. The walls are filled with timelines and posters of the story of humanity. Mesopotamia, the Great Pyramid of Giza, the Ottoman Empire, the Ming Dynasty. And the Black Death.

My history teacher said that the Black Death wiped out thirty to sixty percent of Europe's population. He asked us to imagine what it'd be like to have sixty percent of your world dead. I couldn't imagine it at the time. It seemed so unreal.

In weird contrast, dominating all of these ancient history posters is a picture of an astronaut on the moon with blue Earth rising behind him. Every time I see our ball of blue and white in space, I think it must be the most beautiful world in the universe.

But that seems unreal now, too.

Outside, more trucks rumble into the parking lot. I walk over to the window as Mom starts pushing desks and chairs to one side. I peek outside to see one of the twins leading the dazed newcomers into the school like the Pied Piper.

Behind me, my little sister says, 'Hungry.'

I stiffen and stuff all kinds of ugliness into the vault in my head.

I see a reflection of Paige in the window. In the blurry otherworld of that image, she looks up at Mom like any other kid expecting dinner. But in the warped glass, her head is distorted, magnifying her stitches and lengthening her razor-grafted teeth.

Mom bends down and strokes her baby's hair. She begins humming her haunting apology song.

3

I settle onto a cot by the corner. Lying with my back against the wall, I can see the entire room by moonlight.

My baby sister lies on a cot against the wall across from me. Paige looks tiny under her blanket beneath the posters of larger-than-life historical figures. Confucius, Florence Nightingale, Gandhi, Helen Keller, the Dalai Lama.

Would she have turned out like them if we weren't in the World After?

My mother sits cross-legged by Paige's cot, humming her melody. We've tried giving my sister the two things I could get from the disorganized mess in the cafeteria that is supposed to turn into a kitchen by morning. But she couldn't hold down either the canned soup or the protein bar.

I shift my weight on the canvas cot, trying to find a position where my sword hilt won't jab into my ribs. Having it on me is the best way to keep anyone from trying to pick it up and finding out that I'm the only one who can lift it. The last thing I need is having to explain how I ended up with an angel sword.

Sleeping with a weapon has nothing to do with my sister being in the room. Nothing at all.

Nor does it have anything to do with Raffe. It's not like the sword is my only memento of my time with him. I have plenty of cuts and bruises to remind me of the days I spent with my enemy angel.

Who I'll probably never see again.

So far, no one has asked about him. I guess it's more common than not to have your group break up these days.

I shut down that thought and close my eyes.

My sister moans again over my mom's humming.

'Go to sleep, Paige,' I say. To my surprise, her breathing relaxes and she settles down. I take a deep breath and close my eyes.

My mother's melody fades into oblivion.

*   *   *

I dream that I am in the forest where the massacre happened. I am just outside the old Resistance camp where soldiers died trying to defend themselves against low demons.

Blood drips off the branches and plops onto the dead leaves like raindrops. In my dream, none of the bodies that should be here are here and neither are the terrified soldiers who huddled together back-to-back with their rifles facing outward.

It's just a clearing dripping in blood.

In the center stands Paige.

She wears an old-fashioned flower-print dress, like the ones those girls hanging on the tree wore. Her hair is drenched in blood and so is her dress. I'm not sure which is harder to look at, the blood or the bruised stitches crisscrossing her face.

She lifts her arms toward me as if waiting for me to pick her up even though she's seven years old now.

I'm pretty sure my sister was not part of the massacre but here she is anyway. Somewhere in the forest, my mother says, 'Look into her eyes. They're the same as they've always been.'

But I can't. I can't look at her at all. Her eyes aren't the same. They can't be.

I turn and run from her.

Tears stream down my face and I call out into the woods away from the girl behind me. 'Paige!' My voice cracks. 'I'm coming. Hang on. I'll be there soon.'

But the only sign of my sister is the crunching of the dead leaves as the new Paige shadows me through the woods.

4

I wake to my mom scraping something out of her sweater pocket. She puts it onto the windowsill where morning light filters through. It's yellow-brown goo and crushed eggshells. She's quite careful about it, trying to get every yucky drop onto the sill.

Paige breathes evenly, sounding like she'll be knocked out for some time. I try to shake off the last of my dream, but wisps of it stay with me.

Someone knocks on the door.

The door opens and the freckled face of one of the twins peeks into our classroom. I don't know which one so I just think of him as Dee-Dum. His nose wrinkles in distaste when he smells the rotten eggs.

'Obi wants to see you. He's got some questions.'

'Great,' I say drowsily.

'Come on. It'll be fun.' He throws me an overly bright smile.

'What if I don't want to go?'

'I like you, kid,' he says. 'You're a rebel.' He leans against the doorframe and nods his approval. 'But to be honest, no one has the obligation to feed you, house you, protect you, be nice to you, treat you like a human being—'

'Okay, okay. I get it.' I drag myself out of bed, glad that I slept in a T-shirt and shorts. My sword thuds onto the floor. I had forgotten that I had it with me under the blanket.

'Shh! You'll wake Paige,' whispers my mother.

Paige's eyes open instantly. She lies there like the dead, staring at the ceiling.

'Nice sword,' Dee-Dum says too casually.

Alarm bells go off in my head. 'Almost as good as a cow prodder.' I half-expect Mom to zap her prodder at him, but it hangs innocently on her cot frame.

More guilt hits me as I realize how glad I am that Mom has the prodder in case she needs to defend herself from . . . people.

More than half the people here are carrying some kind of makeshift weapon. The sword is one of the better ones, and I'm glad I don't have to explain why I'm carrying it. But there's something about a sword that seems to catch more attention than I like. I pick it up and strap it across my shoulder to discourage him from trying to play with it.

'Got a name for her?' asks Dee-Dum.

'Who?'

'Your sword.' He says it the way I might say *Duh*.

'Oh, please. Not you too.' I pick through the random assortment of clothes my mom collected last night. She also came back with a bunch of empty soda bottles and other junk from who knows where, but I leave that pile alone.

'I used to know a guy who had a katana.'

'A what?'

'A Japanese samurai sword. Gorgeous.' He clutches his heart like he's in love. 'He called it the Sword of Light. I would have sold my grandmother into slavery for that.'

I nod like that's a given.

'Can I name your sword?'

'No.' I pull out a pair of jeans that might fit and one sock.

'Why not?'

'Already has a name.' I continue digging through the pile for a matching sock.

'What is it?'

'Pooky Bear.'

His friendly face suddenly becomes serious. 'You're naming your collector's-item, kick-ass sword that's made to maim and kill, specifically designed to bring your ginormous enemies to their knees *and* hear the lamentation of their women – Pooky Bear?'

'Yeah, you like it?'

'Even joking about that is a crime against nature. You know that, right? I'm trying desperately not to make an anti-girl comment right now, but you're making it pretty hard.'

'Yeah, you're right.' I shrug. 'I might call it Toto or Flossy instead. What do you think?'

He looks at me like I'm nuttier than my mom. 'Am I mistaken? Do you actually have a purse dog in that scabbard?'

'Oh, I wonder if I can find a pink sheath for Pooky Bear. Maybe with little rhinestones? What? Too much?'

He walks out shaking his head.

He's just too easy to tease. I take my time changing and getting ready before following Dee-Dum out the door.

The hallway feels as crowded as the Oakland coliseum during the World Series.

A pair of middle-aged men exchange a feather for a prescription bottle of pills. I guess this is the World

After's version of a drug deal. Another shows off what looks like a little finger, then snatches it back as a guy reaches for it. They begin whisper-arguing.

A pair of women walk by huddled over a few cans of soup as if they held a pot of gold in their arms. They scan everyone nervously as they weave through the hallway. Next to the main door, a couple of people with freshly shaved heads tape up apocalypse cult fliers.

Outside, the overgrown lawn is eerily deserted with trash blowing in the wind. Anyone who looks down from the sky would assume this building is just as abandoned as any other.

Dee-Dum tells me that it's already a big joke that the Resistance upper echelon has taken over the teachers' lounge and that Obi has taken the principal's office. We walk across the school grounds to Obi's mission-style adobe building, staying on the covered walkway even if it means going the long way around.

The lobby and halls of the main building are even busier than mine but the people here look like they have a purpose. A guy rushes down the hallway dragging cables behind him. Several people move desks and chairs from one room to another.

A teenage kid pushes a cart piled with sandwiches and pitchers of water. As it rolls by, people grab the food and drinks as if they have the right to meal delivery if they work in this building.

Dee-Dum picks up a couple of sandwiches and hands one to me. Just like that, I'm part of the in-crowd.

I gobble up my breakfast before someone points out that I don't belong here. But I almost choke on a mouthful when I notice something.

The gun barrels in this building are extra long. They look like the silencers you see assassins screwing onto their rifles in movies.

If we're attacked by angels, noise won't matter because the angels will already know where we are. But if we're shooting each other . . .

The food in my mouth suddenly tastes like cold, slimy Spam and rock-hard bread instead of the delicious treat it was a moment ago.

Dee-Dum pushes through a door.

'—screwup,' says a male voice from inside the room.

Several rows of people sit in front of computers, totally immersed in their displays. I haven't seen anything like this since before the attack. Some of them are quite a sight with their glasses clashing with their devil-horn gang tattoos.

More people are setting up computers in the back rows and rolling large TVs in front of the chalkboard. It looks like the Resistance has figured out how to get a steady power source, at least for one room.

In the center of all the activity is Obi. A line of people follows him around, waiting for his approval on something. Several people in the room seem to have one eye on him and one eye on something else.

Boden stands beside him. His nose is still swollen and bruised from our little schoolyard fight a few days ago. Maybe next time he'll talk to people like they're human beings instead of bullying them, even if they are petite girls like me who seem like easy targets.

'It was an adjustment in plans, not a screwup,' says Boden. 'And no way in hell was it a "treason against humanity." How many times do I have to explain this?'

Amazingly, there's a basket of candy bars by the door. Dee-Dum grabs two and hands one to me. When I feel the Snickers bar in my hand, I know I'm in the inner sanctum.

'Jumping the gun is not an adjustment in plans, Boden,' says Obi as he looks at a document handed to him by a crusty soldier-type. 'We can't execute a military strategy by letting a foot soldier decide the timing just because he couldn't keep his mouth shut and spilled all the details. Every street pilgrim and hotel whore knew about it.'

'But it wasn't—'

'Your fault,' says Obi. 'I know. You've said it ad nauseam.' Obi glances my way as he listens to the next one in line.

After a moment of fantasizing about the taste of the candy bar, I slip it into my jacket pocket. Maybe I can entice Paige to eat it.

'You're dismissed for now, Boden.' Obi motions for me to come in.

Boden gives me a snarl as we pass each other.

Obi grins at me. The woman who's next in line looks over and eyes me with more than professional curiosity.

'Good to see you alive, Penryn,' says Obi.

'Good to be alive,' I say. 'Are we having movie nights?'

'We're setting up a remote surveillance system around the Bay Area,' says Obi. 'It pays to have so many geniuses in the Valley who can make the impossible possible again.'

Someone in the last row calls out, 'Camera twenty-five is online.' The other programmers continue to tap on their computers but I can feel their excitement.

'What are you looking for?' I ask.

'Anything interesting,' says Obi.

'I got something!' a programmer in the back yells out. 'Angels in Sunnyvale on Lawrence Expressway.'

'Put it on the front screen,' says Obi.

One of the large TV screens at the front of the classroom comes on.

5

The TV lights up.

An angel with blue wings stalks through the rubble of an abandoned street. The road has a giant crack zigzagging down the center with one side higher than the other.

Another angel lands behind the first, then two others. They look around, then walk off-screen.

'Can you turn the camera?'

'Not this one, sorry.'

'Got another one!' says a programmer to my right. 'This one's at SFO.' I always wondered how they got SFO from San Francisco International Airport.

'Put it on-screen,' says Obi.

Another TV comes alive in front of the chalkboard.

An angel rushes in a half-limp, half-run along a field of asphalt. One white wing is off-kilter and dragging behind him.

'We got ourselves a lame bird,' says someone behind me. He sounds excited.

'What's he running from?' asks Obi almost to himself.

The camera has trouble with its picture. It keeps switching from too bright to too dark. It settles on adjusting the lighting to the bright background, making the details of the angel dark and hard to see.

As he gets closer, though, he turns to see whatever is chasing him, giving us a good look at his face.

It's Beliel, the demon who stole Raffe's wings. He's in bad shape. I wonder what happened?

Only one of his stolen wings seems functional. It keeps opening and closing as though reflexively trying to fly while the other wing drags in the dust. I hate to see Raffe's gorgeous wings abused like that, and I try not to think of the abuse they took on my own watch.

There's something wrong with Beliel's knee. He limps and favors it even as he tries to run. He's moving faster than any injured human could, but I'm guessing that it's still less than half his normal speed.

Even from this distance, I can see a vivid red stain seeping through his white pants just above his boots.

Funny that the demon has taken to wearing white, probably since he got his new wings.

As he nears the camera, he turns his head again to look behind him. There's the familiar sneer. Arrogant, angry, but this time, with more than a touch of fear.

'What's he scared of?' Obi asks the question that I'm wondering.

Beliel limps out of the frame, leaving only a cross-section of the empty runway.

'Can we see what's behind him?' asks Obi.

'That's as far as the camera will turn.'

A few seconds tick by, and it feels like the room is holding its breath.

Then Beliel's pursuer shows up on the screen in all his glory.

Demonic wings spread out above his head. Light glints off the curved hooks, sliding down the edge of his wings as he stalks his prey.

'Jesus H. Christ,' says someone behind me.

The pursuer seems to be in no rush, almost as if he's savoring the moment. His head is down, with his wings shading his face, making the details even harder to see than Beliel's. And unlike Beliel, he doesn't turn his head to give us a good look at his face.

But I know him. Even with his new demon wings, I know him.

It's Raffe.

Everything about him – his pace, his arched wings, his shaded face – is the perfect nightmare image of the devil stalking his prey.

Even though I'm sure it's Raffe, my heart stutters with fear at the sight of him.

This is not the Raffe I've come to know.

Does Obi recognize him as the guy who was with me when we first came to the Resistance camp?

I'm guessing not. I'm not sure *I* would have recognized Raffe if I hadn't known about his new wings, even though every feature of his face and body has been burned into my memory.

Obi turns to his men. 'We've hit the jackpot! A lame angel *and* a demon. I want a hunting party on its way to the airport in two minutes!'

The twins are moving before the order is given. 'We're on it,' they say in unison as they run out the door.

'Go! Go! Go!' I've never seen Obi so excited.

Obi pauses at the doorway to say, 'Penryn, join us. You're the only one who's been near a demon.' Everyone still thinks a demon carried me to my family when I was seemingly dead.

I shut my mouth before I can say that I don't know anything. I run to catch up to the group stampeding down the hallway.

6

San Francisco International Airport used to be about twenty minutes north of Palo Alto if there was no traffic. Of course, the highway is clogged now and driving sixty miles an hour is no longer feasible nor a good idea. But no one seems to have told Dee-Dum that. He takes open side roads in our SUV, weaving through abandoned cars and thumping over sidewalks like a drunken race-car driver.

'I'm gonna be sick,' I say.

'I'm ordering you not to,' says Obi.

'Ah, don't say that,' says Dee-Dum. 'She's a born rebel. She'll puke just to make a point.'

'You're here for a reason, Penryn,' says Obi. 'And throwing up in my car is not part of it. Buck up, Soldier.'

'I'm not your soldier.'

'Not yet,' says Obi with a wide grin. 'Why don't you fill us in on what happened at the aerie? Tell us everything you saw and heard, even if you think it won't be helpful.'

'And if you have to get sick,' says Dee-Dum, 'shoot for Obi's direction, not mine.'

I end up telling them almost everything I saw. I leave out all things Raffe, but I tell them about the endless angel party at the aerie with champagne and hors d'oeuvres, costumes, servants and the sheer decadence of it all. Then I tell them about the scorpion-angel fetuses in the basement lab, and the people being fed to the scorpions.

I hesitate to tell them about the experiments on the kids. Will they put two and two together and suspect that these kids might be the low demons who were tearing people apart on the roads? Will they suspect that Paige might be one of them? I'm not sure what to do, but I end up telling them in vague terms that kids have been operated on.

'So your sister, is she all right?' asks Obi.

'Yes, I'm sure she'll be back to herself soon.' I say this without hesitation. Of course she's all right. What else can she be? What choice do we have? I try to radiate confidence through my voice despite the worry that gnaws at me.

'Tell us more about these scorpion angels,' says our other passenger. He has wavy hair, glasses and rich brown skin. He has the air of a scholar who's getting his geek on over a favorite topic.

In my relief to change the subject from Paige, I tell them every detail I can recall. Their size, their dragonfly wings, their total lack of uniformity that's so unlike lab specimens you see in the movies. How some of them seemed embryonic but others looked nearly fully formed. I tell him about the people trapped in the tanks with them, getting their lives sucked out of them.

When I finish, there's a pause as everyone absorbs my tale.

Just as I think this question-and-answer session will be easy, they ask about the demon who carried me and dropped me off at the Resistance rescue truck during the aerie attack. I have no idea what to say so my answer to all their questions is, 'I don't know. I was unconscious.'

Despite that, I'm surprised at how many questions they ask about 'the demon'.

Was he the devil? Did he say anything about what he was doing there? Where did you meet him? Do you know where he went? Why did he drop you off with us?

'I don't know,' I say for the umpteenth time. 'I was unconscious.'

'Can you reach him again?'

That last question squeezes my heart a little. 'No.'

Dee-Dum does a quick U-turn to avoid a backed-up side road.

'Anything else you'd like to tell us?' asks Obi.

'No.'

'Thank you,' says Obi. He turns to look at the other passenger. 'Sanjay, your turn. I hear you have a theory about the angels that you want to share with us?'

'Yes,' says the scholar holding up a map of the world. 'I think that most of the killing during the Great Attack could have been incidental. Sort of a side effect of the angels coming here. My hypothesis is that when a couple of them enter our world, it's a local phenomenon.'

Sanjay pricks a pin through the map. 'A hole in our world is created which lets them come in. It probably causes some kind of local weather disturbance but nothing too dramatic. But when an entire legion comes through, this is what happens.'

He punches a screwdriver into the paper. The handle and his hand also go through, tearing the map.

'My theory is that the world rips when they invade. This is what triggered the earthquakes, the tsunamis, the weather disturbances – everything catastrophic that caused the majority of the damage and deaths.' Thunder rolls through the gray sky as if to agree with him.

'It wasn't the angels themselves who controlled nature when they invaded,' says Sanjay. 'That's why they didn't create a giant tsunami to swallow us up when we attacked the aerie. They can't. They are living, breathing creatures just like us. They may have abilities we don't have, but they're not godlike.'

'You're telling us that they killed this many people and they weren't even trying?'

Sanjay rakes his fingers through his thick hair. 'Well, they did kill a bunch of people after we killed their leader, but they may not be as all-powerful as we initially thought. Of course, I have no proof. It's just a theory that fits what little we know. But if you guys can bring back some bodies for us to study, we may be able to shed some light on this.'

'Want me to confiscate some angel parts from the hallways?' asks Dee-Dum.

I don't joke about how he and his brother are probably dealing in angel parts, just in case it's true.

'There's no guarantee any of those parts are authentic,' says Sanjay. 'In fact, I'd be surprised if any of them are. Besides, it would be much more helpful to study an entire body.' The shreds of the paper depicting our world lie drooping on Sanjay's lap.

'Cross your fingers,' says Obi. 'If we're lucky, we might be able to bring you some live ones.'

I feel a flutter of unease. But I tell myself that they won't capture Raffe. They can't. He'll be all right.

The two-way radio on the dash comes alive and a voice says, 'Something's going on at the old aerie.'

Obi grabs the handset and asks, 'What kind of something?'

'Angels in the air. Too many to hunt.'

Obi takes a pair of binoculars from the glove compartment and looks toward the city. In most places he wouldn't have a clear view, but we're near the water so he has a shot at seeing something.

'What are they up to?' asks Dee-Dum.

'No idea,' says Obi looking through the binoculars. 'There are a lot of them, though. Something interesting is going on.'

'We're halfway to the city already,' says Dee-Dum.

'He said there were too many to capture,' says Sanjay sounding nervous.

'True,' says Obi. 'But it's a chance to find out what they're doing. And you wanted angel bodies to study. The aerie will be the best place to find them.'

'I think it's gotta be one place or the other, boss,' says Dee-Dum. 'If we go to the airport, it'll take everyone we've got to bag our targets, assuming they're still there.'

Obi sighs, seeming reluctant. He speaks into the radio. 'Change of plans. All vehicles head to the old aerie. Approach with extreme caution. Repeat, approach with extreme caution. Hostiles have been sighted. This is now an observation mission. But if you get the chance, bring back a bird specimen. Dead or alive.'

7

The icy rain pelts my face as we race through abandoned cars in a sea of junk. Well, racing is a strong word for an SUV rolling at thirty miles an hour, but these days that speed is neck-breaking – literally, since I'm perched on the window and hanging on for dear life.

'Tank at two o'clock,' I call out.

'Tank? Seriously?' asks Dee-Dum. He strains his neck to see above the debris cluttering the road. He sounds excited even though we both know that the angels would hear a tank from miles away.

'I kid you not. Looks dead.' My rain-soaked hair drips down my neck and traces a finger of ice down my back. It's a light rain, as most San Francisco rains are, but enough to seep through everything. The wet chill freezes my hands and it's hard to hang onto the grab-handle.

'Bus at twelve o'clock,' I say.

'Yeah, that I can see.'

The bus lies on its side. I briefly wonder if it got tilted by one of the earthquakes that shook the world when the angels came, or if it was picked up and tossed by avenging angels when the Resistance hit their aerie. My guess is that it was tossed, since there's a long crater in the road near the bus with an upside-down Hummer in it.

'Uh, giant crater—' Before I can finish my sentence, Dee-Dum swerves the car. I hang on tight as I'm pitched to the right. For a moment, I think I'm going to smash into the asphalt face-first.

He does a crazy zigzag maneuver before he straightens the car.

'A little forewarning would be nice,' says Dee-Dum in a singsong voice.

'A little smoother driving would be nicer,' I say mimicking his tone. The hard metal of the car door presses against my thighs, bruising my muscles as we bump onto the sidewalk.

As if that isn't bad enough, I haven't seen a single hint of batwings attached to an Adonis-like body anywhere along the way. Not that I expected to see Raffe.

'That's it. Glasses or no, it's Sanjay's turn.' I slide down from my perch and sink into the back seat as Sanjay climbs up to sit in the open window on his side.

We're approaching the Financial District from a different direction than Raffe and I had a couple of days ago. This part of town looks like it wasn't the nicest part to begin with, but a few buildings still stand with only their edges singed.

Colorful beads are splashed over the sidewalk in front of a store with a sign reading Beads and Feathers. But there's not a single feather in sight. The bounty that someone has put out for angel parts must still be going strong. I wonder if all the chickens and pigeons have been plucked? Their feathers might be worth more than their meat if they could be passed off as angel feathers.

My stomach feels full of ice as we near the disaster zone that was once the Financial District. The area is deserted now, with not even scavengers looking for bits of usable supplies or scraps of food.

'Where is everybody?'

The Financial District still stands, or at least a few blocks of it does. In the center, there's a gaping hole in the skyline where the aerie used to be. A couple of months ago, it was a high-end, Art-Deco hotel. Then the angels took over and turned it into their aerie. Now it's just a pile of rubble from when the Resistance crashed a truck full of explosives into it.

'Oh, that's not good,' says Dee-Dum, looking up into the sky.

I see it the same time he does.

A funnel of angels swirls from the place where the aerie used to be.

'What are they doing here?' I whisper.

Dee-Dum pulls the SUV over and turns off the engine. Without a word, he takes two pairs of binoculars out of the glove compartment and hands one to me. Obi already has his so I guess I'm supposed to share mine with Sanjay.

Obi grabs his rifle and gets out. I follow with my heart pounding in my chest.

I worry that the angels heard our engines, but they continue to fly without looking toward us. We zigzag on foot from car to car toward the old aerie. It doesn't seem to occur to Obi or Dee-Dum to run away.

An angel with snowy white wings takes off into the blanket of clouds. My eyes follow him even though I know Raffe doesn't have those wings any more.

As we near the destroyed building that was once their aerie, everything is covered in dust. The pulverized concrete fell all over the cars, the streets and the dead bodies. Cars lie strewn upside down and sideways on the sidewalks, on top of other cars and partway embedded in nearby buildings.

Our feet crunch over broken concrete as we dart between the cars and debris. The angels were not pleased about the attack in the middle of their party, and they left the scene the way a child would leave a Lego town after a tantrum.

There are bodies lying in the street and they're all human. I get the sick feeling that the attack didn't do as much damage to the angels as we had initially thought. Where are the angel bodies?

I glance over at Dee-Dum and see from his eyes that he's wondering the same thing. We pause close enough to see what's going on.

The old aerie is just a pile of broken boulders and bent rebar. The steel rods that used to support the high-rise hotel now stand broken and exposed like bloodstained bones.

I expected the aerie to be a mountain of rubble. Instead, the rubble is spread everywhere.

The place is swarming with angels.

Winged bodies lie haphazardly in the wreckage while some are arranged in a row on the asphalt. Angels dig up enormous boulders and toss them away from what was once the aerie. A few of them drag angel bodies and line them up on the road.

My heart is racing so hard I swear I have to swallow to keep it from galloping out of my mouth.

A warrior with spotted wings walks out of one of the nearby buildings with a bucket in each hand, sloshing water with every step. He kicks the nearest body.

The supposedly dead angel groans and starts to move.

The warrior tosses water onto the bodies in the street. They were wet from the drizzle anyway but now they're soaked.

As soon as the bodies get splashed, they begin to move.

8

'What the—' says Sanjay, too startled to remember to be quiet.

A couple of the angels lying on the asphalt immediately resurrect and vigorously shake the drops out of their hair like dogs. The others groan and move sluggishly as if the morning alarm went off sooner than expected.

Some of them are clearly shot up with bullets. Their wounds have ugly entry points and even uglier exit points that look like raw hamburger flowers.

The warrior with spotted wings grabs his other bucket and tosses the water onto the rest of the 'bodies'. He also kicks a few of the wounded still lying on the asphalt.

'Get up, maggots! What do you think this is? Naptime? You're an embarrassment.'

Apparently, Sanjay's not the only one who forgot to be quiet because one of the angels grabs a chunk of broken concrete and throws it at a car the way someone might throw a stone at a rat. And just like rats, two of our men scamper out of the way as it smashes into the car that they were hiding behind.

A couple of other angels grab chunks of broken fixtures and rebar and throw them at us. I barely have time to dive to the sidewalk as the car windows shatter.

I jump up and run so hard I'm hyperventilating by the time I hide in the doorway of a building. I peek at the angels. They're not chasing us any more than we would chase rats in a garbage dump.

Obi and Dee-Dum see me from their hiding place behind a truck and sprint to my doorway. We huddle and peek through our binoculars.

A group of angels digs into the center of the rubble, tossing debris left and right. As they find bodies, they leave the dead humans and pull out limp angels who might wake at any moment.

The angels doing the digging are larger than the ones who are being dug out. The big ones carry swords around their waists, which I assume means that they are warriors. From what I can see, all the victims are smaller and don't carry swords.

Now that I think about it, just how many warriors did
I see at the aerie when Raffe and I walked through it?
There were the guards. A few in the hallways. And that
table full of warriors where that scumbag Josiah the
albino stood. Aside from them, no one else carried
swords. Did they bring administrators and other non-
fighting types to our world? Cooks? Medics? And if so,
where were the warriors when the aerie was attacked?

I groan out loud.

'What?' mouths Obi.

I try to figure out how to talk to them without being
overheard. Dee-Dum must have an idea of what I want
because he pulls out a pad of paper and a pencil and
hands it to me.

I write, 'How many warrior angels did you see at the
aerie last night?'

Dee-Dum shakes his head and puts his thumb and
forefinger only an inch apart, telling me very few.

He glances over at the angels and I can see under-
standing dawning in his face. He writes, 'More here now
than during our strike.'

'Maybe they were on a mission?'

He nods.

By sheer luck, it looks like the Resistance hit the aerie
when almost all the fighters were gone. No wonder so
many of the angels went down without a proper fight. I

remember the chaos in the foyer as both humans and angels ran in every direction at the beginning of the attack. There were angels who ran out into the machine-gun fire to try to take flight. I thought it was sheer dare-devil behavior but maybe it was simply inexperience and panic.

Still, even the civilian angels were a force to be reck-oned with as they grabbed Resistance trucks, tossed soldiers and crushed the frantic crowds.

Now, some of the angels lying on the asphalt look seriously injured. Some of them are so badly off that they can't fly on their own. The warriors yank them by their arms as if annoyed and fly them out.

None of them are dead as far as I can see.

Obi's expression shows that he's beginning to under-stand their healing powers. I told them during the ques-tion-and-answer session that angels could heal even from things that would kill a human, but it looks like Obi's only now beginning to believe it.

When the warriors dig down to ground level, the one in charge signals, and more than half the remaining angels take their injured and fly off. The remaining angels look resentful as they dig. I suspect warriors don't like to do menial labor.

Although I can't see into the pit they're digging, I can hear screeches. I recognize the noise from the thing that attacked and paralyzed me in the aerie basement. There are still a few scorpion fetuses alive down there.

The warrior in charge pulls out his sword and jumps in.

A scorpion screeches. From the sound of it, it's being skewered.

9

It's not long before the streets are quiet. There weren't many surviving scorpions to begin with but now, I'm willing to bet there are none.

Masculine bodies burst out of the pit and disappear into the cloud cover. One of them carries a limp angel, the only one I've seen who looks dead.

Somewhere, far away, thunder rumbles. The wind whistles through the corridor of buildings.

We wait until it seems safe to get up and take a closer look. I'd be shocked if there's even a skin sample of the angels that we could bring back.

We approach the rubble, staying hidden as much as possible even though the coast seems clear.

We're a stone's throw away from the smoking

wreckage when a boulder of concrete clanks down the side of the rubble pile. I freeze, eyes and ears alert.

Another piece falls and rolls into a tiny landslide.

Something is coming up from the rubble basement. We all take cover behind cars, watching carefully.

More rock-sized debris falls and it's some time before hands reach up to the top of the rubble. A head emerges. At first, I think it's some kind of demon that tunneled out from hell. But then, the creature pulls the rest of itself up, trembling and wheezing the entire time.

It's an old woman.

But I've never seen anything like her. She's shriveled, frail and bony. Most striking of all, her skin is so dry it looks like beef jerky.

Dee-Dum and I look at each other, both wondering what she's doing in there. She climbs up onto the peak and begins a shaky trek along the debris pile, moving as if she has arthritis.

She wears a tattered lab coat that's five sizes too big for her. It's so stained with dirt and rust-colored blotches that it's hard to believe it was ever white. She holds it closed as she gingerly steps across the rubble, looking as if she's holding herself together.

The wind blows her hair in her face and she tosses her head to get it out of the way. There's something odd about both her full hair and that gesture. It takes me a minute to figure out what it is.

When was the last time I saw an old woman toss her head to get her hair away from her face? And her hair is dark all the way to her scalp even though the latest post-apocalyptic fashion for older women is at least an inch of gray roots.

She freezes like a frightened animal and looks up at us as we emerge from behind the cars. Even with her dried-up face, there's something familiar about her that's nagging me.

Then a memory tickles my mind.

An image of two little kids hanging onto the fence, watching their mom walk toward the aerie. Their mom turning around to blow a goodbye kiss.

She ended up as dinner in the fetus tank of one of the scorpion angels. I broke her tank with my sword and left her there to fend for herself because I couldn't drag her out.

She's alive.

Only, she looks like she has aged fifty years. Her once beautiful eyes have sunk into her face. Her cheeks are so lean I can almost see the skeleton beneath them. Her hands are talons covered in thin skin.

She scrambles away in abject terror as she sees us getting up from our hiding places. She's almost on all fours as she runs off, and my heart breaks to remember her health and beauty before the monsters got to her. She can't get very far in her condition, and she hides, trembling, behind a post-office box.

She's a tiny slip of a thing, but she's a survivor and I have to respect that. She deserves to get away from the place where she was buried alive, and she'll need energy for that. I dig through my pockets and feel the Snickers bar. I root around to see if there's something less valuable but find nothing.

I take a few steps toward the poor thing as she cringes in her hiding place.

My sister has more experience with this kind of thing than I do. But I guess I've learned a thing or two from watching Paige befriend all those abandoned cats and damaged kids. I put the candy bar on the road where the lady can see it, then take a few steps back to give her some safe space.

There's a moment when the woman watches me like a beaten animal. Then she snatches the candy bar faster than I would have given her credit for. She tears off the wrapper in a split second and stuffs the candy in her mouth. Her strained face relaxes as she tastes the nutty, sweet flavor from the World Before.

'My kids, my husband,' she says in a hoarse voice. 'Where did everybody go?'

'I don't know,' I say. 'But a lot of people ended up at the Resistance camp. They might be there.'

'What Resistance camp?'

'It's the Resistance who attacked the angels. People are gathering to join them.'

She blinks at me. 'I remember you. You died.'

'Neither of us died,' I say.

'I did,' she says. 'And I went to hell.' She wraps her thin arms around herself again.

I don't know what to say. What difference does it make if she actually died or not? She certainly lived through hell and she looks it.

Sanjay walks up to us like he's approaching a stray cat. 'What's your name?'

She glances at me for reassurance. I nod.

'Clara.'

'I'm Sanjay. What happened to you?'

She looks at her jerkied hand. 'I got sucked dry by a monster.'

'What monster?' Sanjay asks.

'The scorpion angels I told you about,' I say.

'The hell doctor said I could go free if I led him to my little girls,' she says with her parched voice. 'But I wouldn't give them up. He said the monster would liquefy my insides and drink them. Said the mature ones wouldn't go all the way and kill if they could help it, but the developing ones would.'

Clara starts shaking. 'He said it would be the most excruciating thing I could imagine.' She shuts her eyes as if trying to keep tears back. 'Thank God I didn't believe him.' Her voice sounds choked. 'Thank God I didn't know any better.' She starts crying in dry heaves as if all the fluid actually was sucked out of her.

'You didn't give up your children and you're alive,' I say. 'That's all that matters.'

She puts her trembling hand on my arm, then turns to Sanjay. 'The monster was killing me. And out of nowhere, she came and rescued me.'

Sanjay looks at me with new respect. I worry about her telling him about Raffe, but it turns out she passed out in the basement as soon as she saw me get stung by a scorpion, so she doesn't remember much.

Clara's plight eats away at me like acid as we pick through the debris. Sanjay sits on the sidewalk beside her, talking gently with her and taking notes. Comforting someone like her is the kind of thing my sister would have done in the World Before.

We find a couple of crushed scorpions, but we find nothing of the angels themselves. Not a drop of blood or a scrape of skin that might help us learn something about them.

'One little nuke,' says Dum, picking through the rubble. 'That's all I ask. I'm not greedy.'

'Yeah, that and the detonation keys,' says Dee, kicking over a boulder of concrete. He sounds disgusted. 'Seriously, did they really have to hide the nukes from the rest of us? It's not like we would have played with it like a toy and blown up a pasture full of cows or something.'

'Oh, man,' says Dum. 'That would have been so awesome. Can you imagine? Boom!' He mimes a mushroom cloud. 'Moo!'

Dee gives him a long-suffering look. 'You are such a child. You can't just waste a nuke like that. You gotta figure out a way to control the trajectory so that when the bomb goes off, it shoots the radioactive cows into your enemies.'

'Right on,' says Dum. 'Squash some, infect the others.'

'Of course, you have to put the cows on ground zero's perimeter, close enough so they'll rocket out, but far enough away that they won't turn into radioactive dust,' says Dee. 'I'm sure, with a little practice, we could get the cows aimed *just* right.'

'I heard the Israelis nuked the angels. Blew them right out of the sky,' says Dum.

'That's a lie,' says Dee. 'No one would blow up their entire country in the hope that a few angels might be in the air when you did it. It's just not responsible nuke behavior.'

'Unlike nuclear cow missiles,' says Dum.

'Exactly.'

'Besides,' says Dum. 'They might turn into radio-active anti-superheroes for all we know. Maybe they'd just absorb the radioactivity and shoot it back at us.'

'They're not superheroes, you idiot,' says Dee. 'They're just people who can, you know, fly. They'll explode into smithereens just like anybody else.'

'Then how come there are no angel bodies here?' asks Dum. We stand in the middle of the debris, looking at the hole that goes down into what used to be the basement.

Broken human bodies lie scattered across the debris but none of them have wings.

The wind picks up, pelting us with cold drizzle.

'They couldn't just have been injured, not with that many bullets and the building collapsing,' says one of the guys who came in another car. 'Could they?'

We all look at each other, not wanting to say what we're thinking.

'They took some bodies away,' says Dee.

'Yeah,' says Dum, 'but they could just be unconscious for all we know.'

'There's got to be a dead angel around here,' says Dee, lifting a concrete chunk and looking beneath it.

'Agreed. There has to be something.'

But there isn't.

10

In the end, the only thing we bring back is what's left of the few dead scorpions that we found scattered beneath the rubble, and their one surviving victim, Clara.

When we park in front of the school, Sanjay walks with her, quietly asking her questions. I don't have to ask her anything to know that she just wants to find her husband and kids. Everyone who sees her moves away, looking like they think she's contagious.

When I get back to our history class, the stench of rotten eggs hits me as soon as I open the door. The windowsills are lined with cartons of old eggs. Somehow, my mother has managed to find a stash of them.

Mom is out. I don't know what she's doing or where she is but that's pretty normal for us.

Paige sits on her cot with her head down so that her hair covers her stitches, and I can almost pretend not to see them. Her hair is as shiny and healthy as any seven-year-old's. She's in a flower-print dress, tights and pink high-top sneakers that dangle over the edge of the cot.

'Where's Mom?'

Paige shakes her head. She hasn't said much since we found her.

On a chair beside her cot is a bowl of chicken soup with a spoon sitting in it. Looks like Mom hasn't had much luck feeding her. When was the last time Paige ate? I pick up the bowl and sit on the chair.

Lifting a spoonful of soup, I move it toward her. But Paige won't open her mouth.

'Aaand the train goes into the tunnel.' I give her a little clown smile as I push the spoon toward her mouth. 'Choo-choo!' It used to work when she was really little.

She peeks up at me and tries to smile. She stops when the stitches begin to crinkle.

'Come on, it's delicious.' There is meat in it. I had laid down the law and declared that Paige could no longer be a vegetarian as soon as we started having trouble finding food. Maybe that's what keeps her from trying the soup?

Maybe not.

Paige shakes her head. She's no longer throwing up, but she's no longer trying to eat either.

I put the spoon down into the bowl. 'What happened when you were with the angels?' I ask as gently as I can. 'Can you talk about it?'

She looks at the floor. A tear sparkles on her lashes.

I know she *can* talk because she's called me 'Ryn-Ryn' like she used to when she was little, and 'Mom' or 'Mommy'. And 'hungry'. She's said that several times.

'It's just us. Nobody else is listening. Do you want to tell me what happened?'

She shakes her head slowly, looking at her feet. A tear drops onto her dress.

'Okay, we don't have to talk about that right now. We'll never talk about it if you don't want to.' I set the bowl on the floor. 'But do you know what you can eat?'

She shakes her head again. 'Hungry.' The whisper is so quiet that I barely hear it. Her lips hardly open to talk, but I can still catch a glimpse of her razor teeth.

My insides churn. 'Can you tell me what you're hungry for?' A part of me desperately wants to know the answer. But the rest of me dreads what she might say.

She hesitates before she shakes her head 'no' again.

My hand comes up without me thinking about it. I'm about to stroke her hair like I've always done. She looks up at me, and her hair falls away from her stitches.

Crude, uneven stitches crisscross her face. The stitches that run between her lips and ears give her a forced grin that cuts her face. Red, black and bruised, they scream for attention. They run down her neck and into her dress. I wish there wasn't one cutting across her neck like they'd sewn her head onto her body.

My hand hesitates over her head, almost touching her hair but not quite.

Then I drop it back to my side.

I turn away from Paige.

A pile of clothes sits on my mother's cot. I dig through for jeans and a jersey. Mom didn't bother ripping off the tags, but she has already sewn a yellow starburst on the bottom of the pant leg for protection from the boogey-man. I don't care so long as it's dry and doesn't smell too badly of rotten eggs.

I change out of my wet clothes. 'I'm going to see if I can find something else for you to eat. I'll be back soon, okay?'

Paige nods, looking at the floor again.

I leave, wishing I had a dry jacket to cover my sword. I consider wearing the wet one but decide against it.

The school sits on a prime corner with a grove owned by Stanford University across one street and a high-end strip mall across another. I wander over to the shops.

My dad always said there was a lot of money in this area and even the strip malls show it. Back in the day, in the World Before, you could see Steve Jobs, founder of

Apple, eating breakfast here while he was still a living resident of Silicon Valley. Or catch Mark Zuckerberg, founder of Facebook, grabbing a bite with his friends.

They all looked like middle managers to me but my dad was into all that. Technocrats, he called them. I'm pretty sure I saw Zuckerberg digging the latrine ditch beside Raffe at the camp a few days ago. I guess a billion dollars doesn't buy much respect in the World After.

I skitter from car to car as if I'm just a random survivor on the street. The parking lot and walkways are mostly deserted, but inside the shops, people mill about. Some are picking out clothes. This is probably as good a place as any to find a jacket, but food comes first.

The signs of burger joints, burrito places and juice shops make my mouth water. There was a time when I could walk into any of these and order food. Hard to believe.

I head for the supermarket. There's a line inside, where people can't be seen from above. I haven't been in a market since the early days of the attack.

Some stores had their shelves emptied by panicked people, while others shut down completely so no one could get in. The established gangs from the World Before took over stores as early as the day after the Great Attack when it became clear that nothing was certain.

The bloody feather hanging on the door tells me that this supermarket is gang-owned. But by the looks of all the people in here, the gang is either generous enough to share with the rest of us, or they lost some kind of fight with the Resistance.

The bloody palm prints smeared on the front door glass make me think that the gang was none too happy about giving up their treasures.

Inside, Resistance personnel give out small amounts of food. A handful of crackers, a scoopful of nuts, instant pasta. There are almost as many soldiers in here as there were during the aerie attack. They stand guard by the food tables with their rifles plainly in sight.

'This is all you get, folks,' says one food worker. 'Hang in there and we'll be able to start making meals soon. This is just to keep you going until we get the kitchens fired.'

A soldier yells out, 'One package per family! No exceptions!'

I guess no one has told them about the food delivery in Obi's headquarters. I look around and scope out the situation.

There are kids my age, but I don't recognize any of them. Even though a lot of them are as tall as adults, they don't stray far from their parents. Some of the girls are tucked under the arms of their moms or dads like little kids. They seem safe and secure, protected and loved, looking like they belong.

I wonder what that's like? Is it as good as it looks from the outside?

I realize that I'm cradling my elbows like I'm hugging myself. I relax my arms and stand tall. Body language says a lot about your place in the world, and the last thing I need is to look vulnerable.

I notice something else. A lot of people are looking at me, the lone teen girl in line. I've been told I look younger than seventeen, probably because I'm small.

There are big guys carrying hammers and bats who I'm sure would prefer to carry a sword like the one on my back. A gun would be better but guns can be tricky to steal, and at this stage of the game, only burly men seem to have them.

I watch the men watching me, and I know that there is no such thing as a safe harbor in the World After.

For no reason, Raffe's chiseled face pops into my mind. He has an unnerving habit of doing that.

By the time I get to the front of the line, I'm pretty hungry. I hate to think of how Paige must be feeling. I reach the distribution table and put out my hand, but the guy takes one look at me and shakes his head.

'One package per family, sorry. Your mom already came by.'

'Oh.' Ah, the joys of fame and misfortune. We're probably the only family who is recognized by half the people in the camp.

The guy looks at me like he's heard it all – any excuse to get more food out of him has already been tried. 'We have rotten eggs in the back if you want more cartons.'

Great.

'Did she just take rotten eggs or was there some real food in there too?'

'I made sure she got some real food.'

'Thank you. I appreciate it.' I turn away. I can feel the weight of eyes watching me walk alone toward the darkening parking lot. I didn't realize how late it was getting.

On the edge of my vision, I see a man nodding to another, who then signals to another guy.

They're all big and carrying weapons. One has a bat across his shoulder. Another has hammer handles sticking out of his jacket pockets. The third has a large kitchen knife stuck into his belt.

They slip out casually behind me.

11

I had planned to shop for a jacket, but no way am I going into an enclosed space at dusk with these goons behind me.

I head for the open parking lot, ducking from car to car as we were instructed to do.

The guys behind me do the same.

My World After instincts scream at me to break into a run. My primal self knows I'm being stalked and hunted.

But my World Before brain tells me they haven't done anything threatening. They're only walking behind me, and where else would they go except to the school across the street?

I'm back in a semi-organized group of people. I can't behave like a savage, like I'm a paranoid schizophrenic.

Right.

I break into a sprint.

So do the guys behind me.

Their feet slap faster and closer to me with every stride I take.

Their legs are longer and stronger than mine. It's just a matter of seconds before they'll be on me. My center of gravity is way lower than theirs so I can zigzag like nobody's business, but that'll only buy me a few more seconds.

I run by several people who crouch behind cars on their way back to the school. None of them looks willing to help.

The standard advice against muggers is to toss away whatever they're after and run like hell because your safety is worth so much more than your purse. That's a no-brainer. Except they're either after me or Raffe's sword. I can't give up either of those.

My adrenaline is pumping and fear is screaming at me. But my training kicks in and I automatically run through my options.

I could scream. Obi's men would be out here in a second. But so might the angels if there are any within hearing distance. There's a reason why we need to be quiet and stay out of sight. I'd be putting everyone at risk by screaming, and the soldiers might shoot all of us with their silencer-enhanced guns to shut me up.

I could run into Obi's building. But it's too far away.

I could stop and fight. But my chances are pretty poor against three men with weapons.

I don't like any of my options.

I run as fast and as far as I can go. My lungs burn and I'm getting a stitch in my side, but the closer I can get to Obi's building, the better the chance that Obi's men will see us and stop the attackers.

When my back prickles, telling me they're getting too close, I turn around and pull out my sword.

Damn, I sure wish I knew how to use it.

The men skid to a stop and fan out around me.

One lifts his bat to striking position. Another pulls out two hammers from his coat pockets. The third pulls out the kitchen knife from his belt.

I am so screwed.

People pause to watch – a few faces through the windows, a mother and child at an open doorway, an older couple under an awning.

'Get Obi's men,' I whisper-shout to the couple.

They grip each other tightly and hide behind a post.

I hold out my sword like a lightsaber. It's about the only sword knowledge I have. I've trained with knives, but a sword is a whole other animal. I guess I could bludgeon them with it like a bat. Or maybe if I throw it at them, I might get a chance to run.

But there's a gleam in their eyes that tells me this isn't just about getting a pretty weapon off an easy target.

I start shifting to the side to line them up in a row so they'll get in each other's way if they rush me all at once. But before I can position myself, one of the guys throws a hammer at me.

I duck.

They pounce.

Then everything happens so fast I can barely absorb what's going on.

I don't have room to swing so I ram one of the attackers with the sword's hilt. I feel the crunch of his ribs as he goes down.

I try to swing the blade at the other men but hands grab me and shove me off balance. I brace for a major hit, hopefully from the bat and not the hammer.

Just my luck, both weapons go up together, one in each man's hand. The bat and the hammer are black cutouts against the twilight sky in that heartbeat moment before they come down for a smashing blow.

A growling blur crashes into the men, knocking them both to the ground.

One of them gapes down at himself. Blood seeps across his shirt. He looks around bewildered.

All our eyes land on the crouching, growling thing in the shadows that looks like it's about to pounce again.

When the thing steps out of the dark, I see the familiar flower-print dress, tights and pink sneakers of my sister.

A zip-up hoodie hangs off her shoulders and her hair streaks down her face, giving glimpses of her angry stitches and razor teeth. Paige stalks around the men like a hyena, bent almost on all fours.

'What the hell,' says one of the attackers from the ground, crab-crawling backwards.

It's freaking me out to see her like this. With all the slashes on her face and the metal shining on her teeth, she looks like a nightmare come to life, one I should be running from. I can tell the others think so too.

'Shh,' I say hesitantly reaching out toward Paige. 'It's okay.'

She growls a low guttural sound. She's about to pounce on one of the guys.

'Easy, kiddo,' I say. 'I'm fine. Let's just get out of here, okay?'

She doesn't even look at me. Her lip twitches as she eyes her prey.

There are too many people watching.

'Paige, put on your hood,' I whisper. I don't care what the attackers think, but I worry about the stories the spectators might spread.

To my surprise, Paige pulls up her hood. Some of the tension eases from my muscles. She's aware and listening to me.

'It's okay,' I whisper inching toward her, fighting my instincts to run from her. 'These bad men are going to go away and leave us alone.'

The men get up, never taking their eyes off Paige. 'Get that freak away from me,' says one. 'That thing's not human.'

My mother has snuck up on the attackers without any of us noticing. 'She's more human than you could ever be.'

She shoves her cattle prod into his ribs. He jerks away from her with a muffled yelp.

'She's more human than any of us.' Mom has a way of whispering that gives the impression of yelling.

'That thing needs to be put down,' says the guy who was holding the bat.

'You need to be put down,' says my mother, approaching him with her prod.

'Get the hell away from me.' Without his bat and his buddies backing him up, he looks like a regular-sized guy with less than regular courage.

My mom jabs her prod at him, zapping it in the air.

He jumps back, narrowly escaping. 'You're all goddamn crazy.' He turns and runs.

My mother runs after him as he scurries into a building.

That dude is not going to have a good evening.

I sheath my sword with hands trembling from the post-fight adrenaline. 'Come on, Paige. Let's go inside.'

Paige walks ahead of me. With her hood up, she looks like a docile little girl. But the couple under the awning isn't fooled. They saw what happened and they stare at Paige with wide eyes, terrified. I wonder how many others are doing the same?

I almost put my hand on her shoulder but can't quite do it. I let my hand drop without touching her.

We walk into our building with the weight of watching eyes on our backs.

12

That night I have a bizarre dream.

I'm in a village made of clay huts with thatched roofs. There's a huge bonfire that lights up the night and everyone is eating, drinking and running around in costumes. Music shrieks and people gyrate around the fire, throwing things into it.

All the hallmarks of a festivity are here but the people are too alert. They steal glances behind themselves into the darkness, and there are only a few shrill laughs. The big bonfire throws long shadows against the hillside that shift and twist like sinister beings.

Maybe I'm getting spooked because people are in monster costumes that are a little too organic for my taste. There's no rubber and plastic to remind me that it's just a costume. These people are wearing pelts, animal heads and claws that look too real for comfort.

Raffe is nearby in the shadows, standing tall with his snowy wings halfway open. It's breathtaking to see his broad shoulders and muscular arms haloed by his own wings. It makes me sad to know that outside of this dream, he doesn't have them any more.

The villagers look at him, especially when they walk by, but their glances are not shocked and fearful like I'd expect. They act as if they're used to seeing angels and don't pay him much attention. At least the men don't.

The women, on the other hand, are gathering around him. Somehow, I'm not too surprised.

The women wear dark dresses that look like stage curtains. Their faces are made up with black circles around their eyes and bloody red lips. One has devils' horns. Some have claws attached to their hands. Others wear goatskins complete with hooves and horns, and makeup to match.

They look bizarrely barbaric, and the shifting light of the fire adds to their savage appearance. Despite his wings, Raffe is the only one who looks 'normal'.

Weirdly, my dream mind picks up on some of Raffe's thoughts. I see humans the way he sees them, alien and bestial. Compared to the perfection of angels, these

Daughters of Men are ugly and smell like pigs. He tries to imagine what his Watchers could possibly have seen in them. He can't see anything worth risking a minor reprimand for, much less the Pit.

Even if he could get past their looks and behavior, they're wingless. How could his angels stomach that?

'Where are our husbands?' asks one of the women. She speaks a guttural language I wouldn't normally understand except that, in my dream, I do.

'They've been condemned to the Pit for marrying Daughters of Men.' His voice is controlled but there's an undertone of anger. They had been his best warriors and good friends.

The women begin crying. 'For how long?'

'Until Judgment Day when they'll finally get their trial. You won't see them again.'

The women cry in each other's arms.

'What about our children?'

Raffe stays silent. How does one tell a mother that he's here to hunt and kill her babies? He came to earth to spare his Watchers the pain of having to hunt down their own children. Even if they were nephilim – monsters who eat human flesh – what kind of twisted punishment is that for a father? He couldn't allow it, not for his soldiers.

'Are you here to punish us?'

'I'm here to protect you.' He wasn't planning to protect the wives. But the Watchers begged him. Begged. He couldn't fathom the idea of his fiercest warriors begging for anything, much less for Daughters of Men.

'From what?'

'The Watchers' wives have been given to the hellions. They'll be coming for you tonight. We need to get you someplace safe. Let's go.'

I look around at all the costumes and the bonfire and realize that this must be some ancient version of Halloween when monsters and demons supposedly roamed the streets. They'll be coming in force tonight.

The women clutch at each other in fright.

'I told you to stay out of the business of gods and angels,' says a gray-haired woman who holds a younger woman protectively. She's dressed in a lamb's skin, complete with the head that drapes over her forehead. It has fangs attached to it like some kind of saber-toothed beast.

Raffe begins walking away from the village. 'Either come with me or stay. I can only help those who want to be helped.'

The older woman pushes her daughter toward Raffe. The others follow, huddling together and rushing to keep up like some weird menagerie.

Music builds near the bonfire as we walk away from it. The tempo speeds up and the beat throbs until the women's breathing matches it.

Just as I think the crescendo will crest, the music stops.

A baby cries into the night.

Then it suddenly stops in the middle of a wail. It ends too abruptly to be natural, and the sharp silence makes the hair on my arms curl.

A woman cries out brokenheartedly. There's no surprise to it, just pain and mourning.

It makes me want to both run to the fire to see if the baby is all right and to run away from these barbaric villagers. They seem mostly unsurprised and unaffected by whatever is happening near the fire, as if this is part of their normal ritual.

I want to tell Raffe that we're not all like these people. That *I'm* not like these people. But I'm just a ghost in my own dream.

Raffe quietly pulls out his sword, on full alert.

They're coming.

Just as the music begins again, this time accompanied by chanting, Raffe spins to look behind him.

The hillside slithers with shadows.

13

Crouched and loping. Stunted black wings. The shapes of emaciated men.

I don't know what they are, but my primal brain recognizes them, because even in my dream, my heart speeds up and my instincts whisper *run, run, run.*

The shadows leap toward us.

Two of them land on a woman, knocking her down. They claw at her. She begs Raffe with her terrified eyes.

One of his warriors loved this Daughter of Man. Gave up his whole life for her. Worried over her even as he was being condemned to the Pit. The why of it is beyond Raffe's comprehension, but that doesn't stop his compassion from blooming.

Raffe kicks off a hellion that lands on him and swings his sword at the demons attacking the woman.

Then a strange thing happens.

Strange even for this dream.

Raffe goes into slow motion.

And so does everything else – except for me.

I've never had a slow-mo dream before. I can see almost every muscle as Raffe shifts his sword and cuts into the hellions that are clawing at the fallen woman.

As one screeches its death cry, I get a decent look. It has a bat-like face, squished and wrinkled, with sharp fangs. Pretty damn ugly if you ask me.

I'm about to put up my hand instinctively to block the slow-mo blood coming my way, when I realize that Raffe's sword is also in my hands even though he is already using it.

Every detail of Raffe slicing the demons as they attack is clear. In slow motion, I can absorb his stance, the shifting of his weight, the way he holds the sword.

When he cuts a swath through the wave of monsters, that part of the dream stops. Then the sequence repeats.

This is like an instructional video of the organic kind.

I must have been seriously frustrated by my lack of sword-fighting skills to make all this up. My dream head hurts just thinking about it.

I put my sword up, mimicking Raffe's stance. Why not? He is a master swordsman, and it's possible that my subconscious picked up details when I saw him fight in real life that my waking brain didn't. I try to swing, mimicking Raffe. But I must be doing it wrong because his swing repeats.

I try it again. Raffe completes his swing, rolls the sword and swings back to complete a figure eight.

I do the same.

Slice to the left, swing up and around, slice to the right and back up and around. He does this a couple of times and then switches his tactic and stabs. Probably not a bad idea to make sure your moves aren't predictable.

The sword adjusts itself here and there to improve my technique. It practically works itself, letting me concentrate on Raffe's footwork. I've learned through years in various self-defense training that footwork is as important as what the arms and hands do.

He glides forward and back like a dancer, never crossing his feet. I mimic his dance.

Sinewy arms burst through the ground, spraying slow-motion dirt everywhere to grab the women. They pull themselves out of the soil, tearing up the earth and spitting it out of their mouths as they climb up.

Some of the women panic and run into the night.

'Stay with me!' Raffe yells.

But it's too late. The hellions pounce on them and their screams intensify.

Raffe grabs the nearest woman as she's being pulled into the ground by demonic hands. The sharp claws hook onto her flesh as she thrashes in slow-motion panic.

Raffe pulls her up out of the dirt, simultaneously swinging his sword while cutting and kicking at the monsters.

This is the way a hero fights.

I copy him, motion by motion, wishing I could help.

We fight, Raffe and I, all through the night.

I wake up trembling in the dark in that quiet time before sunrise. This dream was so vivid that it's as if I was physically there. It takes a few minutes before my heart rate slows back to normal and my adrenaline dissipates.

I shift so my sword's cross-guard isn't poking into my ribs under the blanket. I lie listening to the wind, wondering where Raffe is now.

14

She hasn't eaten in three days.

My sister has drunk some water but that's about all she's managed to hold down. Mom and I coaxed her into swallowing a couple of spoonfuls of venison stew but she gagged that right up. We've tried everything from broth to vegetables. She can't hold any of it down.

Mom is deeply worried. So much so that she's hardly left Paige's side since we found her in the basement lab of the aerie. Paige's skin is corpse white. It's as if all her blood drained through the red-stained holes of the uneven stitches.

'Look at her eyes,' says my mother, as though she understands that Paige's otherness dominates when I look at her now.

But I can't. I keep staring at her stitches while I offer her some cornbread. The cut on her cheek is crooked, as if the surgeon couldn't be bothered to pay attention.

'Look at her eyes,' Mom says again.

I force myself to raise my eyes. My sister does me the favor of looking away.

It is not the eye motion of a beast. That would be too easy. It is the downcast look of a second grader who is all too familiar with rejection. That's the look she used to get when other kids pointed at her as she wheeled by in her wheelchair.

I could kick myself. I force myself to look at her but she won't meet my eyes. 'Do you want some cornbread? I got it fresh from the oven.'

She gives the slightest shake of her head. There's nothing sullen about it, just sadness, as if she's wondering if I'm mad at her or think bad thoughts about her. Somewhere behind her stitches and bruises, I glimpse the lost lonely soul of my sister.

'She's starving,' says Mom. Her shoulders are slumped, her posture dejected. My mother is not exactly a glass-half-full kind of person. But I haven't seen her feeling this hopeless since Paige's accident when she lost the use of her legs.

'Do you think you can eat some raw meat?' I hate asking this. I've gotten so used to her being a strict vegetarian that it seems like I'm giving up on the idea of Paige being Paige.

She steals a glance at me. There's guilt and shyness. But there's eagerness too. She looks down again as if ashamed. Her gulp is unmistakable. Her mouth is watering at the thought of raw meat.

'I'm going to see if I can find some for her.' I put on my sword.

'You do that,' says Mom. Her voice is flat and dead.

I walk out, determined to find something that Paige can eat.

The cafeteria has a line like it always does. I need to come up with a story that convinces the kitchen workers that they should give me raw meat. I can't think of a single reason. Even a dog will eat cooked meat.

So I reluctantly turn away from the food line and head for the grove across El Camino Real. I brace myself to go cavewoman and hope I can catch a squirrel or rabbit. Of course, I have no idea what I'll do with it if I catch it.

In my still-civilized mind, meat comes as packaged food in the refrigerator. But if I'm lucky, I'll find out up close and personal why Paige decided to go vegetarian when she was three years old.

On my way to the grove, I take a detour to do a little shopping first. Joking around with Dee-Dum the other day got me thinking. Guys want a weapon. A badass killing machine whose primary job is to intimidate when you wave it around. But if the same sharp sword was disguised as a cutesy cuddly toy, then the big bad men might look elsewhere for a weapon to steal.

I'm in luck. There's a toyshop in the strip mall. The second I walk into the colorful store full of giant blocks and rainbow kites, I get a tug of nostalgia. I just want to hide in the play corner, surround myself with soft stuffed animals, and read picture books.

My mother has never been normal, but she was better when I was little. I remember running around in play corners like this, singing songs with her or sitting on her lap while she read to me. I run my hands over the soft plush of the panda bears and the smooth plastic of the toy trains, remembering what it was like when bears, trains and moms made me feel safe.

It takes me a while to figure out what to do. I finally decide to slice the bottom of a teddy bear and jam it onto the hilt. I'll just have to pull off the bear if I need to use the sword.

'Come on, admit it, Pooky Bear,' I say to the sword. 'You love your new look. All the other swords will be jealous.'

By the time I cross the street to the grove, my teddy bear is wearing a multi-layered chiffon skirt made of a

wedding veil that I found in one of the boutiques. I
tinted the veil in the bathroom with the stained water
of new clothes so that it no longer has that bridal
white meant to attract the eye. The skirt falls just
below the end of the scabbard, hiding it entirely – or
it will when it dries. The backside is split open so that
I can yank the bear and skirt off without having to
think about it.

It looks ridiculous and says all kinds of embarrassing
things about me. But one thing it doesn't say is killer
angel sword. Good enough.

I weave across the street and scale the chest-high
fence that surrounds the grove. This area feels open, but
there are enough trees to give dappled shade from the
late afternoon sun. A perfect place for rabbits.

I pull off the stuffed bear, satisfied when it comes
off so fast. I stand on the overgrown grass with the
angel sword pointed like a divining rod. A certain
angel, who shall remain nameless because I'm trying
to stop thinking about him, told me that this little
sword is not an ordinary sword. There's enough weird-
ness in my life as it is but sometimes, you just have to
go with it.

'Find a rabbit.'

A squirrel clinging onto the side of a tree laughs in a
series of chirps.

'It's not funny.' In fact, it's as serious as can be. Raw animal meat is my best hope for Paige. I don't even want to think about what will happen if she can't eat that.

I charge the squirrel, my arms loose and ready to be adjusted by the sword. The squirrel takes off.

'Sorry, squirrel. One more thing to blame on the angels.' An image of Raffe's face comes to mind – a halo of flames around his hair, showing lines of grief on his shadowed face. I wonder where he is. I wonder if he's in pain. Adjusting to new wings must be like adjusting to new legs: painful, lonely, and during war, dangerous.

I heave the sword above my head. I can't look and I can't not look, so I do a weird combination of turning my head and squinting while looking just enough to be able to aim.

I swing the sword down.

The world suddenly tilts, making me dizzy.

My stomach lurches.

My vision falters and flashes.

One second, the sword is coming down on the squirrel.

The next second, the sword is being held up to an azure sky.

The fist that's holding it is Raffe's. And the sky is not my sky.

He hovers at the head of an army of angels who stand below him in formation. His glorious wings, white and whole, frame his body, making it look like a statue of a Greek warrior god.

15

Raffe raises his sword into the air. The legion of angels lift their swords in response. A war cry goes up as row after row of winged men take flight.

It's a breathtaking sight to see so many angels lift in formation. The legion flies to battle, led by Raffe.

There's a whisper of a concept in my head.

Glory.

Then, as quick as a heartbeat, the blue sky and winged men disappear.

We're in a field at night.

A horde of scary-as-all-hell, bat-faced demons rush at me like an avalanche, screeching a hellish cry. Raffe steps ahead and starts swinging his sword with perfect precision, just like in my dreams.

Fighting beside him and protecting his back are angel warriors, some of whom I've seen before at the old aerie. They're joking and egging each other on as they fight and defend each other from the monsters of the night.

Another concept echoes in my head.

Victory.

The scene changes again and we're in the sky, only this time it's in the middle of a lightning storm. Thunder rumbles through the dark clouds and lightning lights up the scene in stark contrasts. Raffe and a small group of warriors hover in the rain, watching another group of angels get dragged away in chains.

The prisoners fly with spiked shackles around their wrists, ankles, neck and head. The spikes are on the inside so they're driven into their flesh. Blood washes away with the rain in jagged rivulets down their faces, hands, and feet.

A squat, bat-faced demon with bat wings rides on the shoulders of each prisoner. The demons hold the chains to the collar, using it as a bridle. They jerk the chains one direction, then another, cruelly driving the spikes in and making them fly like drunks. More hellions hang off some of the ankle and wrist shackles that bind the prisoners to each other.

Some of these angels had fought beside Raffe in the field. They had laughed with him and protected his back. Now, they watch him with excruciating pain in their eyes as they're driven like tortured cattle.

The other angels watch with immense sadness, some with their heads bowed. But Raffe is the only one who flies out of the group, brushing hands with a few of the prisoners on his way down toward earth.

As the scene fades, another word takes shape in my head.

Honor.

And then, I'm standing under the trees again in Stanford's grove.

My stomach lurches as I finish my swing and smash the blade into the ground where the squirrel stood a second ago. My hands are clenched so tightly around the hilt that my knuckles feel like they might split.

The squirrel has scampered into a tree and is watching me. It looks puny and insignificant after the things I've just seen.

I let go of the sword and land on my butt.

I don't know how long I sit there panting, but I suspect it's a long time. There's nothing but the blue October sky, the smell of grass, and the unusual quiet that's been everywhere since people abandoned cars.

Could the sword be communicating with me? Sending me the message that it was made for epic battles and glory, not for chasing squirrels and being dressed up as a cutesy stuffed animal?

Of course, that's crazy talk.

But no crazier than what I just saw.

I want to bury my train of thought. Anything that smells remotely insane is a scent I don't want to follow. But I let myself do it just this once.

Raffe said the sword was sort of sentient. If by some truly bizarre chance that's true, then maybe it has feelings. Maybe it has memories that it can share with me.

On the night those men attacked me, did it get frustrated that I had no idea how to use it during the fight? Is it embarrassing for a sword to be wielded by someone who swings it like a bat? Was it actually trying to teach me how to use it through my dreams?

The thing freaks me out. I should switch over to a gun or something that's a little less invasive and has fewer opinions. I actually get up, turn my back on it, and take a couple of steps away.

But of course, I can't leave it.

It's Raffe's sword. He's going to want it back someday.

On my way back, I hesitate near the food line. It's a new group of people but the line is about the same length. The Resistance is setting up a system that includes limiting food to two meals a day. But while that's getting set up, the newcomers are still hoarding and spending a good deal of their time standing in the food line.

I sigh and go to the back of the line.

When I get back to our room, it's empty. I'm not sure it's a good idea for Paige to be out in public but I assume they'll be back soon. I put three burgers on the teacher's desk. I didn't ask what kind of meat it was but I doubt it's cow.

I had asked for the patties to be super rare, specifically mentioning the word 'bloody,' thinking that's as close as I could get to raw without raising suspicions. But I'm disappointed to find that the meat's hardly pink in the middle.

I cut away the cooked portion from the pink center and set it aside for Paige. I can at least try to see if she can hold down pink meat. I try not to think too much about it.

I suspect she hadn't been out of the lab in her new form before we found her, otherwise, she'd know what she could eat. If I had found her a day earlier, could I have saved her from this?

I shut away those thoughts in the old mind vault and methodically eat my burger. The lettuce and tomato are reconstituted from something that's probably not what it's pretending to be, but it reminds me of greens and that's good enough. The bread, though, is fresh out of the oven and delicious. The camp lucked out and found somebody who knows how to bake bread from scratch.

I pull out Raffe's sword and put the naked blade on my lap. I stroke my fingers along the metal. The light hits the liquid folds along the steel, showing the bluish-silver waves that decorate it.

If I relax, I can feel the faint flow of sorrow coming from it. The sword is in mourning. It doesn't take a genius to figure out who it's mourning for.

'Show me more,' I say, even though I'm not sure I can handle more right now. My knees are already weak and I'm feeling drained. Even in a world where angels exist, it's still a shocker to have one of your possessions share its memories with you.

'Tell me about Raffe.'

Nothing.

'Okay. Let's practice fighting,' I say in an enthusiastic voice as if I'm talking to a little kid. 'I could use more lessons.'

I take a deep breath and close my eyes.

Nothing.

'Right. Well, I guess I have nothing better to do now than to decorate the teddy bear with ribbons and bows. What do you think of dusky pink?'

The room wavers, then morphs.

16

Time has a way of being funny in dreams and I'm guessing it's the same with memories. For what feels like a decade, I practice with my sword, fighting enemy after enemy by Raffe's side.

The hellions must have been furious that he snatched some of the wives from their jaws and took what they thought belonged to them. They've been tracking him down ever since, hunting anyone who might have been a companion to him. I'm guessing that demons aren't the type to forgive and forget.

Era after era throughout the world, it's the same everywhere. Medieval villages, World War I battlefields, Buddhist monasteries in Tibet, speakeasies in Chicago. Raffe follows rumors of the nephilim, kills hellions and anything else that terrorize the locals, then disappears into the night. He flies away from anybody he might have connected with in the process to avoid getting them killed.

Alone.

Just Raffe and his sword.

And now he doesn't even have that.

Just when I think the lessons are over, the sword's memory flips to a situation that almost breaks me.

As soon as I arrive, I'm slammed with the intensity of it.

Raffe roars with outrage and agony.

He's in serious trouble. The pain is excruciating. The shock is worse.

My phantom body sways as it loses its boundaries, making me feel totally disoriented. Raffe's experience is so intense, my own thoughts and sensations are overwhelmed by his.

His ragged breathing is all I can hear. It's all he can hear.

Hands and knees hold him down but blood makes their hands slip over his skin. Raffe is drenched in his own blood.

Pain radiates from his back through his entire body. Crushing his bones. Stabbing his eyes. Pummeling his lungs.

Blood spreads over asphalt.

Large hands move something white into the corner of his vision. He desperately doesn't want to look but can't help himself.

Wings.

Snow-white wings.

Severed and lying on the dirty road.

His breathing becomes harsher, and all he can see are those white feathers lying limp on the black asphalt.

A drop of blood from someone's hand drips onto a feather. Beliel the demon stands over Raffe's wings like he owns them.

It dimly registers with Raffe that someone yells, 'Hey!'

He forces himself to look up.

His vision is blurred through the pain and sweat. He blinks several times to try to focus beyond the screaming pain in his back.

It's a skinny Daughter of Man, looking tiny beside one of his attackers. She's half-hidden behind the warrior's burnt-orange wings, but Raffe sees her and knows she's the one who yelled.

That's me. Do I really look that insignificant beside an angel?

She throws something at him with all her little might.

His sword? Could it be?

He doesn't have time to marvel. His sword would do anything for him, even let a human bond with her to help him.

A surge of fury lends him a shot of strength. He bursts out of his attackers' hold and raises his hand. His arm trembles with the effort.

His world shrinks down to his sword, Beliel, and the angels before him.

He catches the sword and in the same motion slices the demon Beliel in the stomach. Raffe almost loses his balance in the process.

He then manages to use his momentum to cut into the angel beside him.

The scene doesn't slow down like the other fights. It doesn't have to. I feel every trembling muscle, every staggering step, every struggling breath.

He's dizzy and barely managing to stay upright. As the attackers fly off, he sees the warrior with the burnt-orange wings smack the girl. She slams against the road, and Raffe thinks she must be dead.

Through the haze of agony, he wonders who she is and why a Daughter of Man would sacrifice herself to help him.

He forces himself to stay on his feet. It takes every-thing he has to hold his sword ready as Burnt assesses him. Raffe's legs tremble violently and he's losing consciousness, but he stays up out of sheer stubbornness and fury.

Burnt, obviously too cowardly to face him alone, gives up and flies off. Raffe collapses onto the asphalt as soon as Burnt leaves.

Lying on the road, the world blackens with only occasional splotches of color. His breath fills his ears, but he concentrates to hear sounds in the surrounding area.

Feet scuffle behind closed doors. Inside the buildings, humans whisper and argue about whether it's safe to come out. They talk about how much Raffe would be worth if they tore him to pieces.

But they're not the ones who worry him. There are more subtle scuffling, slithering noises. Soft clicking, like cockroaches in the walls.

They're coming for him. The hellions have found him. They always do eventually.

But this time, they're in luck. This time, he's utterly helpless. They'll be able to drag him down into hell and slowly torture him over the ages while he lies hopeless and wingless.

He desperately tries to stay alert, but the world melts into darkness.

Someone is calling out for her mother. The voice is strong and determined.

It must be a fever dream because no one would be that stupid in a place full of human gangs. But the footsteps in the building stairwells quiet. The human rats whisper, sure that the girl who calls out for her mom must have her gang nearby. What else would make a girl that bold?

The hellions stop their slithering too. They're not smart enough to figure out much, otherwise they would have gotten to him ages ago by coordinating a real attack rather than just diving at random opportunities. They're confused. Attack or run?

He tries to pull himself away from the exposed road, but black spots bloom across his vision and he fades out again.

Someone flips him over. Pain screams and claws into his back.

A small hand slaps him.

He opens his eyes for a moment.

Against the glow of the sky, dark hair flutters in the breeze. Intense eyes fringed with long lashes. Lips so red the girl must have been biting them.

It takes him a moment to realize she's the Daughter of Man who risked herself to help him. She's asking him something. Her voice is insistent but melodic. It's a good sound to die to.

He fades in and out as she moves him. He keeps expecting her to cut him up or for the hellions to leap on her. Instead, she bandages him and lifts him into a wheelchair that's too small.

When the girl grunts and overacts to indicate that he must be heavy – probably to show how strong she is – he can't help but be amused, even through the haze of pain. She's a terrible actress. Daughters of Men are notoriously dense and heavy compared to angels, and there's something deliriously funny about her pretending.

Maybe his Watchers married their wives because they found them entertaining. Not much of a reason to be condemned to the Pit but it's the first one he's thought of.

Shoes slap on the sidewalk as human rats run toward Raffe. Emboldened by the rats, the hellions slither toward him too.

He tries to warn the girl.

But there's no need. She's already running into the shadows, pushing him as fast as she can go. If she can stay ahead of them long enough, the hellions will get distracted by the juicy human rats.

His last thought before he blacks out is that his Watchers would have liked this girl.

17

The shadows through the windows are long by the time I jerk awake. I'm still shaking from Raffe's experience. I didn't just know what he was thinking; I actually felt what he felt, thought what he thought.

Was the sword really that close to Raffe? Maybe only in extremely intense times. The whole experience was bizarrely freaky at every level.

I run my trembling hand over the warm blade, telling my body that it's okay.

I'm starting to put some pieces together. Some of Raffe's actions make more sense now.

He couldn't jump in to help me during my public fights at the last Resistance camp without rumors spreading about us. The hellions always tracked him down eventually, and it was probably a combination of luck, tracking, and listening to human gossip. A story about a fight like that would definitely be talked about. He bet against me to announce to everyone that we weren't friends, that he didn't care what happened to me.

And he hunted down the low demons in the forest even after they ran because they seemed like they came from hell, didn't they? If any of them lived to tell about how he'd come to the rescue of a Daughter of Man, it'd just be a matter of time before they got to me.

But did he have to go as far as telling me he didn't even like me after our kiss? That was totally unnecessary, in my opinion.

The kiss.

Like a germinating seed, I have the growing impulse to ask the sword about it.

It's silly and embarrassing and maybe even shallow after what I just saw Raffe go through. But because of what I just saw, I want to see him in a different kind of moment. One where he's cocky and in control. One where he's experiencing something other than threats and pain, if only for two seconds.

That, and I'm dying to know what he felt during our kiss.

I know it doesn't matter. I know it won't change anything. I know it's juvenile.

Whatever.

Can't a girl be a girl for, like, five minutes?

'Show me your memories of the kiss.' I close my eyes. The heat creeps up my cheeks, which is silly because the sword was there when the kiss happened and saw the whole thing. So what if I'm curious about what he felt?

'Oh, come on. Do we have to do this again?'

Nothing.

'That last one was totally awful. I need a little comfort. It's just a small favor. Please?'

Nothing.

'Extra ribbons and bows for you,' I try to sound like I mean it. 'Maybe even sparkly makeup on the teddy bear.'

Still nothing.

'Traitor.' I know that's a funny statement since the sword is actually being loyal to Raffe but I don't care.

I slide it back into its scabbard, which has been leaning against my chair, and jam the bear over the hilt.

I slip the strap over my shoulder and step outside to see if I can find Mom and Paige.

The hallway is still crowded, as usual. Two identical guys with blond hair are weaving through the tight space, saying hello to a bunch of people as they walk by. It seems like everyone likes them. It takes me a second to realize that it's Dee and Dum. Their hair is now sandy blond.

Dee discretely shows Dum something in his palm, and Dum almost crosses his eyes trying to hold in a laugh. I'm guessing Dee just pickpocketed someone for something the owner has probably already told them they can't have.

They wave to me and I wait for them.

'What happened to your hair?' I ask.

'We're spy masters, remember?' says Dee.

'As in *masters* of disguise,' says Dum.

'Well,' says Dee rubbing dye off the edge of his hair-line, '"master" is kind of a strong word.'

'So is "disguise",' I say with a half grin.

'Dude, you look great,' says Dum to Dee. 'Handsome as ever.'

'What did you pickpocket?' I keep my voice down in case the owner doesn't have a sense of humor.

'Ooh, you're losing your touch, Bro. She saw.' Dum looks around to see if anyone is listening.

'No way. My touch is like butter.' Dee opens his now empty palms and wiggles his fingers. 'She's just smart, that's all. She can figure things out.'

'Yeah, and that's why we feel so bad about only think-ing of you as a candidate for fights, Penryn. Speaking of which, how do you feel about wearing a nun's habit?'

'Better yet, hot librarian glasses.' Dee nods at me like he's giving me a tip. 'Turns out we have both librarians *and* nuns here.'

'Does it get any better than that?' Dum's eyes are wide with wonder.

They look at each other and simultaneously call out, 'Librarian mud fights!' They shake their hands in the air like excited little boys.

Everyone in the hallway looks over at us.

'See? Look at the interest,' says Dee.

But then the hallway clears as people pour out through the door. Something is happening.

'What's going on?' I ask someone as he peers outside.

'No idea,' he says. He looks scared but excited. 'Just following the crowd to see what's happening. You too, huh?'

A woman brushes past us. 'Someone's been found dead or mangled or something.' She pushes through the doors, letting cold air in.

Dead or mangled.

I follow her.

Outside, a small crowd full of tension hovers on the walkway in front of the main building. The sun may be low on the horizon but the overcast sky simply drains the color, painting everyone shades of gray.

People look across El Camino. On the other side is the fenced grove where I chased the squirrel. During the day it's beautiful and peaceful, with the trees spaced far enough apart to give the area dappled shade without darkness. But as the light dims, the grove starts looking sinister and foreboding.

A few people run straight from the building to the grove, while others hesitate before walking there. Still others linger in hopes of safety near the building, while squinting to see what's going on in the shadows beneath the trees.

I pause to take in the situation, then join those who are running to the grove. I can't help but wonder what draws them there in the dimming light. Snatches of conversation along the way clue me in.

I'm not the only one who worries about someone they love. Lots of people got separated during the chaos of the angel invasion or the aerie attack. Now they're frantically worried that whoever is left in their family might have been hurt or killed. Others are just more curious than smart, emboldened by being part of an organization full of people with purpose, something they thought might never happen again.

In any case, there are enough of us to create a logjam at the fence. It's a metal-framed wire fence that's chest high to me and requires actual climbing. Since the fence borders the grove for several blocks in either direction, there's no choice but to scale it.

Under the trees, a small crowd gathers. I can feel their restlessness and hear the tension in their voices. A sense of urgency shoots through me. Something is seriously wrong here and I'm convinced it has something to do with my family.

I race to the crowd, shoving my way in.

What I see is something I won't be able to blot out of my mind for as long as I live.

18

My little sister struggles under the shadows.

Radiating out from her are ropes pulled by men. One rope is tied around her neck, two others around her wrists and two more around her ankles.

The men struggle against the ropes like they're holding down a wild horse.

Paige's hair is tangled and there's blood in it. There's also blood smeared across her face and staining her flower-print dress. The contrast of the dark blood and the stitches on her pale skin make her look as if she's risen from the dead.

She struggles against the ropes like someone possessed. She lurches when the men yank at her to try to gain control. Even in this light, I can see the bloody chafing of the ropes around her neck and wrists as she's jerked around like a macabre voodoo puppet.

My first instinct is to screech like a banshee and pull out the sword.

But there's something lying in front of Paige.

The shock of seeing her so cruelly tied up like an animal kept me from seeing the rest of the scene. But now I see a shadowy lump, still as rock but shaped like something I wish I didn't recognize.

It's a body.

It's the guy who carried the bat when he and his buddies attacked me.

I look away. I don't want to process what my eyes just saw. I don't want to register the chunks missing from him.

I don't want to think about what that means.

I can't.

Paige's tongue flicks out and licks blood from her lips.

She closes her eyes and swallows. Her face relaxes just for a second.

Peace.

She opens her eyes and looks at the body near her feet. It's like she can't help it.

A part of me still expects her to cringe in disgust at the sight of the corpse. There is disgust there. But there's also a flash of longing. Hunger.

She darts a glance at me. Shame.

She stops struggling and looks right at me.

She sees my hesitation. She sees I'm no longer running to save her. She sees judgment in my eyes.

'Ryn-Ryn,' she cries. Her voice is filled with loss. Tears streak down her blood-smeared cheeks, leaving clear tracks. Her face shifts from looking like a fierce monster to a scared little girl.

Paige starts thrashing again. My wrists, ankles, and neck hurt in sympathy as the ropes chafe against her bloody skin.

The men seesaw at the ends of the ropes so that it's hard to tell whether they have *her* captive or if she's holding *them*. I've seen how strong her new body can be. She's powerful enough to seriously challenge them and give them a real fight. On this uneven terrain, she might be able to throw them off balance and make them fall.

Instead, she struggles ineffectively.

Just enough to get the ropes to cut into her. Just enough to hurt herself in punishment. Just enough so that no one else gets hurt.

My little sister cries in heartbroken sobs.

I start running again. No matter what happened, she doesn't deserve this. No living creature deserves this.

A soldier on my right raises his rifle and points it at me. It's so close I can look right into the dark hole of its silencer.

I stop, almost skidding.

Another man stands beside him, pointing a rifle at Paige.

I raise my open hands.

Men grab my arms, and I can tell by their roughness that they expect a major struggle. We Young girls are getting a reputation.

The men relax when they see that I'm not about to put up a fight. Hand-to-hand is one thing but guns are beyond me. All I can do is stay alive until I get a chance to do something more proactive.

But my mother has her own logic.

She runs out from the shadows, silent as a ghost.

She jumps on the soldier pointing his rifle at Paige.

The other soldier raises the butt of his rifle and smacks Mom in the face.

'No!' I kick the guy holding my arm. But before he hits the ground and before I can get the other guy off me, three of them jump on me. They shove me to the ground like experienced gang members before I get a chance to stabilize.

My mom puts up her hand to deflect another blow of the rifle butt.

My sister ramps up her struggling. This time, it's filled with panic and fury. She screeches into the air like she's calling on the sky to come help her.

'Shut her up! Shut her up!' someone is whisper-shouting.

'Don't shoot!' whisper-shouts Sanjay. 'We need her alive for study.' He has the decency to throw me a quick, guilty glance. I don't know whether to be angry or grateful.

I have to help my family. My brain screams at me about the guns, but what can I do? Lie here while they torture and kill my baby sister and mother?

Three men hold me down. One grabs my arms above my head, another has my ankles, and the third sits on my stomach. Looks like no one's underestimating me any more. So be it.

I grasp the wrists of the guy holding my hands, using him as leverage, making sure he can't get away.

I twist and pump my legs, scrape-kicking my ankle holder's hand off my ankle. It's hard for anyone, big or not, to match the power of a kick with the grip of his hand.

Then I pull back my free leg and kick him full in the face.

With my legs free, I heave and wrap them around the neck of the guy sitting on my stomach.

I slam my legs toward the ground, jerking him backwards. I yank my leg out from under him and kick at his open crotch.

I kick so hard he slides away from me on the grass with a breathless scream. He won't be any trouble for a while.

By now, the guy holding my wrists has started to fight my grip, trying to get away. If I thought he'd just run and let me be, I'd be happy to let him go.

But there's too much of a chance that he'll get ideas about tackling me while I'm down. Guys are sometimes like that when it comes to losing a fight to a small female. They chalk it up to luck or something.

My hold on him is firm. Using him for leverage, I twist and spin on my hip in what someone in my gym has described as looking like I'm running up a wall, only I'm doing it while lying on the ground.

I swing my leg, pivoting on the side of my hip as I kick the guy above me in the head.

I bet he wasn't expecting that little move.

I hop up, scanning the scene around me, ready for another attack.

My mom is on the ground, yanking a soldier by his rifle. She grips the barrel while it's pointed right at her. She either doesn't realize that all he has to do is pull the trigger to blow her away, or she doesn't care.

My sister screeches into the sky like the monster they all think she is. The veins on her neck and forehead stick out like they're going to burst.

Two of the men holding her ropes are on the ground now. A third one goes down as I watch.

I dive toward Mom, hoping the rifle doesn't go off before I can do something.

Luckily, these soldiers are citizen soldiers, newly minted and inexperienced. Hopefully, this one hasn't shot anyone yet and isn't willing to have a desperate mother be his first kill.

19

Without thinking, we all look up. At first, I'm not even sure why I do it.

Then I realize that there's a buzzing coming from the sky. So low that it's barely audible.

But it's growing louder.

Through the gaps in the trees, I can see a dark blotch in the twilight sky. It grows closer at an alarming rate.

The buzzing stays low, just enough to feel it in your bones rather than hear it. It's an ominous sound, like something recognizable at a primal level, a deeply buried unconscious fear turned into sound.

Before I can identify it, people turn and run.

No one screams or shouts or calls out to anyone. People just silently and desperately run.

The panic is contagious. The men holding my mom let go and join the stampede. Almost immediately after, the guys holding my sister release their ropes and run as well.

Paige pants, staring up at the sky. She looks mesmerized.

'Run!' I yell. That breaks her spell.

My sister turns and runs the other direction, away from the Resistance camp. She runs deeper into the grove with her ropes trailing in the dirt like snakes slithering in the shadows after her.

Mom glances at me. Blood trickles from her cut eye. Even in this light, I can see a bruise beginning to form.

After the briefest of hesitations, my mother chases my sister into the trees.

I stand frozen as the buzzing gets louder. Do I go after them or run back to safety?

The decision is made for me when the dark cloud gets close enough for me to make out individual shapes.

Winged men with scorpion tails.

Dozens of them darkening the sky. They're flying low and getting lower.

There must have been another batch of them or several other batches outside the aerie.

I run.

I sprint away from them, which has me running toward the school like everyone else. I'm the last one of the bunch, so I'm an easy target.

A scorpion swoops down and lands in front of me.

Unlike the ones I saw at the aerie, this one is fully baked, complete with shaggy hair and teeth that have matured into lion's fangs. Its arms and legs look disturbingly human except that its thighs and upper arms are extra beefy. Its body, at first glance, is human, but the belly and chest look a little like a cross between defined abs and the sectioned underbellies of grasshoppers.

The teeth are so large the beast can't seem to close its mouth and drool drips from its lips. It growls at me and rears its fat scorpion tail above its head.

Fear grips me in a way that's never happened before.

It's as if I'm reliving the scorpion attack in the aerie basement. My neck becomes hypersensitive, almost twitching in expectation of a stinger jabbing into it.

Another scorpion lands near me. This one has needle-sharp teeth that it bares as it hisses.

I'm trapped.

I snatch off the stuffed bear and pull out my sword. It feels less clumsy in my hand than it did before but that's as far as my confidence will go.

Gunshots go off but mostly the night is filled with the

sound of the thunderous roar of wings and the high-pitched screams of people.

I barely have time to put myself in the ready stance that I learned in my dream before one of the monsters leaps for me.

I swing my blade at a forty-five degree angle, meaning to slice into the juncture of its neck and shoulder. Instead, I slice through its stinger as it whips toward me.

The monster screams, a disturbingly human sound coming out of its fang-filled mouth.

There's no time to finish it off because the second one thrusts its stinger at me.

I shut my eyes and swing wildly in my panic. It's all I can do to keep the memories of being stung from freezing me up completely.

Luckily, my sword has no such issues. The glee rolling off it is unmistakable. It adjusts itself to the right angle. It's feather light on the upswing and lead heavy on the downswing.

When I open my eyes, the second scorpion is bleeding on the ground, its tail twitching. The first one is gone, probably having flown away to nurse its injury or to die in peace.

I'm the only living thing standing in my part of the grove. I slide into the shadow of the nearest tree, trying to calm my breathing.

The scorpions are still landing, but not near me. They're attracted to the mass of people who are logjammed at the fence.

They grab people and sting them repeatedly from different angles, almost as if practicing or maybe just enjoying it. Even when they latch on to their victims with their mouths to suck them dry, other scorpions come and sting the same victims.

People scream and shove each other at the fence, trying to climb over it. They spread out to try to get to a place where they can jump the fence, but they get picked off by the scorpions, too.

The few who make it to the other side seem to be okay. The scorpions are busy stinging the ones in the grove, like lazy predators, and don't pay attention to the ones who manage to get out.

When the victims slide to the ground, the scorpions begin sucking. By the time everyone is either slumped against the fence or running into the school building across the street, the scorpions have lost interest. They take off into the air and swirl like a cloud of insects before they disappear into the darkening sky.

Something rustles behind me, and I spin with my sword ready.

It's Mom shambling toward me.

We are the only people moving on this side of the fence. Everyone else looks dead. I continue to hide in the shadows anyway in case the scorpions come back, but everything remains silent and still.

My mother stumbles past me. 'She's gone. I lost her.' Tears shine on her bloody face. She staggers toward the fence, ignoring the fallen people.

'I'm fine, Mom. Thanks for asking.' I grab the bear and wipe the blood off the sword with its chiffon skirt. 'Are you okay? How did you survive?'

'Of course you're fine.' She keeps walking. 'You're the devil's bride and these are his creatures.'

I slip the blade into the scabbard and put the bear back on top. 'I'm not the devil's bride.'

'He carried you out of the fire and is letting you visit us from the dead. Who else would have those privileges except his bride?'

She sees me once in a guy's arms and she has us married already. I wonder what Raffe would think of my mom being his mother-in-law. 'Did you see where Paige went?'

'Gone.' Her voice breaks. 'I lost her in the woods.' My reaction to that would have been so simple last week. Tonight, though, I don't know if I'm panicked or relieved. Maybe both.

'Did you hide from the scorpion?' I ask. 'How did you survive?' No answer.

If someone told me that moms have magical powers, I'd have no trouble believing that. It doesn't even surprise me much that she somehow survived.

I follow her to the fence. Along the way, I walk past the victims lying in uncomfortable and unnatural positions. Although they're no longer being attacked, they continue to shrivel and dry like jerky. The grove looks like a battlefield with people strewn all over it.

I want to reassure the victims that they'll come out of it, that they'll be okay. But with the viciousness of the attack, I'm not sure that they will.

A couple of scorpion bodies lie among the victims on the field. One shot in the stomach, one shot in the head.

Mom scans through the victims as if she's looking for someone. She picks the one with the most horrified, contorted expression frozen on his face and tugs him to a section of the fence that's been trampled.

'What are you doing?' I ask.

'An offering,' she says, laboriously dragging the poor guy. 'We need to find Paige so we need an offering.'

'You're creeping me out, Mom.' A waste of breath.

As if she knows better than to ask for my help, she heaves the man up against a fence pole. He slides back down in a heap.

I want to stop her, but when she gets a crazy project in her head, nothing on earth will stop her.

Night is starting to fall. The cloud of scorpions is getting farther away, and there's not a single stray one in the sky.

The thought of wandering around the grove in the dark looking for my low-demon sister is not my idea of a good time. But she can't be left roaming by herself, for all kinds of reasons. And it'll be much better if I find her than if the frightened Resistance people find her.

So I leave my mother to do whatever she is doing and return to the shadows of the grove.

20

It's almost full night by the time I get back to the carnage by the fence. There are people walking in a daze around the victims. Some are hunched over a fallen loved one, others are wandering about crying and looking terrified. A few are digging shallow graves.

My mother has finished her project, although she's nowhere in sight. The man she dragged now sits on a stack of bodies with his arms stretched out over the fence like a terrified and terrifying scarecrow. She has tied him in place with bits of rope that she probably found on one of the guys who lassoed Paige.

His contorted, screaming lips are emphasized by ruby red lipstick. His button-down shirt is ripped open, exposing his nearly hairless chest. On it, a message written in lipstick says:

TOUCh mE & YOu'll TaKe mY pLACE

The creep factor of my mother's project is pretty high. Everyone goes out of their way to walk far around it.

As I walk past the bodies, a man bends down to check for the pulse of a woman lying beside me.

'Listen,' I say. 'These people might not be dead.'

'This one is.' He moves on to the next one.

'They may seem like they're dead but they could just be paralyzed. That's what the stingers do. They paralyze and make you seem dead in every way.'

'Yes, well, not having a heartbeat will do that to you, too.' He shakes his head, drops the wrist of the guy he was checking and moves to the next victim.

I follow him while soldiers point their rifles up to the sky on the lookout for any signs of another attack. 'But you might not be able to feel their heartbeats. I think it slows everything down. I think—'

'Are you a doctor?' he asks without pausing in his work.

'No, but—'

'Well, I am. And I can tell you that if there's no heartbeat, there's no chance of a person being alive except for a very unusual situation such as a child falling into a frozen pond. I don't see any children who fell into a frozen pond here, do you?'

'I know this sounds crazy, but—'

Two men pick up a woman wearily and shuffle over to a shallow grave.

'No!' I cry out. That could have been me. Everybody thought I was dead for a while, and if circumstances had been different, they might have dumped me in a hole and buried me alive while I watched, paralyzed but totally aware.

I run over and stand between the men and the hole. 'Don't do this.'

'Leave us alone.' The older man doesn't even look at me as he grimly carries the victim.

'She could be alive.'

'My wife is dead.' His voice breaks.

'Listen to me. There's a chance she's alive.'

'Can't you give us some peace?' He glares at me out of the corners of his eyes. 'My wife is dead.' Tears stream from his red-rimmed eyes. 'And she'll stay dead.'

'She can probably hear you right now.'

The man's face turns red, making it painful to look at him. 'She'll never come back. And if she does, then she won't be our Mary. It'll be some abomination.' He points to a woman standing alone by a tree. 'Like her.'

The woman looks fragile, lost and alone. Even with the brown scarf wrapped around her head and the gloves on her hands, I recognize the shriveled face of Clara, the woman who climbed out of the ruins of the aerie. She wears a dull-colored coat that whispers her desire not to be noticed. I'm guessing people haven't exactly been welcoming.

She hugs herself as if clinging to the husband and children she longs to find. All she wanted was to find her family.

Mary's family drags her paralyzed body into the shallow grave.

'You can't do this,' I say. 'She's fully aware. She knows she's being buried alive.'

The younger guy asks, 'Dad, do you think—'

'Your mother is dead, Son. She was a decent human being and she'll have a decent burial.' He picks up his shovel.

I grab his arm.

'Get away from me!' He shakes me off, trembling in fury. 'Just because you don't have the decency to do what's right for your family doesn't mean you have any right to stop others from doing what's right for theirs.'

'What's that supposed to mean?'

'You should have put down your sister humanely and with love before strangers had to step in to try to do it for you.'

The older man takes the shovel full of dirt and throws it onto his wife in the hole.

It lands on her face, covering it.

21

In the darkening grove, Obi waves over one of his guys. 'Please put Ms. Young with her mother and make sure they're safe and secure for the night.'

'You're arresting me?' I ask. 'For what?'

'It's for your protection,' says Obi.

'Protection from what?' I ask. 'The U.S. Constitution?'

Obi sighs. 'We can't have you or your family loose and causing panic. I need to maintain control.'

Obi's man points his silencer-enhanced pistol at my chest. 'Walk to the street and don't give me any trouble.'

'She's trying to save people's lives,' says a trembling voice. It's Clara, clutching her oversized coat around her as if wishing she could disappear.

Nobody pays her any attention.

I throw Obi a look that says, *Are you serious?* But he's busy waving over another guy.

He points to Mom's victim project. 'Why is that horrible pile of bodies still around? I told you to take them away.'

Obi's man tells two other guys to take the bodies down. Apparently, he doesn't want to do it himself.

The two guys shake their heads and back away. One of them crosses himself. They turn and run toward the school, as far from the bodies as they can get.

As my guard escorts me through the carnage, I hear Sanjay telling people to stow the unclaimed bodies into a van for autopsies.

I stagger away from them. I just can't watch. Maybe these people really are dead. I certainly hope so.

I get tossed into the back seat of a police car parked on the road. Mom is already there.

The police cruiser has a metal mesh between the front and rear seats. There are bars on the back-seat windows. Beneath the rear window, there are blankets and a couple of bottles of water. My foot knocks over a half bucket with a lid, complete with packets of sanitary wipes.

It takes me a minute to understand that they're not taking us anywhere. This is our holding cell.

Great.

At least the guard didn't take my sword. He didn't even pat me down for weapons, so I assume he wasn't a cop in the World Before. Still, he probably would have taken my sword if it didn't look like a post-apocalyptic comfort bear.

I sip on a bottle of water, drinking barely enough to quench my thirst but not so much that I'll need to pee anytime soon.

People frantically rush, trying to finish their jobs before full dark, whether their job is dragging bodies into the autopsy van or burying loved ones. They've been glancing at the sky every couple of minutes, but as darkness slithers over them, people begin looking behind them nervously as if worried something will sneak up on them.

I get it. There's something horrifying about being left alone in the dark, especially with someone you think is dead.

I try not to think about what it must be like for the victims. Paralyzed but aware, left helpless in the dark with monsters and family.

When the last unclaimed body is tossed into the van, the workers slam it shut and drive off.

Those who didn't go in the van trot across the street to the school. Then the families, whether or not they're done shoveling dirt on their loved ones, drop their shovels and run after the workers, obviously not wanting to be left behind.

Mom starts to make animal noises of anxiety as she watches everyone leave. When you're paranoid, the last place you want to be is trapped in a car where you can't run and can't hide.

'It's okay,' I say. 'They'll be back. They'll let us out when they cool off. And then we'll go find Paige.'

She yanks on the door handle, then jumps over to my side to try the other one. She bangs on the window. She rattles the screen separating the front seat from the back. Her breathing becomes a pant.

She's spiraling into serious freak-out mode.

The last thing we need is major hysteria in a space smaller than a sofa.

As the final stragglers run past my window, I yell at them. 'Put me in another car!'

They don't even glance my way as they scramble across the street into the darkness.

And I'm left stuck in a very tight space with Mom.

22

All kinds of worries swirl around in my head.

I take a deep breath. I try to shove all the worries aside and focus on being centered.

'Mom?' I keep my voice quiet and calm. What I really want to do is crawl under the seat to get out of her way when she goes nuclear. But that's not an option.

I hold out a bottle of water. 'Do you want some water?'

She looks at me like I'm mad. 'Stop drinking that!' She snatches it from my hand and stashes it away below the rear window. 'We need to conserve it.'

Her eyes dart around every corner of our jail. Her desperate worry shows in every line of her face, and she is the picture of anxiety. It seems there are more of those lines showing up every day between her eyebrows and around her mouth. The stress is killing her.

She rummages through her pockets. With every smashed egg she finds in her pockets, she gets more frantic. To my relief, someone has taken her cattle prod. I hate to think how much force that took.

'Mom?'

'Shut-up-shut-up-*shut-up!* You let those men take her!' She grips the metal mesh with one hand and the seatback with the other. She squeezes until all the blood runs out of her hands, turning them into white claws.

'You let those monsters do all those horrible things to her! You sold yourself to that devil and couldn't even save your sister?' The ridges between her eyebrows mash together so hard they look nightmarish. 'You couldn't even look her in the eye when she needed you most. You were out there hunting her, weren't you? So you could kill her yourself! Weren't you?' Tears stream down her tortured mask of a face.

'What good are you?' She screams in my face with such intensity that her face turns crimson like it's ready to explode. 'You're heartless! How many times have I told you to keep Paige safe? You're worse than useless!'

She slams her hand against the mesh repeatedly until I think it might bleed.

I try to block it out.

But no matter how many times I hear her raging at me, her words still pierce through.

I curl into my corner, trying to get as far from her as I can. She'll twist anything I say to fit her crazy logic and then throw it back at me.

I brace myself for one of her fury storms. Not something I want to experience in a jail so small that we can't lie down. Not something I want to experience any time, any place.

If it comes down to it, I'm big enough now to beat her in a fight, but she wouldn't stop until I had to hurt her. Best if I can just soothe her.

But I can't think of anything to say to calm her. Paige was always the one who did that. So I do the only thing that comes to mind.

I hum.

It's the song that she hums to us when she's coming out of a particularly bad spell. It's what I think of as her apology song. Sunsets, castles, surf, bruises.

She might ignore me or she might go berserk. It could soothe her or make her angrier than ever to hear me humming her song. If there's one thing you can count on with my mother, it's that she's unpredictable.

Her hand whips up and slaps my face.

She hits so hard I think I'll always carry a palm print on my cheek.

She slaps me again.

The third time, I grab her wrist before she makes contact.

In my training, I've been hit, punched, kicked, shoved, slammed and choked by all kinds of opponents. But nothing hurts as much as a slap from your mom.

I remind myself that it's been several weeks since she's been off her medication, but that does nothing to ease the sting.

I brace myself to subdue her somehow without hurting her, hoping it doesn't escalate too far out of control. But it turns out I don't have to.

Her expression shifts from fury to anguish. Her fingers loosen against the metal mesh. Her shoulders stoop, and she curls into a fetal ball against the door.

She shakes as the tears take over. She cries in big, baby-girl sobs.

Like her husband has abandoned her to the monsters.

Like her daughters have been torn from her by demons.

Like the world has come to an end.

And nobody understands.

If Paige were here, she'd hold Mom and stroke her hair. Paige would comfort her until she fell asleep. She's done that countless times, even after our mother hurt her.

But I am not Paige.

I curl into my own corner, gripping the soft fur of my teddy bear.

23

I dream I'm with Raffe again.

The surroundings look familiar. We're in the guest cottage that Raffe and I slept in the night we left the office. It's the night I learned his name, the night he went from prisoner to partner, and the night he held me in his arms as I shivered in a nightmare.

The tat-tat of the rain against the windows fills the cabin.

I look down at my then-self who is asleep on the couch under a thin blanket.

Raffe lies on the other sofa, watching me. His muscular body stretches languidly across the cushions. His dark blue eyes swirl with thoughts I can't hear. It's as if the sword became self-conscious after telling me so much about Raffe, and now it's keeping his thoughts hidden. Maybe I pushed too hard when I asked about that kiss.

There's a softness to Raffe's look that I've never seen before. It's not that I see naked longing or tender love or anything like that. And if I did, it would just be in my messed-up fantasies.

Not that I fantasize about him.

It's more the way a tough guy who doesn't like cats might look at a kitten and notice for the first time that it can be kind of cute. Sort of a reluctant, private acknowledgment that maybe cats aren't *all* bad.

The unguarded moment is gone in a heartbeat. Raffe's eyes shift to look toward the hallway. He hears something.

He tenses.

I wait, straining to see.

Two sets of red eyes get larger as they creep closer, silent as death. They peer into the living room from the darkness of the hallway, watching me.

Whoa. Why didn't I know about this?

In a flash, Raffe is up and running, grabbing his sword on his way to the hall.

The hellion shadows leap and bound back toward the bedroom, absolute black against dark gray. They dive through the open door where cold air flows out like a river.

Raffe and the creatures drop into slow-mo as they race for the broken window beside the bed. The rain sheets in through the gaping shards as the curtains dance in the wind in slow motion.

I know I'm supposed to copy Raffe's movements as he attacks but I'm too busy watching what's happening. The creatures are running, not attacking.

Were they spying on him? Are they going back for reinforcements?

The hellions would have made it out the window if the first hadn't shoved the second out of the way into the curtains, causing the second to grab the first in its panic.

As they jockey for position, Raffe slices through the one jumping out the window, cutting it almost in half. Then he cuts the second one, slicing its throat.

Raffe looks out the window, making sure these two are the only hellions.

He staggers onto the bed and winces in pain, bending over to catch his breath. The bandages on his back bloom with dark blood stains where his wings used to be.

He had only just awakened from his healing sleep a few hours before and this has been his third fight since then. Once with me, once with the street gang that broke into our office building, and now with these creepy things. I can't imagine how difficult this must be for him. It's one thing to be cut off from your pack and surrounded by enemies, but to be gravely injured on top of that must be the loneliest feeling in the world.

He wipes his blade on the bedding, lovingly polishing it with the sheet. The creatures finally end their death throes as he leaves.

Amazingly, I'm still asleep back in the living room. Of course, I haven't had a decent night's sleep in days and I was practically unconscious from exhaustion. My body is shivering on the couch. The cold seeped in while the bedroom door was open.

Raffe pauses and leans against the sofa, catching his breath.

I whimper in my sleep, trembling below him.

What's he thinking?

That if any of the hellions are watching, it won't make a difference whether we lie on different couches or the same one? Or that I'm already doomed because I've been in his company for too long?

I whimper again, pulling my knees to my chest under the thin blanket.

He leans over and whispers, 'Hush. Shhh.'

Maybe he just needs to feel the warmth of another living being after going through such a traumatic amputation. Maybe he's too exhausted to care if I'm a Daughter of Man, as weird and barbaric as the Watchers' wives.

Whatever the reason, he reluctantly pulls the cushions from the back of my couch. He pauses, looking like he's about to change his mind.

Then he slides in behind me.

At first, his hold is stiff and uncomfortable. But as he begins to relax, the tension in his face eases.

He strokes my hair and whispers, 'Shhh.'

Whatever comfort he's giving me, I'm giving at least that much back just by being a warm body for him to hold at a time when he needs it most.

I snuggle closer to him in my sleep and my whimpering subsides to a contented sigh. It almost hurts to see Raffe closing his eyes and holding me the way a kid might hold a stuffed animal for comfort.

I reach out my phantom hand to stroke his face. But of course, I can't feel him. I can only feel what the sword remembers.

I run my hand along the lines of his neck and the muscles of his shoulder, anyway.

Imagining the smooth warmth of him.

Remembering the feeling of being held in his arms.

24

It's dark when I wake. I float back into reality, still mired in my dream.

I stroke the soft fur of the teddy bear. My dream had more comfort in it than a fighting lesson has any right to have. It's as if the sword picked a soothing memory on purpose and I'm grateful.

It takes a minute before I remember why I'm sleeping in the back seat of a car.

Right. We're prisoners in a police cruiser.

Then the rest of it floods back and I'm wishing I could return to my dream.

Outside, hulks of cars dot the roadway and moon shadows of branches shift back and forth in the wind. Like many places, the streets turn surreal and creepy at night.

Something moves outside the window.

Before I can identify the shadow, it taps on the window.

I yelp.

Silently, my mother clutches my arm, urgently dragging me down into the footwell with her.

'It's me: Clara,' whispers the shadow.

A key turns and the driver's door opens. Luckily, someone has turned the car's overhead light off so we're not a beacon.

Her too-thin form slips into the driver's seat.

'You're the dead woman,' says my mother. 'All shriveled up and looking like you crawled out of the grave.'

'She's not dead, Mom.' I climb up from the footwell and sit on the seat.

'I sometimes wish I were,' says Clara. She turns on the engine, which sounds startlingly loud.

'What are you doing?' I ask.

'Getting you out of here. Away from these horrible people.' The car moves into a wide S-curve to avoid other cars.

'Turn off the headlights,' I say. 'They'll attract too much attention.'

'It's the daytime lights. They can't be turned off.'

As she swerves around the obstacles, our lights hit

Mom's stack of bodies. Apparently, no one wanted to touch them despite Obi's orders.

The gruesome-looking body sitting on top of the stack sluggishly tries to raise his hand to shield against the light.

'The dead are being resurrected,' says my mother. She sounds excited, like she always knew this would happen.

'He wasn't dead, Mom.'

'You were the first to be resurrected,' says Mom. 'The first of the dead.'

'I wasn't dead either,' I say.

'I hope he finds his family and they accept him back,' says Clara. Her tone makes it clear she doubts it.

I try not to think about the rest of the victims.

Ironically, my mother may have saved the only scorpion victims who will survive this night.

Once we put some distance between ourselves and the Resistance headquarters, Clara stops the car so I can sit shotgun. Since my mother doesn't want to be in the back-seat jail any more either, we all cram into the front seat with me in the middle.

'Thank you, Clara,' I say. 'How did you get the key?'

'Dumb luck,' she says. 'Those twins with the funny names dropped it just a few feet away from me.'

'They . . . dropped it?' Those guys are the most skilled sleight-of-hand tricksters I've ever seen. Hard to imagine either of them dropping anything.

'Yeah, they were juggling a bunch of things between them as they walked. The key just fell and they didn't notice.'

'But you did.'

'Sure.'

'How did you know it was the key to our police car?'

She lifts the key tag to show me. It's a clear plastic holder that's probably meant for pictures. This one frames a piece of paper with a note scrawled in little-kid block letters: 'Penryn's police car – Super Secret.'

If I ever see the twins again, it looks like I owe them a zombie-girl mud fight.

'I hope they don't get in trouble,' says Clara. 'They seem like good guys.'

'I'd be surprised if anyone knew they ever had the key. Don't worry, they won't get in trouble.' But I'm guessing one of their archenemies might.

Mom whispers urgently beside me into a cell phone, having a conversation with someone who isn't there.

'So where should we go?' asks Clara.

That darkens my mood. Such a simple question. I can't even begin to think through this. Both Mom and

Clara are older than I am, but somehow they assume *I'll*
figure it out.

Paige is gone. And that dead body she was standing
over . . .

I shut my eyes to try to blot out the image, which only
makes it worse. The blood on her face wasn't hers, I'm
sure of it. Either she will hunt people or people will hunt
her. Maybe both.

I can't bear the thought of either. If they catch her,
they'll treat her the way the Resistance people did – tie
her up like an animal or kill her. If she catches them . . .

Don't think about it.

But I have to think about it, don't I? I can't leave her
out there alone, desperate, and scared.

The Resistance will probably be looking for her in the
morning. If we can find her first, maybe we can somehow
figure out a way to deal with her problems. But how do
we find her?

I take a deep breath and let it out slowly. 'Let's go a
few towns away from the Resistance, then hide out until
we can figure out what to do.'

'Good idea,' says Clara, who is looking at the sky as
much as the road.

'No,' says Mom pointing ahead with one hand and
holding the cell phone in the other. 'Keep going. Paige
went this way.' She sounds sure of herself.

There's something odd about her cell phone. It's bigger and clunkier than normal. It looks vaguely familiar.

'Is that a phone?' I reach for it.

'No!' Mom snatches it away and cradles her body protectively around it. 'It's not for you, Penryn. Not now, not ever.'

My mother has a different relationship with inanimate objects than most of us do. Sometimes, a light switch is just a light switch. Until it isn't.

Out of nowhere, after years of using the same switch to turn on the light, she became convinced that she needed to flip it back and forth to save the city of Chicago. After that, it was just another light switch. Until the day when she needed to flip it back and forth to save New York City.

'What is it?' I ask.

'It's the devil.'

'The devil is a small black box?' It doesn't matter, of course. It never does. But for some reason, I want her to tell me about it. Maybe it will jog my memory about what it is and where I've seen it before.

'The devil talks to me through the small black box.'

'Oh.' I nod, trying to think of something else to say. 'How about we throw it away then?' If only it could be that simple.

'Then how are we going to find your sister?'

The conversation is bound to go in big circles. I'm wasting time.

My mother shifts and I get a glimpse of the phone's screen. It's a map of the Bay Area with yellow arrows pointing to two spots.

I know that display. I remember it from something my dad brought home once. 'That's Dad's prototype.'

Mom shoves it behind her back as if worried that I'll take it.

'I can't believe you stole this and let him get fired for it.' No wonder he left us.

'He didn't like that job anyway.'

'He loved that job. He was totally broken up over losing it. Don't you remember him looking everywhere for this thing?'

'His company didn't need it as much as I did. The devil wanted me to have it. It wasn't theirs to keep.'

'Mom . . .' What's the point?

If he hadn't gotten fired for losing the prototype, he would have gotten fired for something else Mom did anyway. It's hard to be an engineer when your wife calls you every two minutes. And if he didn't answer the call, she called the receptionist or his boss or random coworkers to find out if he was okay. And if nobody answered, then he might get a surprise visit from the police, wanting to talk to him about how his wife freaked out in public, screaming and yelling that *they* had gotten to her husband.

'What is that?' asks Clara.

'A prototype device for tracking pets,' I say. 'It uses a tiny tracker. Waterproof and impact resistant. My dad showed it to us once. Apparently, my mom liked it a lot.'

'He was an engineer?'

'He was,' I say. I don't tell her that by the time he finally left us, he was working night shifts at 7-Eleven, our nearest convenience store, where Mom could sit in the corner while he worked the cash register.

'My husband Brad was an engineer, too,' she says wistfully, almost to herself.

On my mom's device, the arrow blinks and follows a path. Its target is on the move.

'What are we tracking?' I ask.

'Paige,' says Mom.

'How do you know this is Paige?' I ask, pretty sure this is another fantasy. It's one thing to have Dad's tracking device. It's another to actually be tracking Paige, considering she needs to have the transmitter on her.

'The devil tells me.' She lowers her head, looking troubled. 'If I promise him certain things,' she mumbles.

'Okay.' I rub my forehead, trying to be patient. There's a certain art to getting information out of my mom. You need one foot in reality and one foot in her world to get a better picture of what she's talking about. 'How does the devil know where Paige is?'

She looks up at me as if I'd asked the dumbest question in the world.

'The transmitter, of course.'

25

Sometimes, even I make the mistake of underestimating my mother. It's easy to assume that she's not smart and cunning just because she believes in illogical things and makes poor decisions. But her condition has nothing to do with her intelligence. I forget that sometimes.

'Is the transmitter on Paige?' I hold my breath, not daring to breathe.

'Yes.'

'Where? How?' If Mom had put the transmitter in a bag or something, thinking that Paige would have it on her, then we might be following a Resistance trash truck instead of Paige.

'There.' Mom points to my shoe.

I look down and at first I don't see anything. Then I realize that she's not pointing at the shoe. She's pointing at the yellow starburst sewn on the bottom of my jeans. I'm so used to these starbursts that I don't even see them any more.

I reach down to take a good look at the star for the first time. A hard corner beneath the yellow threads pokes into my thumb. It's tiny and unnoticeable, or at least I've never noticed it.

'This is you,' she says, with her finger on the lower arrow in Redwood City.

'This is Paige.' She moves her finger to the upper arrow in San Francisco.

Could she have gone so far in such a short time?

I take a deep breath. Who knows what she's capable of doing now?

I remember Dad showing us a tiny flake of a chip perched on the tip of his finger. He had handfuls of them in the container with the receiver. The chip was covered in plastic coating that made it dirt-free and waterproof, so the dogs could roll in the mud and be sprayed off without affecting the transmitter.

This is how Mom showed up so regularly when Raffe and I were on the road. This is how she ended up at the aerie.

'Mom, you're a genius.'

My mother looks surprised. Then she beams a delighted smile. I haven't seen her this happy since I don't know when. Her face radiates joy like a little girl who just found out she did something right for the first time in her life.

I nod. 'Good job, Mom.' Kind of a disturbing eye-opener to realize that your own parent needs encouragement from you.

We ditch the noisy police car for a quiet electric vehicle that has the keys in the ignition.

I rummage through the police cruiser's glove compartment and trunk for anything useful to transfer into the new car. I score binoculars and a grab-and-go bag full of emergency supplies. If there's one thing Obi's men are good at, it's survival on the run. I suspect all the Resistance vehicles have these.

Clara takes me aside on our way into the new car. 'Don't get your hopes up,' she whispers.

'Don't worry. I know my chances of finding Paige are slim.'

'I don't mean that. I mean about your mom.'

'Believe me, I have no hopes about her.'

'But you do. I can see it. There's a saying, "Just because you're paranoid doesn't mean they're not out to get you." Well, the reverse is true too. Just because someone's out to get you doesn't mean you're not paranoid.'

'I don't understand.'

'The world going crazy doesn't mean your mother isn't still crazy, too.'

I pull back from her. I wasn't thinking that.

Not really.

But did she have to steal that possibility away from me?

'I used to be a nurse. I know how hard this kind of condition can be for a family. It can help to talk about it. I just don't want you to get hurt, thinking your mom might be—'

I kick in the headlights and running lights on the new car to keep it from being a beacon. I smash them so hard the bulbs are practically pulverized.

We don't need those lights. There's enough moonlight to see the hulks of cars on the road even if we can't see much detail.

I slide into the passenger seat.

'Sorry,' says Clara as she slips into the driver's seat.

I nod.

And that's the end of that ugly topic.

She turns on the engine and we head north again slowly toward San Francisco.

'Why are you here, Clara? My mom and I aren't exactly the best traveling mates.'

She drives in silence for a while. 'I may have lost faith in humanity. Maybe they're right to exterminate us.'

'What does that have to do with you traveling with us?'

'You're a hero. I'm hoping you'll restore my faith and show me that we're worth saving.'

'I am so not a hero.'

'You saved my life back at the aerie. By definition, you're my hero.'

'I left you in a basement to die.'

'You broke me out of the grasp of a living horror when I thought all hope was gone. You gave me the opportunity to crawl back to life when no one else could.'

She glances over at me, her eyes shining in the dark. 'You're a hero, Penryn, whether you like it or not.'

26

My mother mutters nonstop at the receiver. Her voice turns into a cadence, and it creeps me out that it's the same cadence as when she prays. Because this time, she's addressing the devil.

It's slow going weaving through dead cars in the dark but we manage. We follow the same route that Raffe and I had when we drove into the city. Only this time, there's no one on the road. No refugees, no twelve-year-olds driving cars, no tent cities. Just mile after mile of empty streets, newspapers tumbling along the sidewalks, and abandoned cell phones crunching under our tires.

Where are the people? Are they hiding out behind the dark windows of the buildings? Even after the aerie attack, I can't imagine that everyone left the city.

I find myself stroking the soft fur of the stuffed bear. There's something especially eerie about the deserted city streets and something especially reassuring about having a kick-ass sword hanging around my shoulders, even if it is disguised as a stuffed toy.

In a couple of hours, we find ourselves working our way toward the piers.

We crest a hill in the dead of night. San Francisco should be a city bustling with sparkling lights, motion, and noise. I used to look forward to and dread coming here at the same time because of all the sensory overload. I almost always got lost wandering around the windy streets the few times I visited with friends or my dad.

Now, it's a wasteland.

The waning moon drips some light onto overturned trash cans and scurrying rats, but the city is so sooty from the raging fires during the Great Attack that it absorbs more light than seems possible. The once-beautiful city has become a nightmare landscape.

Mom surveys the land with a jaded eye. It's as if she always knew it would be like this. As if she had seen things like this her whole life.

But even she takes in a breath at the sight of Alcatraz Island.

Alcatraz is notorious for being the jail that held the most infamous criminals. It sits in the bay, glowing dimly under the moonlight reflecting off the water.

It must have its own generator that someone has fired up. The Alcatraz lights aren't pinpoints of welcoming sparkles. Instead, there's a dull, heavy glow that permeates the island, just enough for it to be visible in the dark bay.

And just bright enough for us to see the swarm of unnaturally shaped creatures swirling in the air above it.

Mom glances at the blinking on her receiver. She points to Alcatraz.

'There,' she says. 'Paige is there.'

Great. How did she get all the way over here in such a short time? Can she really run that fast, or did someone drive or fly her there?

I take a deep breath and let it out slowly.

At least the angels didn't have the sense of humor to take over the neighboring Angel Island instead. That's something Raffe probably would have done if he had been in charge.

Clara parks our car at a random angle on the street, trying to blend in. I grab the binoculars as we get out. We're on Pier 39 near Fisherman's Wharf. In the World Before, it was a major tourist attraction crammed full of T-shirt shops, candy stores and open fish markets.

'My girls used to love this place,' says Clara. 'Every Sunday we'd come here for lunch. The girls thought it was such a treat to eat clam chowder in a bread bowl and watch the sea lions. This place was like happiness in a bottle for them.' She gazes out with a bittersweet look in her eyes.

The sea lions are still here, at least. I can hear them barking somewhere near the water. They're the only things familiar, though.

The docks are skewed and broken like toothpick structures. Many of the buildings have collapsed into piles of driftwood. It looks like the fires didn't reach this area but the angry water sure did.

The fierce surf from the worldwide tsunamis was dampened before reaching into the bay, but that didn't stop the damage. It only kept this part of the city from being swamped and utterly destroyed.

There's a ship lying on its side on the street. Another one sticks out from the roof of a demolished building.

Splinters the size of redwood trees are everywhere. Too bad angels aren't killed like vampires. We could lure them here and have a field day.

There's a surprisingly intact cruise liner docked in the water. I want to run over, take it across to the island, and yell out for Paige. Instead, I huddle behind a pile of broken crates where I can see but not be seen.

I peer through the binoculars at Alcatraz.

The things swirling in the night sky above the island are too dark to see in detail, but I can make out their silhouettes against the moonlit sky.

The shapes of men.

Wings.

Fat scorpion tails.

27

What at first looked like a chaotic swarm turns out to be an ordered flight pattern.

Sort of.

Most of the scorpions follow an angel as he rises, then banks, then dives. The scorpions follow him around like baby birds. Most of them, anyway.

Some lag so far behind that they almost get in the angel's way as he goes through his flight routine. And it is a routine. He repeats his flight pattern to stay near the island. He varies it here and there but it's mostly a predictable pattern.

If I didn't know better, I'd say he's teaching them to fly.

Baby birds are taught to fly and baby dolphins are taught to breathe air. Maybe baby monsters need to be taught how to be monster-like. Usually, babies are taught by their mothers, but these things don't have mothers.

The angel is doing a poor job of teaching, though. Several of the scorpions are struggling. Even I can see that a few of them are flapping their wings too fast. They're not hummingbirds and they're likely to tire out or give themselves a heart attack, assuming they have a heart.

One of them falls right into the water. It flounders there, screeching.

Another scorpion swings down too low to the fallen one. I can't tell which scorpion grabs which – whether the one in the air tries to help its buddy or the one in the water grabs the one in the air – but either way, the second one splashes into the water, too.

They thrash and try to climb on top of each other. Each fights for a few more seconds of air by trying to be the one standing on the other. But the winner only gets enough air for one final screech before they both sink.

The first time I saw these things in the aerie basement, they were suspended in tubes of liquid. But I guess they must have had some sort of umbilical cord, or they changed when they were 'born', because now they're clearly drowning.

Footsteps make me spin and crouch lower. Mom and Clara hunker down beside me behind a broken crate.

There are so many shadows along the pier's old shopping area that an army could be marching toward us and I wouldn't see them. We huddle deeper into the darkness.

More footsteps. Running now.

People dart in and out of the shadows and dash into the open where the moonlight exposes them. A small stampede of people desperately running from something.

A couple of them glance behind them with a look of terror as they run.

Aside from their pounding feet on the buckled wooden planks, they don't make any other noise. No screaming, no calling out to each other.

Even when a woman falls, obviously twisting an ankle, she makes no noise other than the soft thud of her impact. Her face contorts in pain and terror but no sound comes out of her mouth. She gets up and hobbles as fast as she can in a hop-run, frantically trying to keep up with the rest of the stampede.

Their panic echoes in my chest. I have the urge to run even though I have no idea what they're running from.

Just as my leg twitches from indecision, the things chasing the crowd come around the corner.

There are three of them. Two scorpions hover low to the ground, buzzing on their insect wings. In the center limps an angel who looks like he's been on steroids.

The huge angel has snowy wings.

Raffe's wings.

Beliel.

28

Even in this dangerous situation, my heart twists at seeing Raffe's beautiful wings on the demon Beliel.

The last time I saw Beliel, he was limping with an injured wing. Someone must have sewn the wing back into place on him after Raffe ripped the stitches. Must be nice to have evil doctors on hand. Beliel's limp is noticeable but not nearly as bad as it was when Raffe chased him at the airport.

He also has fresh bandages wrapped around his stomach where Raffe sliced him with his sword the first time I met him. It's good to see more evidence that angel sword wounds don't speed-heal like other wounds, just like Raffe said.

The scorpions fly leisurely, swinging back and forth, dipping low enough to look into the windows. One smashes a window – probably the last intact window on the pier.

The shattering noise is immediately followed by a panicked shriek. A family with kids darts out of the shop's door and joins the group running from the monsters.

There's something about the way the scorpions are moving that raises red flags in my head. They're not chasing to catch.

They're flushing out prey.

Before my mind can form the word 'trap', lights blaze on and a fishing net drops from the sky.

That's when the screams start.

One, two, five fishing nets, as big as house tents, fall from the dark sky.

Darker shadows dive down from above. They land on all fours, scuttling along the ground like real scorpions before standing up on human-shaped legs.

Two of them actually slam into the broken dock face-first, as if they haven't quite got the hang of landing yet. One of them shrieks its fury at the trapped people, showing a mouth full of lion's teeth. It viciously yanks the edge of the net, making it whip into people's ankles.

There are dozens of humans trapped under the nets, clawing and squirming, trying to find the edge of their snare so they can escape. A few jabs of the scorpion stingers cause people to crowd together in the middle of their traps. They cry and scream, all their previous silence gone.

Gunshots ring out from one of the trapped groups. A nearby scorpion goes down, screeching.

As if a dinner bell rang, a bunch of scorpions dive onto the netted group where the shot came from. Stingers lash up and down, repeatedly stinging until blood drips from the tips. Their monster heads latch onto the victims to suck on them.

The screams and thrashing quiet after a minute, leaving only a pile of shriveled bodies twitching beneath a shroud of mesh.

I don't know if anyone else has a gun, but after that, no one dares to shoot.

A boy of about eight was separated from his father. They reach for each other under different nets. The kid is crying for his dad but it's the father who looks ashen and utterly terrified at being separated.

The scorpions corral them, half-dragging their nets, half-keeping them moving by threatening with their stingers.

We crouch down farther into the shadows, hardly daring to breathe.

The monsters march the captives to a metal shipping container – the kind that trucks, trains and ships carry.

It's not far from us but with all the debris strewn around, I hadn't even noticed it.

They open the container door. A metal-lattice rollup gate is behind that.

And behind the gate, people cluster together as far from the entrance as they can get.

Half the container is already crammed full of men, women and even a few children. They're terrified and huddling together like the helpless victims that they are.

The scorpions roll up the metal gate, lifting up the nets. The new captives scurry away from the monsters and into the container.

29

The scorpions do a surprising thing. They take off into the night sky, leaving Beliel alone to roll down the prisoner's chain gate and lock it.

He takes his time doing this as if to tease the captives. When he's done, he hangs the key on one of the lamps beside the container.

The mesh of the rollup gate is woven loosely enough to put an arm or foot through an opening, but even a kid couldn't get out.

The old prisoners are quiet but the new ones make a fair bit of noise with their crying and panicked questions.

'What's going on?'

'What are they going to do to us?'

Beliel limps around shutting off the tripod utility lights on the dock. His knee seems to be bothering him more than before. He leaves the lights on only near the shipping container. The circle of light is bright there and I'm glad we're still hidden in the shadows.

As if the fear and hysteria of the prisoners weren't enough for him, Beliel rattles the container gate, then slams his open palm on the metal side. The loud clang echoes through the pier.

Everyone cringes and the crying gets louder. The terror and hopelessness come in such big waves that they swamp me.

Beliel shoves his face into the chains of the gate. Everyone backs away even more. He hisses and growls at them. Then he grabs the edge of the container and shakes it.

Now, even the veteran prisoners are screaming.

What's he doing?

I've seen him in a rage when he's been totally out of control. This is different. There's no passion in what he's doing. It's just a job.

He's on edge, though, and sneaking glances up at the sky.

Is he being watched? Maybe this is more training for the scorpions? Maybe they're still around, watching somewhere? For what purpose?

I look up into the darkness and the remaining roof-lines, suddenly feeling exposed.

I see only the beams of light near the container prison. The lights are a beacon from the bleak landscape of twisted buildings and the lifeless night.

I still can't make sense of it.

Then, a darker silhouette appears against the sky.

Menacing demon wings.

Broad shoulders.

The shape of a Greek god gliding through the sky.

Raffe.

Every nerve in my body comes alive and pulses.

My mind cries trap, trap, trap!

This is why Beliel is alone, making all this noise. The noise would both attract attention and disguise any noises that the scorpions would make. The scorpions are out there. Hiding. Waiting.

Without thinking, I instinctively spring and open my mouth to scream a warning to Raffe.

But vice-like hands grip my arm, knocking me off balance. Hands clamp down over my mouth and all I can see are the huge, terrified eyes of my mother. She looks at me like I have gone insane.

My brain finally catches up to the rest of me.

She's right.

Of course she's right. How bad are things when

your clinically insane mother is more rational than you are?

Raffe.

I nod to show that I'm sane again and shift so I can see what's going on. Mom lets me go.

Raffe lands silently. His wings don't fold all the way. The scythes on the edge of his wings unsheathe and he whips them out. They're retractable. I hadn't realized that before.

I frantically run through my options. What can I do? Yelling will get all of us in trouble. Besides, Raffe thinks I'm dead. Yelling to him might only put him in more danger by shocking him.

The prisoners scream when they see Raffe with his demon wings. It's painful to see that people prefer a bad guy who looks like an angel to a good guy who looks like a demon.

Beliel feigns stage shock like a clown. 'Why, it's Raphael! Oh, how will I defend myself from the great Wrath that is the fallen echo of what once was?' He drops the act. 'Seriously, Raphael, there's nothing sadder than a broken wreck of a has-been obsessed with trying to relive his past glory. Have a little dignity, will you? You're embarrassing yourself.'

'Shall I rip off your arms and legs first and then tear off the wings? Or the other way around?' Raffe's voice is full of raw violence in a tone I haven't heard before. He sounds like he wishes he could have it both ways.

'Why do you want to go back so badly, Raphael? What was so great about being part of the angelic host anyway? So. Many. Rules. I'd forgotten just how many. Maybe you have, too.'

Beliel is stalling. Keeping Raffe in place until the scorpions can descend on him. I'm dying to call out a warning to him. It's all I can do to stay quiet.

'All this theory about how a master warrior race can only survive if every little infraction of the rules is punished in the extreme.' Beliel motions his hand in a gesture that says, *Whatever*. 'It might have made sense once upon a time when there were only a few rules, but now, things have gotten out of hand, don't you think? We, the Fallen, on the other hand, have proven that a master warrior race can survive just fine with the opposite system. No rules. You do what you want. To whoever you want.'

Raffe advances on him, the harsh lights emphasizing the shadows on his face. He looks like the Angel of Death. Or maybe the Angel of Vengeance. Someone I can't imagine approaching.

'You would have saved yourself so much hassle if you had listened to reason and joined us,' says Beliel. 'That little Daughter of Man who died in your arms? She could have been yours. No one would have said no. No one would have dared to try to take her from you.'

With a vicious growl, Raffe attacks.

30

He leaps for Beliel and slaps his wings into him, clearly meaning to slash through him.

Beliel spins out of the way, partly avoiding the hit. He tosses a work lamp in Raffe's direction.

The light crashes onto the pier. It flashes with a loose connection, lighting the fighters in a random strobe light.

Blood drips down Beliel's sneering face and arms. 'Admit it. You like the new wings. Why bother with fluffy and feathery when you can have freedom and power?'

'I could ask the same of you, Beliel.' Raffe stalks menacingly toward Beliel.

'I've had my life of freedom and rampaging. It's time for a change. A little respectability. A little well-deserved admiration, don't you think?' They circle each other like sharks getting ready to attack. Beliel's limp is gone now that he's lured Raffe.

'Respectability and admiration are beyond you,' says Raffe. 'You're nothing but a pathetic minion for angels.'

'I am not a minion!' His face turns red and furious. 'I have never been a minion. Not for devils, not for angels, not for anybody!' The randomly flashing light highlights the stark shadows of his blood-streaked face.

Raffe leaps for Beliel again. But his motion is interrupted by a net falling on him from the night sky.

Raffe rolls on the pier, tangled in the net.

Get up, get up!

All the fight rages inside me. Can I watch as Raffe gets executed? Every fiber of my being chants, No, no, no.

What can I do? What can I do?

Raffe isn't struggling against the net like I expected. Instead, he whisks open his wings. The scythe-like hooks on his wings snag the net.

Then his wings slice up, cutting the mesh.

It falls around him like a dropped veil as he leaps up, ready for a fight.

Scorpions drop out of the sky, a couple of them landing on Raffe. He ducks but their glancing blows shove him off balance.

Raffe's wings, arms and legs whip around him. Three scorpions go down, writhing in pain. That still leaves half a dozen more plus Beliel. As if that isn't enough, three more land on the outskirts of the fight.

I pluck off my bear and pull out my sword, ready to dive in.

Mom grabs my shirt and yanks me so hard that I land on my butt like a little kid.

Luckily, Raffe seems to be able to hold his own. I doubt that he's made peace with his new wings but he's at least learned to control them better than the last time I saw him.

He's also a fearless fighter. I hadn't quite realized just how fierce he could be, but now that I think about it, this may be the first time I've seen him fight when it wasn't immediately after a major injury. The sword's memories only had him fighting with a sword, which was something to see, but this is more of a ferocious dance.

I'm sure Raffe hasn't fully recovered yet, but he's a wonder to watch. He's fast. Faster than the scorpions that keep trying to sting him. A single scorpion is no more a match for him than a fire ant is to a person.

He's far outnumbered, though. Yet, he doesn't seem that concerned as he slowly slashes his way closer to Beliel.

Beliel gets the picture and takes off into the night sky. Apparently, his evil health plan covers wing injuries because his wings seem to work just fine.

Raffe takes off after him.

I watch him get farther from me. He never even knew I was near.

He disappears into the darkness like a fading dream.

I stare at the sky where he vanished for longer than I probably should.

31

The scorpions hesitate before the first ones leave the ground. I assume they're flying after Raffe, but I'm not entirely sure. There's a certain reluctance to the way they take off. Almost half of them stay on the ground, looking at each other, unsure.

These have to be the worst minions ever. Whatever was bred into them, courage wasn't on the list. No wonder Beliel had to fight off Raffe for so long before the scorpions arrived.

Eventually, all the ones who can take off, do. Half a dozen are left bleeding and dead on the splintered dock, while a few writhe and hiss in pain beside them. They don't look like they're capable of much harm any more, but I keep a close eye on them, just in case.

Mom lets out a deep sigh beside me. Clara, though, still seems to be frozen in fear. She's probably going through some post-traumatic stress issues right now after seeing so many scorpions.

It's time for us to get out of here. Somewhere safe for the night where we can cook up some crazy scheme to rescue Paige. But even I can't stir up much enthusiasm for nutty schemes right now.

I am just a girl. I am no match for these monsters. They may have looked weak compared to Raffe, and I may have felt like an equal in some ways during my journey with him, but after seeing what I just saw, reality sinks in.

It would be suicide to sneak onto Alcatraz Island. It's crawling with these monsters and there's no way of getting back out.

Despite my erratic behavior, both Mom and Clara still depend on me to decide the timing of our exit out of here. We're in the shadows and should have a decent shot of making it out unnoticed.

I listen for enemies and monsters. All I hear are the terrified sobs of the people locked in the container. The sounds are muffled now, probably to avoid attention, but the captives can't seem to stop themselves.

The container lights up with the intermittent flashes of the work lamp lying on the ground. Behind the rollup gate, the prisoners crowd together, giving me an impression of despair and grime every time the light flashes.

I get ready to sprint from the pile of crates we're hiding behind. But I can't seem to leave. My eyes keep drifting over to the people locked in the container.

In theory, it would be a no-brainer to run over and let them out. It would only take a couple of minutes to free a bunch of people from whatever horrors await them.

If I had the key.

Beliel hung it on one of the lamps but now, I'm not sure which of the two lamps he used. If it was on the one he threw at Raffe, it could take an hour to find it.

I close my eyes, trying to shut out the sights and sounds of the prisoners. I need to concentrate on Paige and Mom. I can't just be distracted by everybody who needs help, because we all need help now. Desperately.

I glance at Mom and see the terror on her face. She's moving her lips silently and rocking back and forth. These are real monsters straight out of her nightmares. Clara is looking even worse, if that's possible.

I need to get up and get us out of here. I need to take care of my own people.

A heartbroken, terrified sob reaches across the pier and grabs me.

I try to ignore it.

But I can't.

That could have been Paige before those angel monsters got to her. It's almost certainly someone else's sister, daughter or mom. And wouldn't it have been a wonder if someone out there could have helped Paige the way I could help these people?

Ugh. Why can't I shut down that stupid thought?

Yeah, all right already.

I get up from my crouch. Worry and fear intensify in my mother's face when she sees me eyeing the path to the prisoners. I don't have to worry about her following me. Sometimes, being paranoid really does save your life.

There's certainly no chance Clara will follow me. She has excellent reasons to be petrified of the scorpions. But along with the fear, there's something in her eyes I didn't expect.

Pride.

She expects me to rescue them. She still thinks I'm a stupid hero. A part of her would be disappointed if I just walk away.

That almost makes me abandon the whole idea.

But, of course, I don't.

I dash out from the relative safety of the darker shadows.

32

The injured scorpions notice me right away. My heart practically stops when they turn and hiss at me.

I can almost feel the excruciating pain of the sting, the panic of losing control of my body while still conscious. The thought of having to go through that again makes me run so hard I think I might pass out.

In my freaked-out state, I don't pay enough attention to my footing and I slip on blood.

I catch myself from falling by doing an awkward dance of hand and sword balancing.

Focus.

Do not let the scorpions hurt you twice just because you're freaking out over the possibility.

I shove everything – fear, hope, thoughts – into the vault in my head and slam the door shut before they explode back out. It's getting trickier to open that vault door.

The only thing in the world now is my path to the prisoners' container. I rub the sole of my shoe on the ground to wipe off the blood.

For all their hissing and screeching, the injured scorpions stay down. I keep an eye on them to make sure they're not crawling toward me.

Before I walk into the circle of light, I look around to make sure there are no scorpions, angels or winged rats headed my way. It doesn't help that my eyes are already adjusting to the light, making the shadows that much darker.

I dive into the light like I'm jumping into water.

I feel instantly exposed.

Anyone on the pier can see me now. I run as fast as I can to the still-standing light by the metal jail. All the prisoners quiet down as if holding their collective breaths.

The key is not on the standing work light or anywhere near it.

I look back at the flashing lamp that Beliel threw on the pier. The key could have flown off anywhere.

Either I commit to looking for it in this sea of splintered planks, or I give up and make sure Mom and Clara get out of here safely.

Or, I could see if my sword can cut through metal.

It easily cut through bones during my dream training, and it's supposed to be so special. Before I can think about it, I lift the sword and slice down.

The blade easily cuts through the lock and the gate's metal tab.

Whoa.

Not bad.

I lift my sword for the second lock. But before I can cut it, there's a rustling behind me.

I spin with my sword still above me, half-convinced an injured scorpion has crawled over, ready to strike.

But it's not an injured scorpion.

It's a healthy one.

It folds its gossamer wings as if it just landed. It stalks toward me, barefoot on its much too human-like feet. Somehow, I might feel better if they had clawed feet or something else that made them look less human.

Two more scorpion angels land behind the first one.

There's only one more lock. I spin around and chop at it with my blade.

It comes flying off. The chain-link gate hangs open now. All they have to do is roll it up and run.

Instead, the prisoners huddle in the back, frozen in terror.

'Come on!' I slam on the side of the container to shock them into action. 'Run!'

I don't wait to see if they do. I've just put Mom and Clara in danger of a horrifying death. I could kick myself for not convincing them to leave without me.

The gate rattles behind my back.

The freed prisoners begin to run, scattering everywhere, their footsteps pounding on the wooden pier.

I run in the opposite direction of Mom and Clara, hoping to draw the scorpions away from them.

Then I hear my mother.

She screams a bloodcurdling screech of terror.

33

Everyone spreads out, instinctively heading in different directions.

There are only a few monsters and a lot of us. There's a good chance that some of us will get away.

I run toward a mass of shadows where a pink ice cream sign sticks out of a pile of broken planks. If I can get around it, I might be able to disappear into the jagged shadows.

But before I get there, something smacks my head and drapes over me.

I'm tangled in a net.

My first thought is to slice through it with my sword but I'm now surrounded by the people who were running behind me and there isn't enough room. The more we thrash, the more entangled we get.

Shadows fall out of the sky. Shadows with insect wings and curling stingers.

They drop in random places. One on top of the shipping container, making a hollow boom. Several land in front of the old row of shops where half a dozen people were heading before a net came down on them too.

Five, ten, twenty. So many that it starts to sound like we're in a hive.

We're trapped.

Everyone is sobbing again. This time, the despair is so thick I feel like I'm drowning in it.

Even if I could cut through the netting, I couldn't cut my way through all these scorpions. I slide my sword back into its scabbard to make it less noticeable.

The net stinks of fish. At first, I don't think we can walk with it on us, but one of the scorpions grabs the edge of our net and pulls a drawstring. We bunch together as the edge closes around our legs.

The scorpion yanks us along in our net trap like it's pulling a dog on a leash. Its stinger aims for us, hovering just within striking zone. Another scorpion walks beside us, making it clear by the rhythmic jabbing of its stinger that we should do what it wants.

I frantically look for Mom and Clara, hoping against all odds that I won't see them.

But there they are, only two netted groups away from me. My mother clutches my teddy bear to her bosom like it's her long-lost baby, while Clara clutches Mom's arm like she'll die if she lets go. They both look petrified.

I feel sick.

Sick from fear. Sick from anger. Sick from the stupidity of what I've done.

I came here for my sister and instead I've gotten myself recklessly caught. Worse, I've gotten Mom and Clara caught too. And looking at the large number of captives on the pier, I didn't even free anyone either.

Several groups of netted humans converge as we're herded toward the water. At first, I assume the scorpions are taking us to a new shipping container, but instead of a holding cell, they move us toward a boat.

'Brian!' A young woman under my net reaches her hand out to a guy trapped under another as our two groups get closer.

'Lisa!' the guy calls to her with desperation. They strain against the mesh and stretch their arms as far as they'll go to try to touch each other.

For a second, they manage to brush fingertips.

Then our group moves past theirs, breaking their touch. The woman starts sobbing, her hand still reaching for him.

Another group gets shoved in front of Brian and he disappears into the crowd, still reaching for her.

The boat is two stories high and has seen better days. The paint is so scraped that I'm convinced the boat must have been lying on its side on the roof of a ruined building before the bad guys put it to use. Somehow, it still manages to float. And it still sports the words 'Captain Jake's Alcatraz Tours' in blue, although with all the scratches, it looks more like 'Alcatraz ours'.

The engine starts and we're treated to a dark plume of exhaust. The smell of gas pollutes the air almost immediately. A human minion must be running the boat. I kind of hope it's not Captain Jake.

Everyone gets jostled and shoved toward the boat. Scorpions begin releasing us from the nets. We have no place to run, of course, not if we want to live a few more minutes.

As the first captives begin boarding, I manage to get close enough to Mom and Clara for us to shuffle together. Mom hands me the stuffed bear like she's been keeping it safe for me.

I slip the bear onto my sword, disguising it again. I have wild hopes of being able to take it with me and maybe using my fledgling skills to get us out of this mess.

My hopes are dashed when I see that weapons are being taken from prisoners as they board. There's a growing pile of stuff on the dock by the boat ramp. Axes, spiked bats, tire irons, machetes, knives and even a few guns. I would still have hope if the pile only had weapons but it also includes purses, backpacks, dolls, and yes, even stuffed animals.

There are grim-faced people – humans – taking these things from the prisoners. They don't talk and they don't look anyone in the eye. They just grab whatever is semi-visible on the prisoners and toss the objects onto the pile.

I stroke my bear, wondering if this is my best chance at escape. Even if I couldn't get away, maybe I could cause enough of a distraction so that Mom and Clara could. We're in the brief window of time when I still have my sword and we're no longer trapped in a net so it's now or never.

A gunshot explodes so close that we all duck.

A man who apparently didn't want to give up his gun holds it still pointed at one of the women minions who is now bleeding on the ramp. He is instantly surrounded by scorpions with their stingers. Their fangs are so close to his face that I'm sure he can smell their breath.

He trembles so badly that he actually drops his gun and a spreading wetness stains the front of his pants.

The scorpions don't attack the shooter, though. It's as if they're waiting for something.

'Here, take her knife,' says another human minion. His face is lined with grief, his eyes half-dead and shell-shocked. He grabs a kitchen knife out of a prisoner's hand and gives it to the shooter. 'Now, toss it into that pile.'

The shooter's arm spastically jerks the knife onto the pile. He looks so frightened that he probably never considered stabbing one of the scorpions with it.

The scorpions hiss and back off, moving to patrol the crowd again.

We were all so riveted by the drama that none of us thought to escape while it was happening. So much for causing a distraction to let Mom and Clara get away.

The shooter replaces the minion that he shot as he takes weapons and bags from the other prisoners. He doesn't make eye contact and he doesn't say a word. He does occasionally sneak a glance at the woman he shot who is dying at his feet.

After that, there are no more incidents as everyone gets on the boat.

When one of the minions reaches for my bear-disguised sword, I have to force myself to lift the strap over my shoulder and place it on the pile myself. It takes all my willpower to do it, since a part of me wants to yank it out and chop up a few scorpions. But there must be twenty, maybe thirty of them here.

I slip the scabbard into the bottom of the pile, trying to hide as much of it as possible. Someone will eventually find it. What happens after that is anyone's guess.

Mom and Clara pull me up and along with them. I guess I looked like I didn't want to leave it behind. I glance back at the silly teddy bear partially buried under a pile of weapons and bags and can't help but think that maybe I'll never see Raffe or his sword again.

Behind me, the woman who reached for her lover cries softly.

34

The water slaps onto the boat's side while the deck rolls back and forth. We shuffle onto the ship, and before long, we're gliding through the dark waters.

Alcatraz is legendary for being the most inescapable jail of all time. Just the sight of it in the dim light makes me want to run away. I think about diving into the water with Mom and Clara and taking our chances, but others beat me to it.

A couple runs for it. It's Brian and Lisa, the couple who had been separated by the nets. My heart races with hope that they'll make it. We're not so far off that they can't swim to the other side, freezing or not.

But the scorpions are fast.

So fast that three of them zap their stingers to tag the couple on their way out the doors.

They don't chase them though. They just let the pair make their own choices. It takes time to become paralyzed, but I know the excruciating pain and stiffness starts immediately. By the time the couple reaches the edge of the boat, they're dragging their feet.

It would be suicide to jump. They'll be paralyzed long before they can reach shore.

But the other option is to stay frozen among the scorpions, completely at their mercy.

Tough choice. I really feel for them. I'm not sure which I'd choose.

They choose to stay on board. Brian leans against the rail as if thinking about jumping, but he can't seem to commit. Lisa lays her head down on the deck beside him.

I understand. Anyone who is alive now is a survivor. They've done what it takes to make it this far, and they can't help but keep going. Brian slides down the rail and lies beside Lisa, twitching and losing control of his muscles. The scorpions mostly ignore the couple, seemingly bored as they leap off the boat to fly while others land on deck and walk around.

A scorpion bends over and plucks Brian's glasses off his face. It tries to put them on upside down. When they fall, the scorpion picks them back up and tries again. As if it wasn't already weird-looking enough with a man's body, dragonfly wings, and a scorpion tail. Now, it looks around with one cracked lens on its wire-rimmed glasses.

I feel oddly naked without my sword. I keep reaching for the soft fur of my stuffed bear and remember that it's not there any more. I sit between Mom and Clara, three unarmed women surrounded by monsters.

Just a couple of months ago, tourists sat on this boat with cameras and phones, taking photos, yelling at their kids, kissing in front of the city skyline. They probably roamed around in their newly bought sweatshirts, totally unprepared for the cold summer winds of San Francisco.

Now, there are hardly any children and none of them are running around. There are only a couple of older folks mixed in with the others, and only a quarter of the crowd is women. Everyone looks like they've gone too long without a shower or a good meal, and all our attention is focused on the scorpions.

They leave us alone for now. Most of them are not as beefy and broad-shouldered as I imagined monsters would be. Some of them are outright scrawny. They're not made to muscle their prey. They're designed to use their stingers as their main weapon of choice.

They all have tails that look like they've been on steroids. Fat and muscular, unnaturally bulging and grotesque. If I look closely, I can see a clear drop of venom at the tip of each stinger, as if keeping the pipes in working order.

One of the scorpions wears a pair of pants. But the pants are on backwards and hanging with the zipper open to allow for the tail. There's something about it that bothers me but I can't quite put my finger on it.

As the scorpion pulls up its pants with its all-too-human-looking hand, something glints. My stomach clenches in sick dread as I realize what it is.

It's a wedding band.

What is a wedding band doing on a monster's hand?

It must be just some shiny thing that it got from one of its victims. Like an animal playing with a toy. Or maybe it discovered that rings were good for hitting, like brass knuckles.

Yeah, that must be it.

And it's pure coincidence that it's on the ring finger.

In a few minutes, Alcatraz looms in the dim light. I lean back as if I could make the boat slow down. By the time we land, I'm trembling all over.

My imagination keeps wandering to what might happen to us here. I try to corral it back, but I'm not entirely successful at it.

The island seems to be a giant rock. The water is probably hypothermia-cold, not to mention filled with sharks or thrashing scorpions or toothy demons from hell.

So this is how it all ends.

The world destroyed, humans imprisoned, my family scattered.

The thought makes me angry. I hope the anger burns up all other feelings because it's probably the only thing keeping me on my feet and moving right now.

A lot of the prisoners are cringing and sobbing, not wanting to come out of the boat. People and animals aren't that different. We can all tell when we're being led to slaughter.

The island dock is similar to the one on the mainland – spiky, dark, damp. The cold bay winds blow through my shirt, giving me goose bumps. I'm colder than the temperature calls for. I brace myself to face what's coming.

But nothing can prepare me for what's happening beyond the dock.

35

Spotlights blaze along the buildings, lighting up the walkway as we trudge onto the island. Everywhere I look, I see stone and concrete. Peeling paint and rust stains drip down the walls of the nearest building.

Four scorpions work near a shipping container that has a chain mesh gate like the one on the mainland.

They grab glossy entrails and body parts from buckets and toss them onto the concrete. The gore lands just out of reach of the trapped humans in the metal container.

The stench is unbearable. These people have been trapped in that cage for way longer than I want to know. I can tell not just by their stench but also by the fact that they are stretching their emaciated arms to try to grab the entrails and chopped-up body parts just out of their reach.

These people make sobbing, groaning noises. Nothing aggressive, just desperate. Their arms are too skinny, like they're already dead but don't quite realize it yet.

They can't be meant to be turned into new monsters or even to be fed to them. They're too abused, too under-fed. How hungry would you have to be to reach out for raw, chopped body parts?

'Stupid as dirt in so many ways,' says a familiar voice. 'But they still have the devious, twisted instincts of humans.'

It's Beliel, the demon. His stolen white wings spread out behind him, a heavenly backdrop to his oversized body. He stands behind the scorpions who are tossing the chopped-up gore that's plopping onto the ground.

A heart gets tossed onto a broken board, snagging on a giant splinter.

Beside Beliel stands an angel whose toffee-colored hair and gray feathers are windblown. He wears a light gray suit that quietly conveys taste and elegance.

Even without his trophy girls, I recognize Archangel Uriel, the politician. He's the one who secretly orches-trated Raffe's wing switch to keep him from being a competitive candidate in the upcoming angels' election. As if that wasn't enough to make me despise him, he likes to walk around with matching girls who are terrified of him.

'Are you referring to the locusts or their toys?' Uriel's wings spread out partially behind him like a body halo. In the soft light of the aerie hotel, his feathers looked off-white with a touch of gray, but now in the harsh light of the utility lights, his wings look gray with a touch of midnight.

Locusts?

'The locusts,' says Beliel. 'The humans are stupid as rocks, too. But they're too tortured to use instinctive ingenuity. The locusts thought this game up themselves, you know. I was impressed. As devious as any demon from hell.' He sounds almost proud.

He must mean the scorpion monsters. I always imagined locusts to look like grasshoppers, not scorpions, so I don't know why he calls them that.

'You're sure the ones you trained will teach the others?'

'Who can tell, eh? Their judgment is clouded, their brains have shrunk, they're probably insane from the metamorphosis. Hard to predict what they'll do, but this batch did get extra attention and do seem more capable than the rest. They're as close to a leader group as you'll get.'

A scorpion with a white streak in its hair gets tired of the game and walks up to the container of humans. The forest of skeletal arms withdraws back through the chain mesh. The captives' feet scrape the metal floor as they shuffle away from the monster.

The scorpion stands tall in front of the dim interior. Then he tosses a bit of gore into the cage.

The night is instantly filled with metallic scuffling, animal grunting and half-screams of frustration and desperation.

The people inside are fighting each other for the bloody scraps. For all I know, it could have been one of their own who got dragged out and turned into torture bait.

'See what I mean?' Beliel sounds like a proud papa.

I pick up my pace, wanting to get past the container as soon as possible. But the others move at the same speed, careful not to draw attention to themselves.

My arm is clamped in a viciously tight grip and I'm yanked so hard that my neck feels like it's about to snap. A scorpion with greasy hair dripping down to its shoulders pulls me out of the herd.

The white-streaked one who threw the body parts to the prisoners looks at me, interest lighting its face. It walks over to me.

Up close, its shoulders and thighs are massive. It grabs me out of the first scorpion's grasp and drags me behind it, holding both my wrists in one hand.

It's headed for the torture container with its desperate victims.

Skeletal arms reach through the metal mesh with their unnaturally long fingers.

I can't get enough air into my lungs and what I do manage to breathe in makes me gag. The stench up close is ferocious.

I skid on something lumpy and slippery, but the monster's grip is so tight that I stay upright.

My heart has practically stopped with the realization that I won't be going up to the stone building, but instead, will be joining the tortured victims.

I drag my feet and resist. I struggle, trying to loosen one of the monster's hands. But I'm no match for its strength.

A couple of steps before the opening, the scorpion throws me up against the metal mesh.

I slam into it, grabbing the chains to keep myself upright.

The second I hit, the darker shadows in the back of the box scuffle toward me.

Hunched with sharp angles accentuating arms and legs, rags dragging on the floor, they shove each other out of the way to reach me as fast as they can.

A scream tears from my mouth as I frantically push myself back.

Arms reach out like a forest of bones sprouting through the chain mesh.

They grab my hair, my face, my clothes.

I thrash and scream, trying not to see their skeletal faces, their mangy hair, their bloodied nails.

I twist and yank, desperate to get out of their grasp. There are a lot of them, but they're weak, barely standing on their feet as I pull away.

White Streak makes a series of screechy noises that sound suspiciously like a laugh. It thinks this is funny.

It grabs me and drags me toward the stream of people coming from the ferry.

It never intended to dump me into the torture bin. It just wanted to tease the prisoners and, I guess, me.

I've never looked forward to killing anything before. But I'm certainly looking forward to killing this one.

We walk up the paved path toward the main building, which sits at the top of the island. Above us, swarms of scorpions fly in what looks like massive chaos. There are so many of them, they actually create wind that blows in unnaturally changing directions. I know from what I saw earlier that there's a practice pattern to their flight, but from here, it looks and feels as if we're in the middle of a giant insect's nest.

There's not a regular angel in sight. This can't be their new aerie. From what I've seen, angels prefer the finer things in life, and Alcatraz isn't exactly a high-class resort. This must be some kind of human processing center.

I look around to see how Clara and Mom are doing. Clara is easy to spot with her jerky skin and shriveled body but my mother is nowhere to be found. When Clara sees me searching, she looks around too, seemingly surprised to find that my mom is not beside her.

No one seems to be looking for a missing prisoner. I'm not sure if this is good or bad.

I can't hear a thing beyond the insect buzzing of the scorpion wings, but our guards make it clear where they want us to go. We climb toward the stone building on the giant rock that is Alcatraz, following the path walked by so many prisoners of the past.

The weird wind whipsaws my hair all around my head, reflecting what I feel inside.

36

Once we enter the building, the noise and wind quiet down. Instead, there's a low moan that echoes off the walls. Not just the moan of one person but the collective moans of a building full of people.

I am in hell.

I've heard about the horrid conditions of some foreign prisons, places where human rights are a distant dream seen only on television or read about by university students. What I didn't realize is that the guards, the awful conditions and being trapped are only part of the hell.

The rest of it is in your head. The stuff you imagine about the screams you hear from parts unknown. The image you make up of the face of the woman who cries non-stop a few cells from you. The story you piece together incorporating the gurgling, clanging and the high-pitched sound of what can only be some kind of electric sawing.

We're crammed into old prison cells decorated with rust and streaky paint. Only, they don't hold one or two of us per cell the way they were designed to. It's standing room only.

Good thing the cot takes up space, otherwise, the scorpions probably would have crushed more of us in here. As it is, a few of us can sit on the cot at a time, which lets the injured take a break and will come in handy when we're calm enough to rotate for sleep.

As if this place isn't hellish enough, an alarm goes off at random intervals, echoing through the building and putting us all on edge. Also, every few hours, a group of us gets marched down the hallway, which is even more nerve-wracking.

No one seems to know what happens to those who are taken away, but none of them come back. The guards who escort these groups are a couple of humans with a couple of scorpions as backup. The human guards are stoic and talk as little as possible, which makes them even scarier.

Over these fear cycles, I lose track of time as I doze in and out. I don't know if we've been here for hours or days.

When a door clanks, we know another group is leaving.

As they march past us, I recognize a few of the faces. One is the father who was separated from his son. His eyes search frantically for his boy among those of us left behind bars. When he finds him, tears stream down his face.

The boy is in the cell across from mine. The other prisoners gather around him as he shakes with tears, watching his father march away from him.

One of the men starts to sing 'Amazing Grace' in a beautiful, deep baritone. It's a song whose words many of us don't know, including me, but we all recognize it in our hearts. I hum along with everyone else as the doomed group walks past us.

Cigarettes. Who knew they'd be such a problem at the end of the world?

There are a few smokers in our cell, and one of them passed them around. We're jammed together so no matter how hard the smokers try, they can't help but blow into someone's face. In California, you might as well spit on someone as blow smoke on them.

'Seriously, can you please put that out?' a guy asks. 'Don't you think it's bad enough in here without you polluting the air?'

'Sorry. If there was ever a time when I needed a cigarette, this is it.' The woman squashes out her cigarette against the wall. 'A double latte sounds great too.'

Two other prisoners continue smoking. One of them has tattoos on his shoulders and along his arms. The designs are intricate and colorful and were clearly done in the World Before.

There were gangs here in the Bay Area before the angels came. Not many and they stayed in their small territories, but they were here. They're probably the reason the street gangs grew so fast. They were already organized and established. They were the first to take over the stores and then they started recruiting.

My bet is that this guy was one of the original gang members. He gives off an air of the 'hood that Silicon Valley engineers just can't copy, regardless of what they've done on the streets in the past couple of months.

'What you worried about, vegan boy?' asks Mr. Tattoo. 'Lung cancer?' He leans over to the other guy and fake-coughs in his face, exploding smoke all over him.

Everybody tenses up. People shift out of his way, but they can't get far. We're trapped so closely that if there's a fight, we're all going down. It'd be like being caught in a blender. No matter what you do, you can't help but get sucked in.

As if the tension isn't thick enough, the alarm goes off again, scraping our nerves.

You'd think that if there was a real gang member in the group, everyone else would back off. But you'd be wrong.

The valley isn't just filled with mild-mannered, smart engineers. According to my dad, who was once a mild-mannered engineer before he became the most educated convenience store clerk around, the valley is peppered with high-risk, high-octane CEOs and venture capitalists with mega-alpha personalities. Movers and shakers. Entrepreneurs on speed. The kind that the President of the United States came to visit for dinner.

Now, we live in a world where those Ivy-league-educated mega-alphas are jammed up behind bars with the likes of street-schooled gang members like Mr. Tattoo, arguing over who has the right to smoke. Welcome to the World After.

Mr. Alpha is a big, blond, thirty-something guy who probably worked out regularly back when gyms were worth visiting. I'll bet he has a charming smile when he wants, but right now, he looks like his nerves have been stretched about a foot farther than they can go, and the only thing keeping him from breaking is his sheer willpower.

'I'm allergic to cigarette smoke,' says Alpha. 'Look, we all need to work together to survive this.' He grinds out the words between his teeth, clearly trying to keep things cool.

'So I should put out my goddamn smoke for you? Piss off. No one's allergic to smoke. They just don't like it.' Tattoo takes a deep drag of his cigarette.

The third smoker quietly stubs out his cigarette, looking like he hopes no one notices him.

'Put the cigarette out!' There's real command in Alpha's voice that can be heard even over the shrieking alarm. This is a guy who's used to being heard. A guy who used to matter.

Tattoo flicks his still-glowing stub at Alpha. For a moment, everyone relaxes. But then Tattoo pulls out a fresh cigarette and lights it.

The alarm shuts off but the plunge into silence feels worse.

Alpha's face and neck turn a bright red. He shoves the other guy, looking like he doesn't care if he gets beat to a twitching pulp. Maybe he doesn't. Maybe this is an easier out for him than what the angels have in store for us.

The problem is, he's making that decision for the rest of us too. A fight in a cell the size of a coffin means a whole lot of injuries for everyone at a time when we can't afford to have any.

People start backing up.

I'm in the front corner, beside Clara. Bodies are already jostling us against the bars. If the panic gets aimed this way, we could be crushed against the metal bars. We won't be killed but bones could be broken. Not a good time for broken bones.

In the center of the cell, Mr. Tattoo whales on Alpha. Alpha, though, is not to be underestimated.

He grabs a guy's jacket and swings the bottom of the zipper at Tattoo's eyes. It hits a woman in the face.

Tattoo swings his arm back for a sloppy hit and his elbow smacks into an old man's neck.

The man falls back into Clara, making her bang her head against the bars. I'm trying to mind my own business, but this is not going to end well for any of us.

I weave my way to the fighters and grab Tattoo's shoulders.

I jam my knee into the back of his. I'm careful to make sure that I shove his knee straight forward so that I don't knock it out. A broken knee in our situation is a death sentence.

As he collapses down to my height, I pull his shoulders toward me and grab his head in a sleeper hold. I grip his forehead with one arm and clamp his neck with the other.

I squeeze my arms, letting him know I mean it. I'm not trying to choke off his air. Choking off the blood to his brain is faster. He has three to five seconds before he loses consciousness.

'Relax,' I say. He instantly does. This man has been in enough fights to know when it's over.

Alpha boy, on the other hand, doesn't know when to stop. By the look of his bulging eyes and crimson face, his fear and frustration are still slamming around inside him. He swings his leg back, kicking someone else in the process, and gets ready to kick Tattoo like a soccer ball as I hold him.

'You land that kick and I swear to God I'll let him eat you alive.' I lower my voice and try to sound as commanding as I can. But Mr. Tattoo is most likely thinking about how skinny and short my arms are. It's probably registering right about now that my voice is female.

I'll be in a world of hurt if I don't establish control while he's on his knees. Because when he's towering over me and looking down at the top of my head, he might start getting ideas.

So I do something I would never do in the World Before.

Even though he gave in, I choke him out anyway. His body crumples to the floor, head listing.

He'll be out for a few seconds, just long enough for me to take care of Alpha boy. And when these two come back to their senses, lying helpless on the floor with me towering above them, they'll get the message loud and clear: I am dominant here. You live or die at my mercy and I say when you fight and when you don't.

It all sounds good in my head.

Only it doesn't play out that way.

37

I'm about to grab Alpha when we're hit by a force so hard I can only describe it as a cannon full of ice pellets pounding into us. The force slams me back against the wall. But unlike a cannon shot, it doesn't stop.

It takes me a second to realize that it's a bruising spray of water shooting from a fire hose. So icy and intense, it freezes the air in my lungs.

When it finally stops, I am a battered piece of wet cloth lying limp on the floor.

Rough hands grab my arms, and I'm jerked up and dragged out of the cell. In my strained fight for air, I vaguely notice that men with grim faces also drag out Tattoo and Alpha.

I stagger up so that I'm shuffling beside my captors. It's better than having my arms pulled out of their sockets. Once it's clear that I'll walk without resisting, one of the guys lets go of me and helps the two pulling Tattoo. He's become conscious and is struggling in fear and confusion.

My guard walks up to Tattoo and slams a punch into his belly while the other two guards hold him still. I cringe in sympathy. After that, we all shuffle down the center hall without resistance.

The guards lead us into a brick passageway with peeling paint, and we pass through a metal door. A faded sign says:

AUTHORIZED PERSONNEL ONLY

The door opens to a narrow stairwell that makes a hollow metallic clang as we walk down. The space below feels industrial, almost factory-like. A lattice of giant water droplets hangs from the ceiling almost to the floor.

As we get closer, I get a better look. There are things curled inside the water droplets.

People.

Naked and curled in fetal positions. Unconscious and suspended in the water.

There's something familiar and horrifying about them.

I keep expecting to see one sucking his thumb or twitching but none of them are actually doing those things.

'What's this?' asks a man in the middle of the room, glancing our way. He wears a flannel shirt over jeans and holds a clipboard in his hand. With curly brown hair and hazel eyes, he looks like a college student doing research. I'd assume he'd be an okay guy in any other setting except this one.

'Troublemakers,' says my guard.

'Take them to the back,' says the distracted man with the clipboard. 'The last row could use a little help.'

Tattoo, who is now walking on his own without causing trouble, is the first to be led into the field of water droplets. Alpha's guard pulls him along next. Until now, my guard has let me walk on my own without touching me. Now, he grips my arm as if afraid I'll make a run for it.

'Which ones, Doc?' asks my guard.

'Any of them will do so long as they're in the last row,' says Doc as he walks past us toward an office with a window overlooking the droplets.

We enter the water-droplet matrix. The first row contains people.

As we walk to the back of the room, the people inside the droplets begin to change. It's like seeing a time-lapsed video of fetal development.

By a third of the way into the matrix, they have tails.

By halfway back, they've started to grow gossamer wings.

By two-thirds of the way, they look recognizably like scorpion monsters.

The cavernous room is filled with scorpions in various stages of development.

Hundreds of them.

And they all start from humans.

When we reach the last row, the scorpions look fully formed, complete with hair down to their shoulders and teeth that have gone from human's to lion's teeth. The ones in this last row are shifting, alert and watching as we approach.

This lab is several generations ahead of what I saw in the aerie basement. It's more systematic, with the fetuses looking more robust and dangerous. How many of these scorpion factories are there?

Tattoo begins struggling against his guards again. There are three of them, and for all his muscles and attitude, Tattoo's fighting skills are sloppy and untrained.

He yanks his guards, the muscles on his neck and arms straining against their hold. The guards are about to shove him into a droplet when he jerks unexpectedly, knocking one of the guard's elbows into the droplet.

The thing in the water moves so fast I'm not sure what's happening.

One second, the guard is holding Tattoo's shoulder as his elbow breaches the water.

The next second, the guard is halfway into the droplet with his legs kicking the air and the water turning bloody.

We all stare in awe as the guard defies gravity – and I don't know how many other laws of physics – by hanging there, partway in, partway out. Inside the droplet, the monster pumps venom into the guard's neck while it sucks on his face. Clouds of blood swirl around them in the impossible droplet that somehow maintains its shape and contains the liquid despite being punctured by the guard's body.

Tattoo's eyes are huge as he realizes what's in store for him. He looks at me and Alpha. He probably sees the same expression in our faces.

After him, we're next.

Alpha nods to Tattoo like they've just agreed on something. I guess there's nothing like a grisly impending death to make people overlook their differences. They grab one of the remaining guards still holding Tattoo. Ganging up, they shove his head into another droplet.

The scorpion in the droplet slithers around in the water to latch onto him. The guard frantically pulls back, instinctively pushing his hands against the droplet for leverage.

His hands slip right into the water.

Then, he can't get them out either.

His back, neck and arms strain to pull himself out.

His feet slide forward. But not an inch of him comes back out from the droplet.

The guard begins convulsing. Every muscle of his body trembles with his muffled scream as he pushes desperately against the scorpion fetus.

I can't look any more.

The rest of the guards, no longer outnumbering us, run. Two run to the back door while my guard runs in the other direction.

The gurgling of the bubbles and scuffling of the victim's shoes against the floor grates against my raw emotions. But before long, both victims quiet down as they become paralyzed.

The place is suddenly too quiet.

'Now what?' asks Tattoo. Despite his muscles, he looks like a lost little boy.

We all look around at the forest of monsters suspended in droplets.

'We get out of here,' says Alpha.

The hissing of a scorpion comes from the back door.

We run through the matrix toward the front stairs, careful not to bump into any of the droplets.

38

A rumbling echoes through the cavernous room. Rows of droplets sway, threatening to fall. I hate to think about what will happen if they drop. In my mind, the water is already splashing on the floor and the monster fetuses are uncurling as we run past.

The structure on the ceiling that dangles the rows of droplets slowly shifts back. Is that water splashing behind us or is that my imagination?

The matrix moves back one row, then stops.

The eerie feeling of running through transparent wombs makes me feel even more surreal as the scorpion fetuses change in every row back to humans. By the time we reach the new first row of empty droplets, a hollow clanging of footsteps echoes down the stairs ahead of us. We skid to a stop, looking around.

The only place left to go is the raised office that over-looks the monster matrix. We run up the few steps to the office and rush in.

Doc, the guy in the flannel shirt and jeans, looks up from taking notes on his clipboard in front of an ancient TV set.

Alpha grabs a pen with one hand and grabs Doc's hair with the other. He points the pen near Doc's eye, ready to stab.

'I'm going to poke this through your eye unless you get those monsters off our backs,' whispers Alpha. I still think he used to be a company guy, but he looks like he really means it. Maybe life in an office is tougher than I thought.

'One human is as good as another to them,' says Doc staring at the pen. 'They won't be searching for you.'

As if to prove his point, he shifts his eyes toward the large window that overlooks the lab. A group is coming into the factory below us. Several scorpions usher in a line of dirty, naked people.

In front of them is the new row of empty water droplets.

One of the human minions stands in front of the group. We can hear him below us through the open door as he says, 'It'll be better for you to just do as you're told.' He actually sounds like he believes it and is doing them a favor by letting them in on a secret. 'Otherwise, this could be you.' He nods to two of the other minions.

They grab the nearest person and drag him down a few rows, where they shove him into a droplet.

Even from here, I can hear his gurgled scream of muffled terror. The half-formed scorpion jerks as if trying to sting its prey with the stinger it doesn't yet have, then it latches on with its still human mouth.

I look away while I can.

The naked people in front of the door stand frozen, both mesmerized and horrified.

'Your choice,' says the guy who I assume is the foreman. 'You can be like him.' He points to the scorpion victim. 'Or you can choose to step into one of these water thingies without any trouble. The first fifteen people to volunteer to go into the water get it.'

Everyone steps forward.

The foreman starts picking people at random and they slip into their watery cages.

'How do I breathe?' asks a large man whose body is already in the droplet with his head sticking out.

One of the human minions shoves the man's head the rest of the way in without answering.

The question seems to occur to all of them as soon as they're in the water. I guess the whole situation was so weird and surreal that the victims must have figured these details would be taken care of for them. Or maybe they just assumed they could pop their heads out to breathe.

When they realize that they're trapped and can't push back out, their faces shift from anxiety to panic.

The front row of droplets swings and jerks erratically as the new inhabitants freak inside their watery cages. Bubbles fill the droplets as the last of the victims' precious air seeps out of their mouths. A few scream underwater. Muffled echoes bounce off the walls of the lab.

The remaining people back away, now clearly regretting their decision. But the minions grab them and shove them into the droplets. It's an easier job for them because I realize now that all the first people they picked were the biggest and strongest of the victims.

By the time it becomes obvious that this is no bargain, only the weakest of the group are left.

39

Tattoo quietly closes the office door, shutting out the noise below.

Alpha yanks Doc's head back, still holding the pen to his eye. 'How can you live with this on your conscience?' growls Alpha.

'Asks the man who's threatening to stab a fellow human being in the eye,' says Doc.

Tattoo leans over Doc. 'Your human privileges are being revoked, asshole.'

The office has a desk, a chair and old-fashioned bell jars of flesh-colored blobs that I don't want to look at. I wouldn't be surprised if this stuff was used back when Alcatraz was a real jail for real criminals.

'I'm a prisoner here, just like you,' says Doc through

gritted teeth. 'I do what they make me do, just like you. And just like you: I. Have. No. Choice.'

'Yeah,' says Alpha, 'only unlike us, you're neither monster Gerber food nor bio-mass for whatever these things are.'

Behind Doc, there are several rectangular boxes the size of books. Each one has a picture taped to it with a name written below. I'm about to scan past them when one of them catches my eye.

The felt-tip letters on one of the boxes read PAIGE. The grainy picture is as bad as it gets, but the dark eyes and pixie face are unmistakable.

'What are these?' My heart is thumping fast, telling me to forget about it.

'The human race is being wiped out and you think I'm happy about it?' asks Doc.

'What's this?' I hold up the box that says PAIGE.

'Let me guess, you're bravely fighting to free us,' says Alpha.

'I'm doing what I can.'

'Behind the scenes, no doubt,' says Alpha.

'Way behind the scenes, bro,' says Tattoo.

'Hey!' I say. 'What is this?'

They finally look at me holding up the little box with Paige's name and picture.

'It's a video,' says Doc.

The alarm bells shriek again, echoing off the walls.

'The hell is that?' asks Tattoo. 'And why does it keep going off?'

'There's some crazy lady on the loose,' says Doc. 'Keeps propping open emergency exits. Triggers the alarm. Are you going to let me go?'

Well, at least my mom must be doing okay.

'I want to see this video,' I say.

'Seriously?' asks Tattoo. 'Want popcorn too?'

'I think that's my sister.' I lift the video. 'I need to see this.'

'Paige is your sister?' asks Doc. He seems to really notice me for the first time.

It sends a jolt through me to know that this man knows Paige.

Doc tries to come to me but Alpha yanks his hair back.

'Stab me in the eye or let me go.' Doc busts out of Alpha's grip, looking ready to punch him.

'I need to see this video.'

'If that little girl was your sister,' says Doc, 'I'm afraid she died in the aerie attack.'

'No, she didn't,' I say.

He blinks at me in surprise. 'How do you know?'

'I was just with her yesterday, or however long it's been since I got here.'

Doc's eyes focus so intensely on me that it's as if I'm the only one in Doc's world right now. 'She didn't attack you?'

'She's my sister.' As if that answers the question.

'Where is she now?'

'I think she came here. We followed.'

The alarm turns off and we all relax our shoulders a little.

'Don't got time to watch a video, sweetheart, are you crazy?' asks Tattoo. 'Take it with you.'

'It's Betamax,' says Doc. 'This is probably the only Betamax player left in the Bay Area. It's ancient, like everything else that was left around here.'

'What's Betamax?' I ask.

'Obsolete video format,' says Alpha. 'Older than you.'

'So you can't see it anywhere but on this machine,' says Doc.

'What's your plan?' I ask Alpha and Tattoo. 'Is there any way I can watch this and meet you guys?'

They look at each other, and it's clear neither of them has a plan.

'We take him captive and walk out of here,' says Alpha.

'Then we all die,' says Doc. 'I mean no more to the locusts than you do.'

'Locusts?'

'Those things.' He nods toward the window. 'That's what the angels call them. Not sure why. These things will be the end of humanity.' He fades into his own world for a minute as he looks out over the scorpion factory, then seems to remember us. 'Look, if you want to escape, tonight is the time to do it. There's something scheduled that will have all the locusts flying off on a mission.'

'And we believe you why?' asks Tattoo. He's found a letter opener from somewhere and is checking out the edge.

'Because I'm a human being and so are you. That puts us on the same team, like it or not.'

'How long will the creatures be gone?' asks Alpha.

'Don't know.'

'What time will they leave?'

'I only know what I just told you. Tonight will be your best and only shot.'

'If they're gone, we could free everybody,' I say, thinking of Clara and Mom and everyone who sang 'Amazing Grace' when those people were marched to their deaths. Now I know where they went.

'Hard to sneak out with everybody in tow,' says Alpha.

'There's no sneaking with that boat,' I say. 'Unless you plan to swim with the sharks to get out of here. The more people, the better chance that some of us will make it.'

'If everyone's running,' says Alpha, 'it's guaranteed a lot of us *won't* make it.'

'If we leave people behind, it's guaranteed that *none* of them will make it,' I say.

'Girl's got a point,' says Tattoo.

Alpha takes a big breath and lets it out slowly.

'Cell keys are in the guard room,' says Doc. 'Convince the human guards that you'll free everyone, including them. They'll get the keys, spread the word and unlock the cells for you.'

'You're lying,' says Tattoo.

'I'm not. You think there's a single person here who wants to be here? You think we wouldn't all bust out if we could? You just need to convince them their chances of survival are greater with you than against you. That's the part that's going to be tougher than you think.'

'Why aren't you all leaving tonight if the guards are gone?' asks Alpha. 'Why wait for us to break everyone out?'

'Because there's only one boat. And when they leave, it'll be docked in San Francisco, not here. This is Alcatraz, gentlemen. They don't need guards. They have the water.'

'Can we swim it?' asks Tattoo.

'Maybe. For the right athlete who has trained for it and isn't afraid of sharks. Someone in a wet suit and swimming during the day, with a backup team on a boat. Know anyone like that?'

'There's a way out,' says Tattoo. 'Think, little man. Or I'll make sure you're the first one to get thrown into the water tonight.'

Doc watches me. I can almost see the gears in his head cranking into overdrive. 'I've heard the boat driver is locked up on the pier when the boat docks there. I might be able to get this girl onboard.' He nods toward me. 'Maybe she can free the driver and talk him into bringing the boat back.'

'I'll go,' says Tattoo. 'I'll take one for the team.'

'I'm sure you will but it needs to be her,' says Doc.

'Why?'

'There's a team here recruiting females for the aerie. When they leave, I might be able to make sure she's included. So unless you're a young female, you can't have a ride out.'

Tattoo assesses me. He's trying to decide if I'll bolt the second I get to the mainland.

'My mom is here and so is my friend,' I say. 'I'll do everything I can to help with the escape.'

The guys look at each other again as if having a silent conversation.

'How do we know the ferry driver is going to risk his life coming back for us?' asks Alpha. 'Is his mom here too?'

'She'll just have to be persuasive,' says Doc.

'And if she isn't?' asks Tattoo.

'Then we'll find someone else to drive the ferry,' says Doc confidently.

'If you're so sure, why haven't you done this already?' asks Alpha.

'This is the first time all the creatures and angels have been scheduled to leave. What makes you think we wouldn't have done it without you?'

The guys nod. 'You up for this?' Alpha asks me.

'Yeah. I'll drive the boat back myself if I have to.'

'It'd be great if the boat doesn't sink on its way here,' says Alpha.

'Right,' I say. 'I'll talk someone into it who knows what they're doing.' I sound more confident than I feel.

The alarm shrieks again, echoing off the walls and assaulting our ears.

'Maybe you can get that woman to help you,' says Doc. 'She can show you all the exits.'

'Go,' I say. 'Get the cell doors open when the time comes. I'll free the boat captain on the mainland.'

Tattoo and Alpha eye each other, both looking unconvinced. The alarm shuts off again.

'Unless you have a better plan?' says Doc.

The men nod to each other. 'You better be telling the

truth, Doc,' says Tattoo. 'Or you'll be shark bait by morning. You get me?'

Alpha looks like he's about to ask if I'll be all right, but then, maybe remembering where we are, he turns to leave.

'If you see that emergency-exit woman,' I call after him, 'tell her Penryn sent you. Take care of her, okay? I think that's my mom.'

Tattoo gives Doc one last glare and leaves.

40

'Were you really telling them the truth?' I ask.

'Mostly,' says Doc as he inserts the video into the rectangular machine below the TV. They both look ancient. Even though the screen is small, the rest of the TV is fat and heavy looking, like something out of one of my dad's old photos. 'It was the fastest way to get them out of here so we can talk about what really matters.'

'And what's that?'

'Your sister.'

'Why is she so important?'

'She probably isn't.' He glances at me sideways, giving me the impression that he thinks otherwise. 'But I'm desperate.'

He's not making much sense, but I don't care as long as I can see the video. He presses a button on the machine below the TV set.

'That thing really works?'

He scoffs. 'What I wouldn't give for a computer.' He fiddles with the dials and buttons on the old TV.

'It's not like anyone is stopping you. Computers litter the Bay Area, ready for the taking.'

'Angels aren't exactly a fan of man's machines. They prefer playing with life and the creation of new and hybrid species. Although I get the impression they're not really supposed to be doing that.' He says this last part in a mumble, like he's talking to himself. 'I've snuck some equipment in but the infrastructure on this rock was far from state-of-the-art to begin with.'

'The stuff out there looks pretty cutting edge.' I nod toward the window. 'Way more than what was in the aerie basement.'

Doc raises his eyebrows. 'You saw the aerie basement?'

I nod.

He cocks his head like a curious dog. 'Yet, here you are. Alive to tell me about it.'

'Believe me, I'm as surprised as anyone.'

'The aerie lab was our first,' he says. 'I still clung to the old ways back then – the human ways. It required test tubes, electricity and computers, but they wouldn't let me have a lot of what I needed. The angels' resistance to human technology hampered me in ways that made that lab into some kind of 1930s Frankenstein basement.'

He presses PLAY on the video machine. 'Since then, I've grown to like the angelic ways. They're more elegant and effective.'

A grainy, gray picture of a dismal room appears on the screen. A cot, a bedside table, a steel chair. It's hard to tell if it used to be a jail cell for solitary confinement or sleeping quarters for a sad bureaucrat.

'What is this?' I ask.

'Somewhere along the line, somebody installed a surveillance system on this rock. Not surprising, considering it was a busy tourist attraction. I added sound in some of the rooms. The angels obviously don't know they're being watched, so don't go around announcing it.'

On the screen, the metal door of the room slams open. Two shirtless angels shuffle in holding a giant between them. Even through the grainy video, I recognize the demon Beliel. He has a bloody bandage wrapped around his stomach.

Behind them is another angel who looks familiar. I can't tell the color of his wings in the grainy video but

I'm guessing it's burnt orange. I remember him from the night Paige was taken, the night he and his buddies cut Raffe's wings. He holds little Paige in one arm like a sack of potatoes.

Her face is uncut and her legs dangle, atrophied and useless. She looks tiny and helpless. This must be the night Paige was kidnapped.

'Is that your sister?' asks Doc.

I nod, unable to say anything.

Burnt angel tosses Paige toward the shadowy corner of the room.

'You're sure you want to see this?' asks Doc.

'I do.' I don't. I want to throw up at the thought of anything that might have happened while I wasn't around to protect her.

But I have no choice. I'm compelled to watch the rest of the video.

41

The blurry blob flying into the corner resolves into my sister again when she lands with a thud. I cringe as she bounces off the wall and crumples on her useless legs.

A tiny squeal of pain escapes from her, but no one in the room seems to notice.

Burnt angel has already forgotten about her as he lifts Beliel's legs. They toss him onto the cot. Beliel comes down onto the squeaking springs. He looks dead. I wish it were true.

Behind them, my baby sister drags herself further into the shadowy corner and cringes there. She pulls up her legs with her hands to curl them against her chest in a fetal position as she watches the angels with huge, terrified eyes.

Beliel's unconscious head lolls at an uncomfortable angle against the metal bar that serves as a headboard. All they'd have to do is pull him down a little and he could lie in relative comfort. But they don't.

Another angel comes in with a plate of sandwiches and a large glass of water. He lays the food and water on the bedside table. While he does that, two of the angels exit, leaving Burnt and the delivery guy.

'Not so bossy now, is he?' says Burnt.

'I wonder how deep that cut went into his stomach muscles?' says the one who brought in the sandwiches. 'You think he can reach the food?'

Burnt casually pulls the rickety table just out of Beliel's reach. 'Not any more.'

The angels give each other sly grins. 'We brought food and water like we're supposed to. Is it our fault if he can't sit up and reach it?'

Burnt curls his lip like he wants to kick Beliel. 'He's got to be the bossiest, nastiest, most self-important reject I've ever had to work with.'

'I've worked with worse.'

'Who?'

'You.' The angel laughs as he shuts the door behind them as they leave.

Page huddles in the dark, apparently completely forgotten. She must be getting hungry and thirsty herself.

If she could walk, she could have snuck over and snagged a sandwich. But without her wheelchair, she would have had to slowly drag herself across the floor, grab it, and drag herself back. It could be done but I can see why she wouldn't try. It's hard to feel like you can steal something when you can't run.

The video fades out.

When it turns back on, there's light coming into the room, probably from a small window somewhere off camera. Time has passed. It's hard to guess how much.

A painful growl rises to a howl of angry frustration. Beliel is awake and trying to sit up. He flops back onto the cot with a disgusted grunt.

He lies there panting, seemingly unaware of Paige still curled on the stone floor in the corner. Bright blood stains the bandages wrapped around his waist. He turns his head and stares at the water. He reaches out without leaning forward. The table with the sandwiches is just beyond reach.

However hungry and thirsty he is, Paige must be hungrier and thirstier. She's tiny. She doesn't have much stored up.

Beliel drops his hand and slams it against the cot. He grunts in anger and pain as the motion tears at his wound.

He lies back, trying to stay still. He gulps a dry gulp and looks at the glass of water on the table.

He takes a deep breath as if to brace himself and reaches out again. This time, he manages to stretch a little farther but not far enough. He pants through gritted teeth as he inches forward toward the water. The pain must be enormous. If it had been anyone else, I would have felt sorry for him.

He gives up with a frustrated grunt and slumps back down. His face is contorted in pain.

Paige must have moved or made a noise because he suddenly glares into the corner.

'What are you doing here?'

Paige shrinks back against the wall.

'Did they send you here to spy on me?'

She shakes her head.

'Get out.' He practically spits out the words. 'Wait. Make yourself useful and bring me the water and sandwiches from that table.'

Paige stares at him in fear. Poor baby. A part of me wants to shut the video off. Whatever happened happened. My watching it won't change anything.

But I'm mesmerized by this window into my sister's past. If she had to go through this because I wasn't there to protect her, then I don't deserve to be protected from watching what she went through.

'Do it now!' Beliel bellows at her. He's so loud and forceful that I jump.

Paige shrinks back even more.

Then, she lies on the concrete floor and drags herself toward him. Her eyes look huge and her pant legs lie almost empty as they drag.

42

'What's wrong with you? Are you broken?'

'No. I just can't walk like other people.' She puts her arm out and drags herself forward a few more inches.

'That means you're broken.'

She stops on the hard floor, propped on her elbows. 'It means I move in a different way.'

'Yeah, like crawling on the floor like a worm. Show me, Little Worm. Entertain me. Crawl over here and I'll let you have some of my water.'

I want to punch my fist through the TV screen at him.

Where were you when she needed you?

My little sister looks at the water and takes a dry gulp.

'I can see you want it. The thirst is probably cracking your throat right now.' His own voice sounds dry and cracked. 'Soon, you'll get a headache and start feeling dizzy. Later, your tongue will swell and every instinct you have will be whispering at you to bite it so you can drink your own blood. Ever been thirsty enough to want to kill a man for his cup of water? No? You'll know that feeling soon.'

He touches the bloody bandage as if wanting to share the pain. 'Come over here, Little Worm. Show me how the broken and abandoned "walk" in a different way, and I'll give you something to drink.'

'I'm not abandoned.'

Beliel scoffs. 'Name one person who didn't abandon you.'

She looks at him with her wide eyes and pixie face. 'My sister.'

'Really? Then where is she?'

'On her way here. She'll come and get me.'

'That's not what she said.'

'You talked to her?' The hope in her face breaks my heart.

'Sure, I talked to her. Who do you think gave you to me?'

I clench my fist so hard my knuckles feel ready to split.

'You lie.'

'It's the truth. She said she feels bad about it, but she can't handle the responsibility of taking care of you any more.'

'You're lying.' Her voice wavers. 'She didn't say that.'

'She's exhausted. So tired of waking up every morning, knowing she has to find food for you, carry you, wash you, do everything for you. She tried, but you're such a burden.'

All the strength drains out of me and I have to stagger back and lean on the wall to stay up.

'They're all like that.' Beliel's voice is not unfriendly. 'In the end, they always abandon us. No matter how much we love them or how much we do for them. We're never good enough. We're the rejects, you and I. The abandoned.'

'You're a liar.' Her face crumples and her words blur. She hiccups as she cries, lying there on the stone floor, utterly helpless. Her tone almost begs for this monster to comfort her.

My chest feels like there's a heavy weight on it, and I have trouble breathing.

'You'll see. Nothing will ever be given to us freely the way it is for other people. Not love, not respect, not even friendship. The only way we'll get any of that is to put them all in their rightful place beneath us. The last thing we can afford is to be helpless and weak. You have to be strong and beat them into submission. And if they beg and behave, then maybe we'll let them be our lap dogs. That's the closest outsiders like us will ever come to feeling wanted.'

It's bad enough that he's crushing the fragile hopes of an innocent seven-year-old. But what kills me is that we proved him right. The image of her tied and yanked like a wild animal will be burned forever into my memory.

'Would you like some water?' Beliel's voice is neutral. Not nice but not overly cruel either.

My sister gulps and tastes her parched lips with her tongue. Desperately thirsty even though she's crying.

'Crawl over to me, Little Worm, and I'll give you some.'

She lies still on the floor with her upper body resting on her forearms. She looks at him with distrust. I absolutely dread her falling for his game, and yet there's a part of me that wants her to go to him because she needs to drink.

Paige slowly puts her arm out and drags herself laboriously. Once, twice, until she gets a slow rhythm crawling across the room. Her dead and dried-up legs drag behind her.

Beliel claps in a slow beat. 'Bravo, Little Worm. Bravo. Such a miniature likeness of your kind. You monkeys are so cleverly desperate to do whatever it takes to survive. Compared to your people and the things some of them will do, I'm practically a nice guy.'

Paige reaches the table that holds the plate of sandwiches and glass of water. She crawls up the metal chair that sits beside it.

'I didn't say you could have that,' Beliel growls. 'I told you to come to me, not to the table.' He starts to lean forward in anger but eases back in pain with his hand on his bleeding stomach, letting out a deep breath.

She reaches out to the glass, looking at the water with obvious longing and thirst.

'Of course, you're just like the rest.' His lips sneer. 'There isn't a creature alive who looks out for anyone but himself. Even a little worm like you. So you learned a lesson from your sister, did you? The only thing that matters in the end is your own survival. It's what humans and cockroaches are best at.'

Paige looks at the water. Then at Beliel. A battle is raging inside her, and I know her well enough to know what she's debating.

'Don't do it,' I whisper. 'Take care of yourself first.' Just for once.

Without taking a sip, she holds out the glass of water to Beliel where he can reach it.

I groan in despair. I want to snatch it away and make her drink.

'My sister is coming for me.' Her voice breaks, like she's not sure. Her face scrunches as she fights the tears.

He stares at the water.

He stares at her.

'Aren't you thirsty, Little Worm? Why not drink it yourself?' Suspicion fills his voice.

She sniffles. 'You need it more.' She's being stubborn. Clinging on to who she is even under these circumstances.

'Don't you know you'll die if you don't get some water?'

She holds it out steadily.

He reaches out his arm without moving his body and takes it. He sniffs it as if suspicious that it might not be just water.

He takes a sip.

Then a gulp.

Then he downs two-thirds of it.

He pauses for a breath. He glares at Paige as if she insulted him. 'What are you looking at?'

She just blinks at him.

Beliel puts the glass to his mouth, but this time he takes just a sip. He glances at Paige as if considering giving the rest to her.

Then he drains it in one big gulp.

'That's what happens when you're nice. You might as well learn that lesson early. Nice may have worked for you in the past but no more. That strategy only works when you're wanted. But now, you're no different from me. Ugly. Rejected. Unloved. I understand.'

I cannot wait to kill him.

He hands her the glass. She takes it, desperate. She tips it over in her mouth.

One small drop drips into her mouth.

43

Her face crumples but no tears come this time. She's probably too dehydrated.

'Hand me the sandwiches.'

She glares at him.

'They won't do you any good. You'll just get thirstier if you eat them.'

She pauses, then grabs the sandwiches. She throws them at him.

He chuckles as they bounce off his chest and land in pieces on his bloody bandage. He puts a sandwich back together and takes a bite. 'Not too smart, are you?'

She puts her head down on her arms on the tiny table and slumps there like she's given up.

The video goes dark.

I catch myself before asking whether she came out of that all right. For a moment, I forgot what she's like now. Of course she's not all right.

Doc hovers his finger over the eject button. 'Had enough?'

'No,' I say through gritted teeth. 'Not yet.'

He drops his hand. 'It's your punishment. Who am I to argue?'

The screen comes back on again.

Time has passed. The light has dimmed and the shadows are longer now. The door opens and an angel comes in. It's Burnt.

Paige raises her head. When she sees who it is, she scrambles off the chair and frantically crawls under Beliel's cot.

'Ah, so that's where it went,' says Burnt watching Paige.

'And where did you go?' asks Beliel.

'You didn't seem to need us, so we brought you some food and water and left you to sleep it off. How are you feeling?' Burnt bends over to look at Paige.

'Just fantastic, thank you for asking.' The sarcasm in Beliel's voice is unmistakable. 'What are you doing?'

Paige screams as Burnt drags her out from under the cot.

'Let her go,' Beliel bellows.

Burnt lets go in surprise.

'You don't do anything without my permission.' Beliel grabs Burnt by the arm and yanks him to his face. It must hurt like hell in his condition, but Beliel doesn't show it. 'You don't touch that girl. You don't even breathe without my permission. Uriel gave you to me to command. You think he'd spend a second of his illustrious life wondering what happened to you if you ended up as a splatter on the wall?'

Burnt looks back at him defiantly but with a touch of nervousness. 'Why would you do that?'

'You really thought I wouldn't notice that you were trying to starve and drain me with thirst?'

'We left you food and water,' Burnt grunts through his teeth as he tries to jerk his arm out of Beliel's grasp. The demon holds tight despite the pain. 'We brought you back, too, when we could have left you on the streets to die.'

'Uriel would have plucked you alive if you hadn't. You boys still don't have the nerve to lie to him, do you? Afraid you'll get some divine punishment. Well, his punishment would feel playful compared to what I'll do if I ever wake up to dinner out of my reach again. Understood?'

Burnt nods resentfully.

Beliel lets him go.

Burnt takes a step back.

'Get me some decent food and water. Fresh meat, cooked to body temperature. I'm not a child who can live off peanut butter and jelly sandwiches.'

Burnt turns to go with a sneer.

'Bring a few sandwiches for her, though.' He tips his head toward Paige. 'Nothing like a dead broken thing in the corner of your room to stink up your day.'

Burnt glances at Paige who has scrambled back under the bed, then at Beliel like he's lost his mind.

'Problem?' asks Beliel.

Burnt slowly shakes his head.

'Too bad. Now, I'll have to wait to finger-paint the walls with your blood.'

Burnt turns to go.

'Bring a pitcher of water and some milk for the girl too. Pronto, feather boy. I don't have all week to lounge around. The sooner I can fly to talk to your precious archangel, the sooner you might be set free from your duties.'

Burnt leaves.

'Come out, Little Worm. The big bad angel is gone.'

Paige peeks out from under the bed.

'That's a good pet.' He closes his eyes. 'Sing me a little song while I drift into a nap.' He grimaces with the pain he refused to show the angel. 'Go on. Any song.'

Paige hesitantly starts humming 'Twinkle, Twinkle, Little Star.'

The screen goes blank.

44

'That's it,' says Doc as he turns off the TV.

I have to swallow tears before I can ask, 'What happened next?'

'Beliel kept her in the room as his pet until he recovered enough to go to the aerie. He had to report to Archangel Uriel. Something about a legendary angel who has been away for a long time.'

Raffe. Beliel must have reported that Raffe got away.

'Whatever it was,' says Doc, 'Uriel was displeased. Beliel was in a seriously bad mood after that, and he took it out on your sister. After treating her like a pet for days – feeding her, confiding in her, taking her with him everywhere – he abandoned her to the medical team. He tossed her our way and didn't look back.'

He pops out the video. 'She kept asking for him until we – they – turned her into what she is now.'

'She asked for him?'

He shrugs. 'He was the only one familiar to her in her new environment.'

I nod, wanting to throw up.

'And what exactly did you turn her into?'

'Don't you think you've had enough punishment for the day?'

'Don't pretend you give a damn. Tell me.'

He sighs. 'The kids were Uriel's pet project. Sometimes, I think he just likes playing God – something people used to accuse me of doing a lifetime ago. He wanted the kids to look like something he couldn't even describe. Said he'd never seen the things that he wanted the kids to mimic but that no one who mattered had.'

I'm scared to ask but I do anyway. 'What did he want them to be?'

'Abominations. They were to look like unnatural children who ate people. They were to roam the earth and terrorize the population as part of the angels' endless political machinations.'

So he could pass them off as nephilim and blame Raffe for not doing his job. So he could ruin his competitor's reputation and win the election for Messenger.

'You purposely made kids into abominations?'

He sighs, like he never expected me to understand. 'The human race is about to come to an end and I, for one, am scared out of my skull. Unless we can figure out a way to stop it, this is it for us.'

He sweeps out his arm as if inviting me to look around at the scorpion factory. 'I'm in a very special place to make a difference, to help figure out a way to stop it. I have access to their facilities and knowledge. I have their trust and a small degree of freedom to work under their noses.'

He leans back against the wall as if he's tired. 'But the only way I can help the human race is if I do what they tell me to do. Even if it's horrific. Even if it's goddamn soul-shredding.'

Doc pushes off from the wall and paces the office. 'I'd do anything not to be that guy who has to make choices that haunt him night after night. But here I am. It's me and no one else. Do you understand?'

What I understand is that he chopped up my baby sister and turned her into an 'abomination'. 'And just how are you helping the human race?'

He looks at his shoes. 'I've tried a few experiments that I kept secret from the angels. Stole some angel science, or magic, or whatever you want to call it, and implemented it here and there. They'd kill me if they knew. But all I have so far are tantalizing possibilities. No confirmed successes yet.'

I'm not interested in making this butcher of children feel good about his job. But accusing him won't get me answers.

'Why did you make my sister move like a machine?'

'What do you mean?'

'She sits with her back straight, moves stiffly with every motion, turns her head as if her neck doesn't work the same any more, you know – like a machine.' Except when she's attacking, of course.

He looks at me as if I've lost it. 'The girl has been cut and stitched everywhere like a quilted doll. And you have to ask why she moves stiffly?' The guy who did that to her looks down at me like *I'm* the insensitive person.

'She's in pain.' He says it like he's saying *Duh*. 'Just because she's fully functional doesn't mean she's not suffering from excruciating, soul-shattering pain. Imagine being cut up everywhere, having your muscles ripped out and replaced, stitched up, every fiber of your body altered. Now imagine that no one gives you painkillers. That's what it's like for her. I guess I can safely assume that you didn't even give her aspirin?'

It's like he's punching me in the lungs.

'If that never occurred to you, then it's no surprise she left, is it?'

I can't even think about what it must be like for her without feeling like I'm breaking.

I even offered Raffe aspirin when he was unconscious before I ever got to know him. I offered the enemy pain relief but never considered it for my own sister. Why?

Because she looked like a monster, that's why. And it never occurred to me that monsters might feel pain.

'Do you have any guesses as to where she might be?' Hearing the tremble in my own voice sucks out my confidence.

He glances at the dark TV. 'She's not here. I would have heard about it by now. But if you're right and she was here even briefly, then she's looking for something. Or someone.'

'Who? She's already come to me and Mom. We're all she has in the world.'

'Beliel,' says Doc with certainty. 'He's the only one who would understand. The only one who would accept her and not judge her.'

'What are you talking about? He's the last one she'd run to.'

He shrugs. 'He's a monster. She's a monster. Who else is going to accept her without considering her a freak, much less understand what she's going through?'

'We . . .' The words shrivel in my mouth.

The thought of Paige turning to Beliel astounds me.

But if it had been Paige and Beliel together at the Resistance camp, wouldn't people have tried to corral them both as a monster team? As if they belonged together and not with the rest of us humans?

'She might even have a touch of Stockholm syndrome.'

I don't like the sound of that. 'What's that?'

'It's where a kidnapping victim forms an attachment to the kidnapper.'

I stare at him, dumbfounded.

'It's not common but it can happen.'

I grab the back of the chair and sit down shakily like an old woman. The thought of little Paige feeling like she has no one to turn to but a nightmare like Beliel breaks me in a way that the end of the world couldn't.

'Beliel,' I say breathlessly. I shut my eyes and will myself not to let the tears out. 'Do you know where he is?' My own words stab me.

'He should be at the new aerie by now. Something big is going on there, and Beliel has a job to do for the archangel.'

'What job?'

'Don't know. I'm just the lab monkey. Need-to-know-only basis.' He watches me. 'Talk to the ferry captain about rescuing the Alcatraz prisoners, then go to the aerie.'

'What if—'

'Whether you can talk the captain into the rescue or not, go to the aerie. The number of people dying here is no worse than what's happening out there. Your sister is more important than releasing prisoners into a bigger slaughter house, which is what the world will be if we can't figure out a way to stop it.'

That jars my brain into thinking. 'Why is Paige so important?' I can't help the distrust that laces my voice.

'She's a very special girl. She may be helpful in our fight against the angels. If you find her at the aerie, bring her back to me. I'll work with her. I'll help her if I can.'

'Help her how?'

He rubs the back of his neck, looking half-ashamed, half-excited. 'To be honest, I'm not sure yet. I altered the kids in this latest batch in the hope that I might be able to increase our chance of survival as a species. A desperate move in desperate times. The angels would tear me to pieces if they knew about it. But the altered kids got wiped out during the attack on the aerie before I even got a chance to see if any of it worked.'

He paces around the small office. 'Now, you're telling me there's one left. We need to find her. I don't really know what she can do, or even if it works the way I think it does. But it's a chance for humanity. A tiny one but that's better than what we've got now.'

I don't trust him any more than I trust a rabid angel. But if he can help me find Paige, I'll go along with his plan for now. 'Okay. Help me find Paige and I'll bring her back to you.'

He looks at me as if he knows I don't trust him. 'Let me make this very clear. We cannot have someone like Beliel in control of your sister. Do you understand? Under Beliel's control, she could end up being a major instrument of our destruction. You have to lure her away from him. She could be our last hope.'

Great.

Before this all goes down, I could really use another Saturday morning where Paige and I eat cereal and watch cartoons in our condo during the peaceful lull before Mom gets up. Our biggest concern on mornings like those was whether we still had our favorite cereals left at the end of the week or if we'd have to settle for the non-sugar kind.

'If I don't make it off this island, or if you can't find me—' Doc pauses as if dwelling on all the terrible things that could happen to him— 'it'll be up to you to figure out what she can do and if she can help people. If your sister can't help humanity, I'm just an evil doctor doing horrific deeds for the enemy. Please don't let me be that person.'

I'm not sure I'm the one he's pleading with, but I nod anyway.

He nods back. 'Okay. Come with me.'

45

We walk out of the heart of the monster factory, down the brick passageway and into another room. I assume this was once a gift shop by the look of the postcards and key chains on a forgotten stand by the door.

Inside, several human minions mix with prisoners. The minions stand out with their clean faces, groomed hair, and fresh clothes. There's also an air of confidence about them that the prisoners don't have.

'Madeline,' says Doc.

A woman with the strong lines and the aging-model looks of a ballet instructor saunters over. Every motion is graceful and fluid, as if she was used to being on stage or on the catwalk. The tight bun of her gray-streaked hair only emphasizes her emerald eyes.

'Can you find a place for her?' asks Doc in a low voice.

Madeline looks me over. She's not just glancing at me to get a quick impression of who I am. She assesses, taking in my hair, my height, every curve and plane of my face. It's as if she's memorizing me, cataloging aspects of my appearance. She glances back at the collection of prisoners.

The prisoners are all female and they stand in pairs. There's a pair of twins with matching strawberry hair and freckled pink skin. The rest of the pairs are probably not twins, but at first glance, they look like it. A set of curvy women with chocolate skin, a set of skinny girls with honey hair cascading down their shoulders, a set of tall women with Mediterranean eyes and skin.

Madeline looks around the room, then back at me.

'Wrong body type, wrong age,' she says.

The door opens and a man ushers in a pair of teen girls. Dark hair, high cheekbones, petite like me.

'How about these?' asks Doc.

Madeline swings her laser focus onto the girls. Then she looks at me.

'These two are better matched,' says the tanned guy who brought them in, gesturing to the girls beside him.

'We'll have to make do with this one.' Madeline nods her head toward me.

'You're going to tell the archangel that this is the best match we could find?' asks the guy.

My skin prickles at the word 'archangel.'

'Same coloring, same body type,' says Madeline. 'After a makeover and haircut, they'll look like twins.'

'If they don't, it's all of our necks on the line, not just yours,' says the guy.

Madeline looks at Doc who nods.

'Switch them.'

The guy's face darkens. 'Just because he's got your husband holed up in a jail cell doesn't mean you can trade our lives for his whenever the good doctor snaps his fingers.'

'Daniel, please just do as you're asked.' Madeline's voice is commanding with a hint of threat.

Daniel takes a deep breath. Everyone stares at us, feeling the tension.

He assesses the two girls, then takes one by the arm and ushers her out.

The cold part of me says don't ask. As far as I can tell, it's to my benefit. And it could help my sister. 'You're holding someone hostage?'

One of these days, I'll learn to keep my mouth shut.

'We're all hostages here,' says Doc. 'I'm doing what I can to keep someone alive.'

That sinks in.

I take him aside and whisper, 'If the prison break doesn't go down the way it's supposed to, will you see that my mother is safe?'

'Your mother, the lady running around triggering the alarms?'

I nod.

'I don't think I can promise that.'

Surprisingly, I feel better about his answer than if he *had* promised to take care of her because it's more honest.

'Will you try?'

He doesn't look happy about it.

'Paige will listen to her, too.' Not entirely true considering some of the things my mother tells us to do, but no need to get into details with him.

He thinks about it, then nods. 'I'll try.'

That's as good as I can expect.

'And there's a woman named Clara—'

He shakes his head. 'I'm not a magician. I can't make the hell that is Alcatraz go away. One is all I can promise to try to keep safe.'

He steps back from me and takes Madeline aside. They whisper in the corner, giving me a chance to absorb the situation.

The dark-haired teenager steps closer to me. She's my height. We have the same figure and the same shade of dark hair and eyes.

Matching pairs of girls.

Archangel.

An image of Uriel the politician walking through the aerie's club with his matching terrified women comes to mind.

I instinctively reach to stroke my bear-sword, trying to get some comfort from the soft fur, but there's nothing there but empty air.

46

The ferry ride to San Francisco is as quiet and gloomy as the one that took me to Alcatraz. The big difference is that humans are guarding us instead of scorpions.

Madeline and her crew go around asking the two dozen of us if we can sew or design costumes, or if we know how to make jewelry. If we answer yes, they write stuff down on their clipboards. I don't know how to do any of these things but they don't seem to care.

I've lost track of how long it's been since my last ride on this ferry. It's dawn now. The sky is tinged with what I always thought of as rosy pink, but this morning it looks more like the color of a fresh bruise.

I try to see if I can talk to the captain, but the guards firmly redirect me to the bathrooms. On my way back, I find a pen and paper on a clipboard hanging on the wall in the stairwell. So I spend the rest of the ride writing down what I want to say to the boat driver, just in case I have to slip him a note instead of being able to talk to him.

I carefully word my argument to try to be as persuasive as I can. When I'm done, I fold the paper and slide it into my pocket, hoping I won't need it. It'll be much better if I can persuade the driver in person.

Once we dock, we walk out into the sunlight, unable to believe we're free from Alcatraz. The scorpions that were injured on the night we were captured are nowhere to be seen. Blood streaks across the splintery dock and into the early morning shadows.

Our human guards don't veer from their intended course even though there are no scorpions or angels around.

'Why don't you run?' I can't help but ask one of the guards.

'And do what?' he says loud enough for all the prisoners to hear. 'Fight to scrounge for scraps in the garbage bin? Not be able to sleep because I'm so afraid angels will hunt me down?'

He looks around at all the prisoners. We all look unsure, tentative and lost. 'Angels might hurt others but not me. Their creatures get out of my way when I walk by. I eat three full meals every single day. I stay warm

and protected. And you can too. You've been chosen.
All you have to do is follow instructions.'

He must have been a spin doctor in the World Before,
the way he turns my simple question into a propaganda
moment. I notice he doesn't say he's free.

The piles of weapons, bags and other precious items
that were left on the pier look like they've been hurriedly
picked through and are scattered near the dock. The
only things that remain are the weakest of weapons,
upended bags, and toys. I scan the stuff until I see the
two things I'm looking for.

Mom's tracker lies beside a purse, looking like a clunky
cell phone. And Raffe's sword lies near it, just where I
left it, half-hidden under a rummaged backpack with
clothes spilling out of it. The teddy bear that still hides
the sword stares at the sky as if looking for Raffe to fly
down and rescue it.

Huge relief floods through me. I run to grab the tracker
and sword, hugging the bear like a long lost friend.

'You'll have to leave them here,' says Madeline. 'You
won't be allowed to bring anything into the aerie.'

I should have known. I hate to leave them but at least
I might be able to hide them. The other guards leave me
alone, probably realizing that Madeline has an agenda
with me, and they don't want to get into trouble with
her.

I look at Mom's tracker. On the screen, my arrow points to San Francisco's piers. Paige's arrow points near Half Moon Bay on the Pacific coast.

'Where is the new aerie?' I ask Madeline.

'Half Moon Bay,' she says.

Is Paige really looking for Beliel? I close my eyes, feeling like I've been stabbed in the stomach.

I shut off the tracker. I badly want to take it and the sword with me but I don't have a choice. As much as I want to hide the tracker, I want my mother to have it if I can't keep it.

The world is littered with abandoned phones. The odds of people leaving the tracker alone are very good. I shut it off and put it back where I found it, forcing myself to turn away.

The sword, on the other hand, needs to be hidden. I got lucky that the looters were probably in a huge rush, otherwise, they would have noticed that the bear's dress is too long. I can't resist giving the bear a final caress before hiding it with the sword under a pile of wood and shingles that were once part of a shop.

I'm about to let go of the sword when my vision wavers and fades.

The sword wants to show me something.

*　　*　　*

I'm in the glass-and-marble hotel suite of the old aerie where Raffe and I spent a few hours together. This must be the time after visiting the speakeasy club and before his wing transplant.

The shower is running at the other end of the suite. It would be peaceful and posh here except for the panoramic view of San Francisco's charred cityscape dominating the living room.

Raffe walks out of the bedroom, looking fantastic in his suit. With his dark hair, broad shoulders and muscular build, he looks better than any movie star I've ever seen. He looks like a guy who belongs in a thousand-dollar-a-night hotel suite. Every move, every gesture conveys elegance and power.

Something catches his eye and he walks to the window. A formation of angels flies past the moon. He leans toward the glass, almost pressing his face to it as he looks up at the angels. Every line of him tells me he longs to fly with them.

I suspect it's more than just wanting his wings back. We once had exotic fish in a bowl that Paige and I had decorated with seashells. My dad told us that we always had to make sure there were at least two fish in the bowl because some species needed to belong to a group. If one of them was left alone long enough, it would die of loneliness.

I wonder if angels are like that.

When the angels disappear into the night sky beyond the moon, Raffe turns sideways and looks at his reflection in the window. The wings peeking through the slits in his suit jacket look like other wings I've seen on angels at the club downstairs, but they're not. The severed wings are strapped under his clothes and arranged to look normal.

He closes his eyes for a moment, swallowing his sadness. I'm so used to seeing Raffe with his game face on that it's hard to see him like this.

He takes a deep breath and lets it out slowly. Then he opens his eyes. He's about to turn away from the window when he sees something on his white shirt.

He plucks it and holds it up. It's a strand of hair. He runs his fingers along it. It's dark and long and looks like mine.

His lips twitch as if it's funny to think about how my hair might have ended up on his shirt. My guess is that it must have happened when I kissed him in the hallway downstairs by the club. He thinks it's amusing.

If I had a body in this dream, my cheeks would be burning. It's embarrassing just to think about it.

He walks over to the marble bar lined with bottles of wine. He looks beneath it and comes up with a small hotel sewing package. Why anyone who can afford a room like this would want a set of emergency thread and buttons, I don't know, but there it is. He rips open the package and pulls out the thread. It's the same snowy white as his wings.

He holds the thread and hair together and twirls them with his thumb and forefinger so that the two strands intertwine.

Holding the ends together, he steps over to the sword that lies on the counter and wraps the strand around the sword's grip.

'Stop complaining,' he says to the sword. 'It's for luck.'

Luck. Luck. Luck.

The word echoes in my head.

I put my hand on the splintery dock to steady myself. The world comes back into focus as I take deep breaths.

Did Raffe really keep a strand of my hair?

Hard to believe.

I look carefully at the sword's hilt. Amazingly, there it is, on the grip at the base of the cross-guard. Snow-white thread mixed with midnight dark.

I run my finger over the hair-thread and close my eyes. I think about Raffe doing the same thing as I feel the alternating texture of thread and hair against my fingertip.

Was the sword wishing me luck?

I know that it misses Raffe. If I don't come back, I guess it has no chance of ever seeing him again. Even if it bonds with someone else, that person will have no connection with him and no knowledge of what it is. So maybe it does have a reason to wish me luck, along with a little reminder of Raffe.

I hate to leave the sword but I have no choice. I cover it, bear and all, with broken shingles and splintered boards.

I get up and walk away, feeling naked. I hope the looters don't have the luxury of digging through piles of debris for hidden treasures.

47

By the time the captain gets off the boat, our group is being shepherded into a small caravan of vans, SUVs and a short school bus. Madeline escorts the captain to one of those hateful shipping containers. I casually join them.

'There's an escape planned for tonight,' I say in a low voice.

He looks at me, then at Madeline, then back at me. He's younger than I expected – probably no more than thirty – with a clean face and a completely bald head. 'Good luck to you.' His voice isn't unfriendly, but it isn't inviting either.

Madeline unlocks the shipping container and swings the metal doors open. It has shelves stocked with canned soup and vegetables, along with rows of liquor and books. Battery-powered lights stand in the corner and an overstuffed chair sits beside a small side table. By World After standards, it's downright cozy.

'They need you to take the ship back and pick up the prisoners,' I say. His expression is skeptical so I rush on before he can say no. 'It'll be totally safe. All the scorpions and angels will be gone. They have a mission tonight.'

He steps into the container and turns on the lights. 'Nothing is totally safe. And that ferry keeps me alive and fed. I can't risk it. I won't rat you out but I won't let anyone touch that ferry, either.'

I glance at Madeline for help. 'Can you talk to him? I mean, you have someone imprisoned on the island too, right?'

She looks down, refusing to meet my eyes. 'The doctor will keep him safe so long as I help him with his little projects.' She shrugs. 'We need to get going.'

I glance from Madeline to the captain who is now pouring himself a drink. 'This is your chance to make a difference,' I say. 'You can save all those lives. Make up for whatever it is you felt you had to do to survive. You know what goes on there.'

He bangs the glass onto the table. 'Where did you find her, Madeline? Isn't what we go through bad enough without Little Miss Pain-in-the-Ass lecturing us?'

'It's the right thing to do,' I say.

'The right thing is a luxury for rich and sheltered people. For the rest of us, the only right thing is staying out of trouble and surviving as best we can.' He sits in the chair and opens a book, pointedly not looking at me.

'They need you. You're the only one who can help them. My mom and my friend—'

'Get out before you convince me to rat you out just to get rid of you.' He has the decency to look uncomfortable about it.

Madeline closes the door. 'I'm leaving it unlocked.'

'That's fine,' he says in a voice that makes it clear he's done with the conversation.

I had completely underestimated how hard it would be to talk someone into risking his life for others. Whatever issues the Resistance has, they would have rallied around a cause like this.

'Can anyone else drive the boat?' I ask Madeline.

'Not without sinking it while trying to back it out from the dock. You can't make someone be a hero. I've left the door open for Jake in case he changes his mind.'

'That's not good enough. I need to find someone to take the boat back tonight.'

Daniel, Madeline's assistant, sticks his tanned face out of the bus window. 'Let's go!'

Madeline takes my arm and pulls me toward the bus. 'Come on. It's not our problem any more.'

I yank out of her grasp. 'How can you say that?'

She pulls a small pistol from her pocket and points it at me. 'I told the doctor I'd take you to the aerie and that's what I'm going to do. I'm sorry, but my husband's life depends on it.'

'A lot of lives can be saved, including your husband's, if we can just—'

She shakes her head. 'There is no one else who can drive that ferry. And even if we found someone, he wouldn't risk his life any more than Jake would. I'm not throwing away my husband's life for a pie-in-the-sky escape plan. Let's go. Now.' She has a determined gleam in her eyes like she's ready to shoot my arm and drag me into the bus.

I reluctantly head toward the bus with Madeline.

48

We weave through the abandoned cars onto I-280 and head south. The further we get from the piers, the worse I feel about the Alcatraz escape plan. Captain Jake looked like he was pretty comfortable with his position as slave captain. Is there any chance he might throw away the one asset that's been keeping him alive and risk his life to rescue the same people he ferried to their doom?

There's a small chance that he might. He is human and humans sometimes do things like that.

But it's more likely that he'll drink steadily all day until he's in a guilt-induced stupor when the scorpions take off on their mission.

This is too much. Mom and Paige are too much. The sword and Clara and all those people on Alcatraz . . .

I shove everything into the vault in my head and mentally lean hard to shut the door. I have a whole world in there now. I can't afford to open it without the serious risk of being crushed by all the stuff that'll spill out. Some of my friends had therapists in the World Before. What I have in that vault could take a therapist's entire career to untangle.

Sitting in the back of the bus, I gaze out the open window without really seeing anything. It's all a blur of dead cars, junk, broken and burnt buildings.

Until we drive cautiously by two black SUVs.

The SUVs have drivers in them even though they're parked. They're keeping watch, and they look ready to move at a moment's notice. Three men are fiddling with something on the ground by the side of the road. It's so small I can't see it clearly.

As we drive by, I get a good look at the drivers. At first, I don't recognize them because of their newly blond hair. But there's no mistaking the freckled faces of Dee and Dum.

I remember the letter I wrote to the ferry captain in case I didn't have enough time to talk to him. I yank it out of my pocket and stare hard at the twins, willing them to see me. They're watching us carefully as we go by, and their gazes snag on me.

I shift my body to block the guards from seeing what

I'm doing. I hold up the letter to make sure Dee and Dum see it and then I slip it out the window.

It falls to the ground, but their eyes don't follow it. Instead, they keep their cool and continue their surveillance of the rest of the bus. They don't get out of their cars to pick it up, even though I'm sure they saw the letter drop.

I casually glance at the guards to see if anyone noticed what I did. The only one watching me is my girl look-alike sitting beside me, and she doesn't look like she's about to tell anyone. Everyone else is watching the Resistance group with an intensity that borders on paranoia, if anything could be called paranoid any more.

We all watch the guys by the side of the road until they shrink to a dot. My guess is they are setting up cameras of some kind for their surveillance system around the Bay Area. It makes sense that they might want a few cameras along the highways.

It takes a while for my heartbeat to return to its normal pace, and I actually have to suppress a smile. I never thought I'd think good things about the Resistance again. But if anyone is going to risk their necks and pull off a major rescue, it'll be those guys. No guarantee it'll happen but it sure beats counting on Look-Out-for-Number-One Captain Jake.

49

Half Moon Bay is bordered by a crescent-shaped beach on the Pacific coast. The earthquakes and sea storms have trashed the coastline to the point of being unrecognizable. Half Moon Bay now looks more like Crater Moon Bay with all the recent dents and bumps along the coast.

The new aerie is a posh hotel that used to sit on the bluffs overlooking the ocean. Now it sits on a piece of the land that miraculously didn't get washed away with the rest of the cliffs surrounding it. A narrow land bridge connects what's left of the bay with the hotel island, making the whole place look like a keyhole.

The land bridge isn't the old road that used to go to the hotel. It must have once been part of the golf course.

Whatever it was, the drive is as bumpy and jittery as my emotions as we approach the sprawling, estate-like hotel. Being this close to the sea, it's amazing the hotel is intact.

We drive past the main entrance, which faces a big circular driveway with a colored-light fountain that is oddly still running. The driveway is at the end of a road that now leads off a cliff.

We drive onto the grounds from the side, where the pavement is still solid and most of the golf course sprawls over the spectacular view of the ocean below. The grass is both green and mowed as if it was still in the World Before.

The only thing marring the illusion is an empty swimming pool hanging halfway off the cliff on the edge of the grounds. As we drive by, a freakishly large wave crashes against the cliff, fanning into a spectacular spray and taking a chunk of the pool with it as it recedes.

The main building looks like a country estate from a Regency romance novel. Once we park, we're herded into the rear entryway. We walk up the stairs and into a cream-and-gold banquet hall that's been turned into what feels like the backstage of a play.

Wheeled racks of costumes are everywhere. Flapper dresses, demi-masks with peacock and ostrich feathers, 1920s hats and sparkly headbands, zoot suits, pinstriped suits and elegant tuxes. As if that isn't enough, there are gossamer fairy wings of every color hanging from all the racks and fixtures around the room.

An army of people in hotel uniforms fuss over the costumes and shell-shocked females. Women and girls sit in front of mirrors, putting on makeup or sitting mutely while someone else works on them. There are also females being dressed and then paraded in front of the staff in glamorous speakeasy dresses and old-fashioned heels.

Makeup artists rush from mirrored station to station with powder and brush in hand. One station has so much hairspray and perfume in the air that it looks like a fog has moved into that spot.

Costumes are being rolled around so fast it's amazing they're not crashing into each other. They give the impression of feathers and sequins zipping across the room with nervous energy. Everybody is visibly jittery.

There are far too many women here to serve as Uriel's twin trophies. Although there must be at least a hundred people, hardly anyone is talking. The tension is more like that of a funeral home rather than a prep room for an elaborate party or play or whatever this is.

I stand by the entrance, staring. I have no idea what I'm supposed to do. I like the chaos. It might give me a chance to sneak away and look for Paige or Beliel. It gets even better when Madeline seems to forget about us and marches off to give orders to a group of hairdressers.

I drift around the room among the ribbons and sparkles. The only whispered conversations I hear repeat the same mantra: 'Get yourself an angel protector, or else.'

I find myself melting into the group of matching females who are being prepped in one corner of the ballroom. My look-alike is already there. The women are made up in pairs to look like identical twins, which several of them are.

So this is why Uriel's trophy women looked so terrified when I saw them at the last aerie. They'd been drafted from the jail cells of Alcatraz and had probably known about the horrors awaiting them if they didn't please Uriel. I thought the aerie club scene was surreal when I was there, but now I realize how insane the whole thing must have been to the girls who came from that nightmare factory.

Just when I think we've been orphaned enough for me to sneak off, Daniel, Madeline's assistant, rushes in to talk to her. His voice carries over the eerie quiet.

'"Brunettes. Small, but well-proportioned," he says.' Daniel gives her an I-told-you-so look.

Madeline scans the group of girls standing in pairs. Everyone freezes like a rabbit waiting for a hawk to swoop down. The girls all try to escape Madeline's notice by shrinking and looking anywhere but at her.

She looks at me and my matching pair, Andi. We're the smallest of the brunettes. Her lips thin out into a stubborn line.

'You're not really going to risk all of us, are you?' asks Daniel. He sounds as if he thinks she will. 'We have to give him the closest thing we've got to what he wants. You know that.' Fear vibrates off him through the intensity of his eyes and the tension of his shoulders.

Madeline closes her eyes and takes a deep breath. Whoever Doc is protecting must be very special to her.

'Okay,' she breathes out. 'Get them ready.'

Daniel looks over at us. Everyone follows his gaze and watches us. I don't like the mix of sympathy and relief in their eyes.

We get special attention even though the workers look frazzled and harried. After a whirlwind of showers, lotions, perfumes, haircuts, dresses and major make-overs, we stand in front of Madeline.

Our masks are sparkly makeup rather than a plastic disguise. Playful ribbons of blue and silver makeup tease each other from our temples and curve around our eyes and over our cheekbones.

We wear matching dresses with silky drapes of burgundy that cling to every curve. Headbands with plumes of peacock feathers. Thigh-high nylons with elastic bands to keep them up. Shapely, sparkly, gorgeous but uncomfortable heels.

People are fighting for their lives on the streets, and I'm here minding my p's and q's in four-inch heels that pinch my toes.

Madeline walks in a slow circle around us. I have to admit, we look like twins. My hair has been cut to Andi's shoulder length, and there's so much gunk in it that it would take hurricane-force winds to tweak a strand from the matching curled halos around our heads.

'Nice touch with the eyelashes,' says Madeline. We wear shockingly long fake lashes tinged with silver at the tips. I doubt that Uriel would remember me from his brief glimpse in the old aerie basement, but it's reassuring to know that even my own mother probably wouldn't recognize me now.

Madeline nods after she finishes her inspection. 'Come with me, girls. You'll get the next shift with the archangel.'

50

Uriel's suite is spectacular. The living area is enormous – the kind of thing you see in Hollywood movies. Two of the walls are lined with large windows that give a stunning 180-degree view of the ocean. A bank of fog is rolling in over the horizon, curling and tumbling above the water. The view is breathtaking, and we can't help but slow down to gawk as soon as our heels hit the plush carpet.

'Over here, girls,' says Madeline. She walks to the grand desk that sits on one side of the room beyond the tan leather sofas and chairs. She points to either side of the desk by the wall. 'While the archangel is in his suite, you stand in these two spots. Do not move unless he tells you to move. Not *like* a statue – you *are* a statue. You're allowed to breathe but that's it. Understood?'

We walk to our spots. There is a subtle piece of tape on the floor that marks where we're supposed to stand.

'You are living art. You are the archangel's trophies, and you'll remain on either side of him while he sits.'

We take our positions. Madeline stands tall, pushing out her chest, dropping one shoulder and emphasizing her curves to show us how we should look. We mimic her. She comes over and adjusts us, putting a hand on my thigh, tilting my head, arranging my hair. I've seen storekeepers do this with their mannequins.

'When the archangel leaves his suite, you follow. Flow around the desk and all obstacles in unison. Walk two steps behind him at all times. If you find yourselves falling behind, do not run. Gently pick up your pace until you are caught up. Grace at all times, ladies. Your lives depend on it.'

'What if we need to go to the bathroom?' asks Andi.

'Hold it. Every few hours, you'll get a quick break for food and bathroom runs. Someone from our team will come for you with food and makeup kits to freshen your hair and makeup during those times. Sometimes, the archangel will remember to give you a break before a long meeting. He can be good with his pets as long as they do what they're supposed to do.' Her voice makes it clear this is a warning and not a reassurance.

She walks to the far side of the desk and eyes us critically as we hold our unnatural positions. She nods and tells us to go hit the bathroom. When we come back, we assume our poses without her help. She looks at us again and makes minor adjustments.

'Good luck, ladies.' She sounds grim.

She turns and leaves the suite.

We stand there for almost an hour before the door opens. It's enough time for me to worry about every possible reason why Uriel wants us here. I'm in the middle of another poorly thought-out, harebrained scheme that risks not only my life but all the other lives around me. How am I supposed to sneak out and find Paige while I'm being a decoration for Uriel?

We wilt over time as the minutes drag by. But as soon as we hear voices outside, I can see out of the corner of my eye that Andi perks up as much as I do. My heart hammers so fast that I can actually see my chest fluttering.

The door swings open and Uriel walks in. His friendly smile seems genuine, reaching his eyes. In the ocean glow coming through the windows, his wings look off-white again. What had looked like a touch of darkness on the Alcatraz dock now looks like a blush of warmth in this rosy light. I guess the late afternoon sun reflecting off the water can make even a killer like him look mellow. No wonder everyone wants to live in California.

'—should have the reports from the secondary labs tomorrow.' A woman walks in behind him. Gold-spun hair cascading over her shoulders. Perfect features. Large blue eyes. The voice of . . . well, an angel. Laylah.

Every one of my muscles tenses and I worry I'll tip over in my high heels from all that tensing. Laylah. The head doctor who operated on Raffe. The one who should have sewn back his feathered wings and instead sewed demon wings onto his back. I wonder if the satisfaction of a major punch to her perfect jaw would be worth dying a horrible death.

'What's taking so long?' asks Uriel as he closes the door.

Laylah gives him a wide-eyed stare, looking both wounded and angry at the same time. 'It's a miracle we're as far along as we are. You know that, right? In only ten months, we've managed to get an entire apocalyptic machine running.'

Ten months?

'Most projects would barely be getting started in that time. A normal team would still be experimenting with their first batch and it would be years, maybe decades away from having a horde of mature locusts that are ready to pounce on the world. My team is almost dead from exhaustion, Uriel. I can't believe—'

'Relax,' says Uriel. His voice is soothing, his expression gentle.

The angel invasion happened less than two months ago. Had they set up labs months before the actual invasion?

He guides her to the leather sofa and sits her down. He lounges on the chair beside the sofa and puts his feet on the marble coffee table.

His black soles look dirty beside the bottle of wine and flowers arranged on the table. Otherwise, they make a beautiful picture. Two exquisite angels lounging on expensive furniture.

Uriel takes a deep breath. 'Breathe. Enjoy the wonders of God's Earth.' He proudly sweeps his hand toward the windows overlooking the spectacular surf as if he had something to do with it. He takes another deep breath as if to show her how it's done.

Laylah follows his lead and breathes deeply a couple of times. So far, neither of the angels has glanced over at us any more than they looked at the dining table. We're just furniture to them.

I keep my eyes staring at a point on the bookshelves, as befitting a statue. The last thing I want is to have them notice that I'm watching them. According to my sensei, you're better off watching your enemies through your peripheral vision anyway.

'If I didn't think you could lead this project, I wouldn't have asked you to head it.' Uriel picks up the bottle of wine and removes the foil at the top. 'There is no greater chimerologist than you, Laylah. We all know that. Well, everyone but Gabriel knew that.' His voice holds a hint of sarcasm when he mentions the Messenger. 'He should never have appointed that doddering idiot, Paean, as the realm's Lead Physician. It should have been you. And it will be as soon as I'm elected Messenger. Maybe we'll even change the title to Lead Creator.'

Laylah's perfect lips part in surprised pleasure. Oh, she'd like that.

'If Paean had been in charge of this project,' says Uriel as he works the corkscrew deeper into the cork, 'he would have started with cellular cultures and we'd be waiting years before anything happened.'

'Centuries,' says Laylah. 'He thinks everything should start with cellular cultures just because that's his specialty.'

'His methods are eons outdated. You, on the other hand – I knew you'd slam through this. You're a genius. Why bother with building a species from the ground up when we can mix and match what's already out there? Not that that's not enormously complicated.' He pops the cork. 'Your work is absolutely brilliant. And I know that this project is progressing at unbelievable, record-breaking speeds.'

He nods. Pins her with a look.

'But I need it to go faster.' His friendly features harden into something unrelenting. He pours a glass of red wine. It looks like a stream of blood pooling into the glass.

'And I know you can do it, Laylah.' His voice is soft, encouraging, but with an undertone of command. 'I wouldn't have given you the job if I didn't think you could make it happen. Triple your staff, cut corners, birth the locusts prematurely if you have to.' He hands her the glass and pours one for himself.

'Triple my staff with whom? More humans? I might as well try to train dogs to work with us for all they know about species creation.'

'This area of the globe is the best that humans have to offer. That's what you said. That's why we're here in this soulless place instead of Mecca or Jerusalem or Vatican City, where the locals would have gotten down on their knees and treated us with proper, old-world respect. Instead, we opted for the equipment, the labs, the highly trained biologists. Remember?' He takes a drink. 'You're the one who wanted to come here. So make it work, Laylah.'

'I'm doing my best.' She takes a sip, staining her lips with dark red. 'The latest batch of locusts have the lion's teeth and women's hair that you requested, but they can't work their mouths properly. If you want them closer to the biblical description, we need more time.'

He takes a cigar from a box on the coffee table and offers it to her. 'Cigar?'

'No, thank you.' She crosses her model-long legs, which emphasizes her graceful curves and lines as she lounges on the sofa. She looks like an artistic rendering of the perfect feminine form, more like a goddess than an angel.

'Try one. You'll like it.'

I assume she'll say no. Even I can tell that a fat, ash-tipped cigar wouldn't make a good accessory for her. But she hesitates.

'Truly, who knew that the nectar of the gods was meant to be smoked rather than sipped? It's no wonder so many of our upper echelon have taken to it.'

She leans forward to take it. Her back becomes stiff. Her legs look uncomfortable in her new position. Her fingers look unsure and clumsy as she lights the brown tip.

'The locusts don't need to be perfect,' says Uriel. 'They just need to put on a good show. They don't even need to survive long – just long enough to wreak havoc, torture humans in good old-fashioned, biblical style, and darken the sky with their numbers.'

Laylah takes a puff. I expect her to cough like an amateur but she doesn't. She does come close to wrinkling her nose, though. 'I'll try to speed things up.'

'Trying is not a commitment.' Uriel's voice is smooth but firm.

She takes a deep breath. 'I won't let you down, Archangel.'

'Good. I never doubted it.' He blows smoke. It must be a good cigar. He looks satisfied. He gets up and Laylah follows. 'I must make the rounds at the party. Things are probably about to get a little wild down there. When will you be joining the festivities?'

Laylah looks even more uncomfortable, if that's possible. 'I need to get back to work. My staff needs me.'

'Of course they need you. But they'll have to manage without you for an evening. Part of the job of being Lead Physician is attending major ceremonies. And believe me, this one will go down in history. You won't want to miss it.' Uriel ushers her out the door. 'The monkey named Madeline will see to your appearance.'

'Yes, Your Grace.' Laylah almost bolts out.

51

For the next couple of hours, Uriel gets dressed for the party. It's apparently another period costume party, only this time, it seems like the point is to actually be semi-disguised.

'Make the masks and wing coverings available everywhere,' he tells his assistant angel as Madeline and two other people cover his gray-tinged wings with a gauzy white material. Even though it would be Madeline and her team who would put the costumes out for the angels, Uriel only addresses his angelic assistant. 'I want all the angels to feel anonymous. And the Daughters of Men – make sure they're wearing wings.'

'Wings?' asks the assistant. His wings are sky blue and I can understand why the angels would need to cover their wings if they really want to be disguised. 'But, Your Grace, if I may, with all the wine and costumes, the Daughters of Men may be mistaken for angels by some of the drunk soldiers.'

'Wouldn't that be a shame?' Uriel's tone implies that it wouldn't be a shame at all.

'But if some of the soldiers were to make a mistake . . . ,' he breaks off delicately.

'Then they'd better pray that I become the Messenger and not Michael. Unlike Michael who is off on one of his endless military campaigns across the world, I am attending the party. I will be right here to understand how such a terrible mistake could be made. And as for Raphael, even if they don't accept that he has fallen, they'll certainly remember how preachy he got about fraternizing with the Daughters of Men after his Watchers fell doing exactly that.'

Madeline and her assistants place a layer of black feathers over Uriel's wings so that the white material peeks out between the feather gaps.

'What are you doing?' asks Uriel irritated.

Madeline stares wide-eyed at Uriel's assistant, looking terrified that Uriel just addressed her. Then she bows and tries to shrink into herself. 'I, um, thought you wanted to be in costume. Your Grace.' I'm beginning to suspect that only the Messenger gets to be called 'Your Grace', and that his toadies call him that to flatter him.

'I'll wear a mask and wing coverings but I need to be recognized, even from afar. It's the masses who need to be anonymous. Do I look like the masses to you?'

'Absolutely not, Your Grace.' Madeline sounds breathless with terror. She and her men whisk off the black feathers and gauzy material with shaking hands. 'We'll be right back with a more appropriate outfit.' They scramble out, trailing feathers.

'My apologies, Your Grace.' The assistant bows.

'I suppose intelligence is too much to ask of them.'

They launch into a discussion about wine and liquor. By the sound of things, they must have cleared every bar in the Bay Area to provide a constant flow to the angels tonight. It hits me once again how we are at war but they are not. To them, we humans are just incidental.

Despite our attack on their last aerie, they're more concerned about drinks and costumes than they are about defense against the humans. Of course, the fact that virtually all the angels were just injured and will fully recover, if they haven't already, probably just bolsters their outrageous confidence.

I discreetly rub my fingers against the fabric on my hip where my bear sword would have been. The fabric feels flimsy and vulnerable.

Before long, Madeline sweeps back into Uriel's suite with an entire crew, complete with rolling racks of costumes circa the 1920s crammed full of sparkling feathers. They get to work on Uriel.

He ends up in a white suit with wings of sparkling gold and a matching mask that's more of a crown than a face cover. It extends above his forehead, giving him the illusion of additional height, and curls around his eyes without actually hiding his features.

When he looks at himself in the full-length mirror, he orders Andi and me to stand behind him. Our makeup has been refreshed and we now wear shimmery gauze wings, more fairy than angel. We are the perfect accessories to his costume.

I understand now why he wanted petite brunettes. Our small bodies make him look large. His wings look giant, his height seems endless. We are the dark silk background to his gold and diamond regalia.

We arrive just as the party is getting started. Winged men and glamorous women mingle on the multi-tiered terrace and on the golf course below. Torches and fire pits blaze against the golden glow of the sky before sunset, lighting up the grounds.

Colorful lanterns are strung up and blowing in the wind like tethered balloons. Tall bistro tables are scattered around the party with gold-and-silver corkscrew ribbons and shiny confetti, accenting the whole scene with a festive atmosphere.

The surf pounds the cliffs at the edge of the golf course while waves splash gently on the beach on the other side. The rhythm of the water blends elegantly with the music of the string quartet.

I glance at the ocean and wonder how the escape plans are going on Alcatraz. Is the Resistance on its way there? Will Captain Jake get off his recliner and do the right thing? Then I sweep my gaze over the glittery, glamorous crowd and wonder how I'm supposed to find my sister here.

Uriel shines, clearly in his element as he greets his people. At first, Andi and I walk exactly two paces behind him, but after a while, the crowd gets tighter and we only have room to stand a single pace behind him. It gets a little tougher when he walks down to the golf course. Nothing like heels on grass to make a girl feel clumsy.

Bits of conversation spill over as we walk by. The two words I hear repeatedly are 'apocalypse' and 'Messenger'. 'Apocalypse' is said loudly with relish while 'Messenger' is said quietly with an undertone of wariness.

The women are dressed as whimsically and colorfully as we are. Delicate wings, hair curled and scalloped, demi-masks sparkling and colorful on their faces. Some are draped in long silk while others are in tasseled flapper dresses.

The angels have slicked hair and are dressed in old-fashioned tuxes or suits. They wear half masks and wing disguises that change the colors and patterns of their wings. Some, like us, have makeup or tattoo designs around their eyes instead of masks. Others wear zoot suits with looping chains and hats.

The women hang all over the angels, laughing and flirting. Their eyes, though, are far from relaxed. Many of them look grimly determined to get themselves an angel, while more than a few look outright scared. They're obviously taking their instructions to get an angel protector seriously.

At this party, Uriel's matching pair of girls are not the only ones who are screaming-on-the-inside terrified.

There are a lot of women, but there are way more angels at this party than there were at the last one at the old aerie. And unlike before, this party is crammed full of hard-muscled, hard-eyed warriors.

It turns out that most of the women are in wings that are more fairy than angel. Even the feathered wings are little cherub wings rather than the true angelic kind. No way could anyone mistake these women for angels.

If an angel gave way to temptation tonight, there would be guilt in the morning. And the knowledge that he couldn't convince the others that it was just a mistake.

And Uriel would be his only chance for salvation.

I guess I already knew that Uriel is a manipulative bastard. I suspect he'd been building up to this over weeks of parties, slowly introducing the Daughters of Men to the angels, the unlimited drinks, the costumes. And now, the masks and wing disguises that allow for anonymity so the angels can do whatever tempts them without feeling like someone is watching. It would have been outright weird if Uriel had suggested such a thing as soon as they arrived on earth.

The word 'premeditated' comes to mind.

The fact that I'm allowed to overhear enough to start piecing this stuff together makes me worried.

Very worried.

52

From what I can gather from snippets of conversation among the hotel staff, it's not just a party, it's a banquet. On the agenda are drinks, scantily clad Daughters of Men and more drinks. Then dinner with more drinks. Then dancing with Daughters of Men and more drinks.

Basically, there's a whole lot of drunkenness planned for the evening. I guess, if the angels don't break their own rules tonight, Uriel's backup plan must be to make sure they don't remember that they didn't break the rules.

Uriel glides from one group to the next, clasping hands and making sure everyone is having a good time. He offers Andi and me to those without girls on their arms, but they all politely decline without even looking at us.

I get a better notion of Uriel's monumental task. This is not an easy crowd to manipulate. Already, a lot of the soldiers are turning down extra drinks and refusing the attentions of the women.

Some of the crowd welcome him warmly and with a brief fanning of wings. It seems like the equivalent of a salute – not so much that it takes up too much space, but enough to show respect. They didn't do that at the old aerie. He must have made progress in his campaign. They hadn't called him Your Grace then either.

I'm glad to see that other groups greet him only with simple nods and polite smiles. They call him Uriel, Archangel, and occasionally Uri rather than Your Grace.

'Do you really think we're nearing Judgment Day, Uri?' asks a warrior. He hadn't saluted with his wings and doesn't address him with much respect, but there's genuine interest and – hope? – in his face.

'I absolutely do,' says Uriel. His voice has real conviction. 'Archangel Gabriel brought us here for a reason. Bringing two other archangels to Earth along with a legion of warriors is nothing short of apocalyptic.'

Ain't that the truth.

I wonder what Raffe would think of this party.

Before Uriel can go on with the conversation, others intervene, and Uriel goes back to nodding greetings and stretching his mouth with an over-bright smile.

My feet are already hurting and the party has just begun. My toes feel like they're in a vice that gets tighter by the minute, and my heels feel like electric drills are boring into them.

I fantasize about stepping into the crowd and losing myself in it. Could I drift out to the edges and disappear?

Just as I'm thinking that, a woman screams from the beach, followed by an unnatural growl. The piercing sound gets swallowed quickly by the roar of the waves, the conversation and the music.

Andi and I exchange a quick glance before going back to our matching poses. We mold our faces into mannequin faces – plastic and aloof. But I'm sure that if someone really looked, they could see the alert fear in our eyes.

Uriel works his way to a makeshift stage at the edge of the party. As he meanders along, he looks over at someone for a second longer than usual. I hadn't even realized how closely I'd been watching him until I notice a change in his attitude. His shoulders and expression freeze on autopilot as his mind switches over to something else.

The change is so subtle that I'm sure no one else noticed it, except maybe for Andi who has been watching him as closely as I have.

Uriel looks at an oversized angel on the edge of the crowd. He has snowy wings peppered with gold feathers and a matching gold mask over his eyes. He looks angelic in every sense except for the sneer on his lips.

He holds his snowy wings out a little as if insecure that he belongs here. One of his wings has the scissor notch that's now forever etched in my memory.

Beliel.

I also recognize two angels beside him from the video Doc showed me. Their wings are shimmery bronze and copper, but I'd bet my next meal that one of them has burnt orange wings beneath that costume. It's Burnt, the Kidnapper of Little Girls.

I clench my fists automatically and have to force them to relax.

Beliel and Uriel exchange a look. Beliel nods ever so slightly at Uriel. The archangel glances away without responding but he smiles brightly at the next person and seems more relaxed.

I do a sweep of the people around Beliel. Of course, Paige is nowhere to be seen in the sea of angels and neither is Raffe. I'm not even sure I believe what Doc said about Paige being drawn to Beliel, but apparently my heart does.

Uriel steps into another group of warriors. This one is part of the 'Your Grace' crowd. Smiles and wing-fanning all around. As Uriel makes his way through the various masked and disguised angels, one of them catches my eye.

He's a warrior with the required broad shoulders and Adonis body. This one has white-feathered wing covers flecked with silver that sparkles in the twilight. A matching mask swirls and curves with feathers, ornately covering everything but his eyes and mouth. Even his forehead is partially hidden by his tousled dark hair.

There's something about him that makes me forget about my heels pinching my toes, the too-close crowd, and even the monstrous Politician. Something feels familiar about him, although I can't say exactly what. Maybe it's the proud way he holds his head, or the way he cuts through the crowd with utter confidence, as if it's assumed that everyone will get out of his way.

Although he doesn't observe Beliel any more than anyone else, he moves when Beliel moves, stops when Beliel stops.

All my attention is drawn to the warrior as I look for the slightest proof of him being Raffe. If he had been in a crowd of human men, it'd be easy to pick him out as a god among them. Just my luck that we're in a crowd of walking mountains of muscle and the kind of studliness that females all over the world would die for. Too bad there's too big a risk of actually dying around them.

My intense study of him must tickle his spy sense because he looks over at me.

I know that, as a soldier, he probably sized up all the others around him, the weapons they carry, the best escape route. But as an angel, I doubt that he bothered to take much stock of the humans.

When he looks at me, it's the look of someone noticing a person for the first time, proving yet again that an angel's arrogance knows no bounds. Which, now that I think about it, increases the likelihood that this is Raffe.

He does a full evaluation of me, taking in the cut and curled hair accented with peacock feathers, the blue and silver makeup ribbons chasing around my eyes and cheekbones, the silky dress that clings to every part of my body.

But it's not until his eyes meet mine that a jolt of recognition passes between us.

I have no doubt that it's Raffe.

But he fights his recognition of me.

For a second, his defenses fall and I can see the turmoil behind his eyes.

He saw me die. This must be a mistake.

This glittery girl doesn't look anything like the street waif he traveled with.

Yet . . .

His step falters and he pauses, staring at me.

53

The river of people mills around him as he stands like a rock in the channel. He stares at me, seemingly oblivious to the traffic of sparkling fabric, plumage of all colors, masked faces and flutes of champagne flowing around him.

Time may have stopped for him but it hasn't stopped for the rest of the world. Beliel continues to move farther into the crowd while Uriel walks closer to Raffe. If Raffe doesn't move soon, he'll be stuck having to greet Uriel.

The angels around Raffe fan their wings as Uriel approaches. If Raffe doesn't fan his wings, too, Uriel is bound to notice him. Maybe he'll stop to talk to him. Will he recognize Raffe's voice? Walking into an angel party with demon wings is a little like walking onto a shooting range disguised as a target.

I try to warn Raffe with my eyes as we drift over to him, but he seems to be in a trance as he stares at me.

Only when it's practically too late does he blink out of it and finally glance at Uriel. He ducks his head and turns away, but he gets caught trying to go in the wrong direction as the angels around him move forward to greet Uriel.

I can't think of any way to help Raffe that doesn't involve getting my head chopped off or something equally horrendous.

But if I do something to distract Uriel, he'll likely wait until we're in private to chop me up and feed me to his scorpion-tailed hounds.

At least, I hope so.

I take two small steps out of sync with my matching twin. I trip.

I careen into Uriel, bumping him harder than I intended.

Uriel stumbles into one of his sycophants and champagne sloshes onto his hand. He spins to look at me with a scowl. There is the promise of eternal torture in his eyes.

I almost expect scorpion monsters to jump out and grab me on the spot, dragging me into the depths of some dungeon where death minions will scuttle out to chop me to bits in the lonely darkness. I don't need to fake my terror when Uriel looks at me.

But just as I suspected, he'll wait to deal with me until he's done stroking feathers or whatever it is that angel politicians do. I have until then to figure out how to get out of this mess.

By the time he composes the raw violence in his face into something more suitable for a politician and turns back to his admirers, Raffe is nowhere in sight.

It takes a few minutes before my heart slows down to normal. I keep my eyes forward and behave like a model accessory, ashamed to glance over at Andi and see the fear in her face. She's not very useful to Uriel without me, is she?

I hope Raffe made it to a shadowy corner somewhere. I hope Paige is okay and that I'll soon find her. I hope Mom and Clara are doing all right and are successfully escaping. And now, there's Andi, who I clearly need to take with me when I leave because it'll be a death sentence for her if her twin walks off or gets killed. And then there are all those people on Alcatraz. . . .

Too many.

Being responsible for Mom and Paige is nearly crushing me already. I take comfort in reminding myself that I am just a kid, not a hero. Heroes have a tendency to die in horrible ways. Somehow, I'll get through this, and then I'll lead the quietest life anyone could possibly have in the World After.

We follow Uriel as he works the crowd and makes his way to the makeshift stage at the ocean side of the lawn. The stage has a long table with a white tablecloth on it. The cloth shivers in the ocean wind, held down by plates and cutlery. Angels are seated on either side of an empty center chair like disciples at the Last Supper.

Uriel walks in front of the table and stands in the center, looking down at the party below him. I wonder if we should find seats, but Andi and I both hesitate long enough that we just assume our trophy poses on either side of him.

As if on cue, the roar of the party quiets down and all eyes are on us. On Uriel, of course, but I'm close to him so it feels like everyone's staring at me, even though no one is.

I find myself scanning the masses for a certain sarcastic angel.

I take a deep breath. Am I really wishing that Raffe is still here? He almost got caught already. It'll be suicide for him if he doesn't get out of here fast.

But I can't help but wonder if he sees me.

I should be staring at a spot above the crowd as my pose dictates, but my eyes keep drifting back to scan the faces below us.

'Welcome brothers and sisters,' Uriel says as everyone quiets down. 'We are gathered tonight to unite in a single cause and to celebrate. I have news both appalling and amazing. First, the appalling.' The audience listens with hushed curiosity.

'Until the humans attacked our aerie, we assumed that they'd been behaving as well as could be expected. But now it has come to my attention that they've been up to sinister things that we cannot abide.'

Uriel motions for someone to come forward. An angel drags a cowering man onto the stage. He wears faded jeans, a Rolling Stones T-shirt, and glasses. He's shaking and sweating, clearly terrified. The angel hands over a rolled cloth to Uriel.

He unrolls it, letting its contents fall onto the stage.

'Tell us, Man,' says Uriel. 'Tell everyone what you had hidden in this cloth.'

The man starts hyperventilating in loud, raspy breaths, looking wildly at the crowd. When he doesn't say anything, his guard grabs his hair and yanks his head back.

'Feathers,' the prisoner gasps out. 'A . . . a handful of feathers.'

'And?' asks Uriel.

'Ha . . . hair. A lock of golden hair.'

'And what else, Man?' asks Uriel in a freezing voice.

The prisoner's eyes dart around, looking trapped and desperate. His guard yanks back his head again so that his neck looks like it's about to snap.

'Fingers.' The man sobs. Tears streak down his face, and I wonder what he did for a living before the civilized world came to an end. A doctor? A teacher? A grocery clerk?

'Two . . . severed . . . fingers,' he says between gasps. His guard lets him go. He huddles on the stage, shaking.

'What was the source of these feathers, hair and fingers?'

The guard raises his hand and the man cringes, shielding his face.

'I got them from someone else,' says the man. 'I didn't hurt anybody. I swear. I never hurt anybody.'

'Where did they come from?' asks Uriel.

'I don't know,' cries the man.

The guard grabs him by the arms, and I can almost hear his bones crunching.

The man cries out in pain. 'Angel.' He falls to his knees, crying. His eyes dart around the hostile crowd in terror. 'They're angel parts.' He almost whispers, but the audience is silent and I'm sure they can hear him.

54

'Angel parts,' says Uriel in his booming voice. 'The monkeys are slicing up our injured brethren before they can recover. They are trading our feathers, fingers and other parts for currency. And you all know how long and painful it can be to grow back fingers, not to mention the parts we can't grow back.'

Angels roar, restless with violence.

Uriel lets the righteous anger build with the masses. 'For so long we have waited. For so long we have let monkeys infest this beautiful land, letting them believe that *they* are the most favored species in God's universe. They still don't understand why they've had unprecedented free reign over Earth for so long. They're so arrogant and stupid that they don't even realize that no one else is dumb enough to make a legendary battlefield their home.'

The crowd chuckles and hollers.

Uriel smiles at them. 'But I have amazing news, brothers and sisters. News that will put humans like this in their rightful place. News that will allow us to punish them with God's blessing.'

The crowd quiets.

'You've heard the rumors,' says Uriel. 'You've heard the speculations. I'm here to tell you that they are true. The signs are here. We have definitive *proof* of the reason why Gabriel the Messenger brought us here to Earth.'

The audience murmurs excitedly.

'We don't have to wonder any more, brothers and sisters. We don't have to argue and debate about whether this is a drill or a skirmish with the Fallen or just another warning to the humans while they peck at us with their pebbles and rocks.' He pauses for dramatic effect.

The crowd quiets.

Uriel sweeps the crowd with his eyes. 'Biblical locusts are here.'

A low murmur quickly bursts into an excited roar.

He lets the noise build before putting up his hands to quiet them. 'As many of you know, part of my job is to visit the Abyss. Yesterday, I opened the Bottomless Pit. From it, black smoke rose and darkened the sun and the air. Out of the smoke came locusts upon the earth. Just as it was foretold, their faces were the faces of men and they had tails like powerful scorpions. Thousands upon thousands. Pouring into the sky.'

As if on cue, all the angels in the crowd turn the same direction to look up at the sky. I see the dark cloud on the horizon before I hear what they hear.

The cloud explodes, spitting out more darkness, growing ever larger. A low buzzing quickly turns into a thunderous roar.

I've heard this before.

The sound of swarming scorpions.

Everyone is silent and still while we all watch the roiling cloud rush toward us.

Uriel raises his arms like he's ready to hug the crowd. 'We have our confirmation, brothers and sisters. What we have been waiting for. What we have been *bred* for. What we have *lived*, *breathed* and *dreamt* of is finally here!'

Uriel's voice feels like a booming command in my head.

'We will be like—'

Gods.

'—Heroes of Old!'

He takes a deep breath. 'Finally.' Another breath, his chest swelling with satisfaction. 'It's time for Judgment Day. The legendary apocalypse is HERE!'

55

As everyone takes a moment to absorb what he's saying, the horde of scorpion locusts hurls toward us.

I want to shout that he's lying. That the scorpions are his creations, not biblical locusts. But I lose my chance because the crowd goes nuts.

Warriors raise their swords and stab the sky. They shout war cries that shatter the twilight.

Their wings flex, bursting out of the sheaths that disguise them.

Madeline's carefully placed feathers fly everywhere. Glitter and fluff float into the air and drift like a scene in an old-time ticker-tape parade.

I shrink back, wishing I could disappear. Ironically, Andi does too, so that we continue to look like a matching set.

Bloodlust pulses in the air like sprays of pheromone. The air is thick with it and getting thicker.

Then the terrible thing happens.

Beside us on the stage, a warrior grabs the angel-parts dealer and lifts him above his head. The guy squirms like a kid as his glasses fall off. The angel heaves him into the crowd.

A hundred arms grab the poor man and pull him down into the engulfing center of the angelic masses. The man screams and screams.

The multitude shoves each other to try to reach the man. Bloody bits of cloth and bigger, wet chunks I don't want to think about fly out of the place where he landed.

The warrior angels rage and yell as they restlessly jostle each other, cheering on the ones tearing at the man who is drowning in their violence.

The crowd is peppered with humans.

From here, the humans look small and terrified as they realize what's going on. Most of them are women, and they look especially vulnerable in their scanty dresses and heels.

The scorpions thunder above, darkening the sky as they fly by. The wind gains force from countless wings, mixing with the shouts of the crowd. The frantic energy whips up the bloodlust in the drunken warriors.

People panic and run.

And like cats whose instincts get triggered by a flee-ing mouse, the warriors pounce.

It's a massacre.

The ones trapped in the center of the crowd have no place to run, although they try. It's too crowded for the angels to use their swords. They grab the humans with their bare hands.

Screams fill the night as the center of the crowd tightens in on itself while the edges disperse as people fan out. The angels seem to enjoy the chase as they let humans run away from the crowd before tackling them.

One warrior punches his fist into a waiter's stomach and pulls out a stringy, bloody mass that can only be his intestines. He drapes them over a screaming woman like fine jewelry. The angels around him roar their approval and punch their fists into the sky in a crazed frenzy.

From the stage, I can see the color of blood spreading across the crowd in a spill that just won't stop.

Andi is screeching in panic. She turns and runs, hopping down from the stage and into the night.

My instincts yell at me to do the same but the stage is the least crowded, the safest of all the areas I can see. But being on stage during a riot is like being under a ten-thousand-watt spotlight when every cell of my body needs to be hiding in the dark.

Even Uriel seems to be at a loss as to what to do. The jerky motions of his head and the tense expression on his face when he turns to talk to his aides tell me this isn't part of the plan.

He meant to get everyone drunk, excited and riled up enough to break taboos tonight. But he clearly didn't expect this. Maybe if he was a warrior instead of a politician, he would have predicted their response. He would have known that their veneer of civilized behavior was just waiting for an excuse to be shredded.

In pockets of the crowd, angels who've been shoving each other in the race to catch a human start throwing punches at each other.

It's turning into a brawl as well as a massacre. Some of them take to the air to get more room and the chaos becomes three-dimensional.

56

My peripheral vision has been tracking a movement that's just now coming to my attention. Someone is hurrying through the throng toward the stage.

I try not to let my imagination leap to where it wants to go. But I can't help it. I'm not usually a girl who hopes for a damsel-in-distress rescue but no matter the odds against it, this would be a freakin' fantastic time for Raffe to come and sweep me into the sky.

But it's not him.

It's Beliel. His giant shoulders cut through the chaos as he shoves his way forward. My eyes search the crowd behind Beliel for Raffe but I see no sign of him.

Disappointment kicks me so hard, I want to start crying.

I need to find a way out of this.

Alone.

Lots of distraction – that's good. Murderous angels everywhere – that's bad.

That's about as far as my frozen brain will go.

Beliel climbs onto the stage and shoves his way through the angels surrounding Uriel.

The screams, the yells, the smell of blood all assault me. My brain and muscles want to seize up and it takes everything I've got to keep myself from vaulting into the lethal crowd like Andi did. My choices are to stand here until angels converge on me or run into the slaughter and hope against hope that I can sneak out of here.

I've never had a panic attack and I'm hoping I'm not about to now. But I'm hyper-aware of what a flimsy, inconsequential creature I am compared to these demi-gods. Did I think for a second that I could have my own agenda among them? That I could beat any of them? I'm a little nobody, a nothing. By all the laws of nature, I should be crawling under a table and crying for mommy.

Only, relying on mommy is what other people do.

I get cold comfort from that. I've always been on my own and I've managed okay so far, haven't I?

In my head, I run through a list of vulnerable body parts that makes size and strength irrelevant. Eyes, throat, groin, knees – even the biggest, toughest men have vulnerable spots that take very little force to damage. This thought soothes me enough that I can start looking for a way out.

As I survey the scene with a little less panic, I notice someone new on the stage stairs.

Raffe stands on the steps, as still as a statue, watching me.

In the twilight, his white-wing covering sparkles like stars in the summer sky. I never would have guessed that beneath that covering lies a pair of scythe-edged demon wings.

Does he recognize me yet?

Uriel's group begins leaping off the stage and taking to the air like a multi-winged organism. Beliel is the last to leave. He opens his stolen wings to their full glory and starts to beat the air.

Raffe leaps and tackles him.

They slam onto the stage with a bang, but no one notices one more pair of warriors fighting.

We are now the only ones left on stage. Below us is the shrieking slaughter. Above us is the seemingly never-ending mass of scorpions thundering through their flyby. In between, it's a drunken angel free-for-all with some even having mid-air collisions.

A bloodied angel thunks onto the stage from above.

So much blood streaks from him that it splashes onto my dress. His shoulder is badly ripped like he got scraped against the pointy tip of a lamppost. But he doesn't seem to notice as he jumps up, instantly ready for more.

I become acutely aware that I'm the only human around.

57

What I wouldn't give for Raffe's sword right now.

The bloody angel takes a step toward me.

I snatch a high-class steak knife from the table and kick off my heels.

Or I try to.

One of my heels refuses to come off without a helping hand. Either my foot has swelled or the shoe was too small for me.

I don't know a single fighting art that doesn't require good footwork, and I'm pretty sure that having one bare foot and one in high heels is not a recommended technique.

My dress is also a problem. It's full length and shapely. It looks great but doesn't exactly give me enough room to kick. My legs are the strongest part of my body and I'm not about to hobble myself in a fight for the sake of modesty. I slit my knife through a seam, ripping the skirt all the way to my thigh.

I angle the knife so it'll slip between his ribs when I stab.

The throat is a better target but I'm too short to go for that with this beast. At least not on the first thrust. The second move, after he's taken a hit, is another story.

He almost smiles at my knife as if that just adds more fun. He raises an eyebrow when he sees that I'm holding it like I know how to use it. But his sword stays untouched in its scabbard as if this massacre and brawl don't merit the use of his sword.

His eyes are focused on my knife and face. Easy to do since my hands are up near my face in a fighter stance.

But my heel is still on my back foot, several inches higher than my front foot. No way can I have decent footwork limping around like this. So I do the only thing I can do.

I kick him in the face point blank with my high heel.

He wasn't expecting that.

The angel flies back off the stage.

'It really is you,' says Raffe.

He's staring at me, stunned. His fist is mid-air but paused in the middle of pummeling the hell out of Beliel who is bloody and staggering.

He starts a slow smile that melts my bones.

Beliel interrupts the moment by butting him in the head.

Raffe staggers back.

Beliel takes a good look at me. He smiles like he now knows a secret. His teeth are covered in blood dripping from his gums.

He jumps off the stage, sweeping his wings.

Raffe leaps and grabs Beliel's leg. He yanks back, keeping him from taking flight. Raffe is about to get his wings back.

I yank off my remaining shoe, ready to dive in and help him.

Before I can move, though, the bloody angel I kicked off stage drags himself back up from the mass of seething bodies.

Boy, does he look pissed.

My heel caught him in the nose, which now looks exploded on his face. His once festive mask is now like something out of a horror flick.

I back away, quickly glancing at Raffe. He's pulling with all his might to keep Beliel from flying off. This is the perfect opportunity to get his wings back. Who would question one more act of brutality among so many? He might not get a chance this good again.

Raffe glances over at me and our eyes meet.

The wind blows my hair across my face and billows my split dress around my legs.

I'm not sure which is more mortifying – that my thigh-high nylons are showing all the way to their tops or that my fairy wings are fluttering in the wind right before a fight.

My opponent draws back his fist for a punch that may flat-out kill me if it connects.

I get ready to deflect and stab. I tell myself I can take him on but I can't escape the fact that I will only be delaying the inevitable. I know when I'm outgunned.

His fist comes flying at me.

Before I can react, it's deflected by a forearm just as big as his. Raffe punches him so hard, he lands flat on his back and stays there.

Beliel, poised on the edge of the stage, watches us with his bloody grin as if he likes what he sees.

He leaps into the air.

On Beliel's back, Raffe's beautiful snowy wings beat back and forth. Once, twice. Waving a graceful goodbye.

The giant demon disappears into the fist-throwing, flight-hopping crowd.

58

Raffe rips the tuxedo jacket off my dazed attacker and drapes it over me. It covers my entire upper body including my head. I can peek through the slit of the collar as I hide in the oversized jacket.

A warm arm enfolds me like a shield around my shoulder and turns me toward the side of the stage.

'Stay with me,' says a familiar masculine whisper from above my head. Even over the yelling of the mob and the roaring of the waves, something unfurls in my chest at the sound of that voice.

I look up to say something but he puts his finger to my lips and whispers, 'Don't talk. You'll just spoil my fantasy of rescuing an innocent damsel in distress as soon as you open your mouth.'

I'm so relieved I might laugh hysterically if I open my mouth anyway.

My vision shrinks down to a sliver between the jacket collars as I trot along in the warmth of his cocoon. He holds me tightly against him, guiding and shielding me with his body. I shuffle beside him, trying to become invisible.

We descend four steps into the seething mass of violence.

As soon as we step down, we get jostled. I grip my knife even tighter, trying to be ready for whatever might come next. Raffe freely shoves and jostles right back in a very dominant way. He holds me behind him as he plows through the crowd in front of us.

We're near the edge of the masses but we still have to work our way through to reach open space. We step over bodies and I try not to look down.

Most of the crowd is too busy with their own fights to bother with us. It's now mostly angel-on-angel but there are still a few humans on the ground with their arms raised protectively against pummeling fists and kicks. Some warriors shake their heads in disgust at the sight but it's not much of a consolation. A part of me wants to slash at the attacking angels while another part of me wants to run and hide.

Raffe drags me along too fast for me to dwell on it. I can't see much in the crush of bodies and I knock into him as he suddenly stops.

We're on the outskirts of the crowd with most of the fighting behind us. Ahead of us is the bluff that drops down to the dark beach. The only thing between us and freedom is a brawl.

Two angels go at it while two others circle each other. Neither of them have their swords drawn. These fights aren't meant for real damage, at least not to each other. They're like drunk Viking warriors with a hellacious vicious streak that Uriel thought he could control.

One of the angels gets thrown our way. His arm grazes me as he whizzes by. I half-spin and stagger, my head accidentally popping out of the oversized jacket.

'What's that you got there?' the one still standing asks. 'There's still one left?' He swaggers over and grabs for me.

Without warning, Raffe throws a punch into his face, followed by two hits so fast that his fists are almost a blur.

I duck out of the way and step out from his shadow. When the other angel lurches back, Raffe doesn't follow. He hovers near me.

I'm fully out in the open now. I drop the jacket, step into a defensive stance, and lift my knife in front of me.

Like the previous one, this angel smiles when he sees my blade. He's up for more of a challenge than squashing an ant. At least this ant has a sharp knife and an attitude.

My back feels exposed but I'll just have to assume the angels will be more sportsmanlike than to attack from behind while I'm fighting, since this is nothing but sport to them anyway.

Beside me, Raffe is already exchanging blows with an angel. He slams his attacker with the force of a head-on collision.

My own opponent makes the first move. His grin is so wide, you'd think I was cooking up a treat for him.

Males – they've all trained against each other. They expect attacks to certain zones on their bodies and from someone who's used to relying on upper-body strength. And they always, always underestimate women.

Me, I don't have much upper-body strength, nothing compared to most men, much less these guys. Like many women fighters, my power comes from my hips and legs.

He dives for me, hands out to grab my knife, expecting me to go straight at him.

I duck, crouching with bent knees, letting him almost sail over me.

I leap up at the last second and stab my blade into his crotch with all the force of my springing legs.

Why bother attacking their strengths when you can go straight for their weaknesses?

He rolls around on the sand just like any other guy who gets kicked in the nuts. He'll heal. But he won't be breaking taboos anytime soon.

An angel gets tossed past me head first. I spin to see Raffe pummeling the last one. More are coming our way from the crowd, attracted to a good fight.

Raffe looks over at the bloody knife in my hand. 'If I still had any doubts that it was you, that would do it.' He gestures toward my opponent rolling on the ground with his hands cradling his package.

'He should have been polite and just let us by,' I say.

'Way to teach him some respect. I always wanted to meet a girl who fights dirty,' says Raffe.

'There's no such thing as dirty fighting in self-defense.'

He huffs. 'I don't know whether to make fun of him or to respect you.'

'Come on, that one's easy.'

He grins at me. There's something in his eyes that makes my insides melt a little, like something deep inside us is communicating without me being fully aware of it.

I'm the first to look away.

I slip the blade into the elastic band of my thigh-high stockings. If they're tight enough to keep the nylons up when I fight, then they should do a decent job of holding my knife. I'm glad these things are good for something.

I look up and see Raffe watching me. I feel a wave of awkwardness.

Raffe grabs me around the waist and lifts me into his arms like in an old-time movie. His arms cradle my back and knees.

I reflexively wrap my arms around his neck. For a moment, I'm confused, and the silliest thoughts flood through my head.

'Don't let me go,' he says.

He runs with me toward the bluff. Two steps into it, his wings burst out from their wing coverings. Madeline's sparkly white feathers explode behind us as giant bat wings spread out.

Freedom in the shape of demon's wings. I want to laugh and cry at the same time.

I'm in Raffe's arms, flying.

59

We're in the air.

I cling tighter, and he shifts me so that I'm holding on like a kid with my legs wrapped around his middle. He's warm even as the ocean wind blasts against my back. We pick up altitude to a frightening height, but his arms around me are secure and I can't help but feel reassured.

That feeling doesn't last long. Between Raffe's wings, I get glimpses of what's behind us.

Tipsy or not, the angels have no trouble lifting off into the air. The sight of demon wings must have incited them because there are more of them chasing us than we saw on the beach. They fly up through wisps of fog lit by pinpoints of firelight as we glide over the black waves.

Angels are supposed to be beautiful creatures of light but the ones chasing us look more like a cloud of demons spewing forth from the mist. Raffe must be thinking something similar because he tightens his grip around my waist as if to say, 'not this one.'

He banks into a turn, flying farther away from the shore to where the mist turns into a blanket. He glides lower toward the water where the fog is thicker and the waves are louder.

We're so low, the sea sprays over me as it surges. Water swells, turning into whitewater and rolling below us. It feels like mile after mile of black and raging surf.

Raffe zigs one way, then the other. He makes sharp, unexpected turns after going straight for a while. Escape maneuvers.

The fog is so thick that there's a chance the angels are chasing shadows. The roar of the waves and wind means the angels can't hear Raffe's wings as they pump powerfully through the air.

I'm shivering against his body. The icy spray and ocean wind are freezing me to the point of not being able to feel my arms around his neck or my legs around his torso.

We glide along in silence, slicing through the night. I have no idea how close the angels are or whether they're even on our tail any more. I hear and see nothing in the fog glow. We take another sharp turn toward the ocean.

A face pops up in the fog.

Behind it, giant wings with feathers the color of mist.

He's too close.

He slams into us.

We spin out of control, bat wings tangling with feathered ones.

Raffe whips his wing with its extended scythes and gouges into the feathered wings. The blades rip through the layers of feathers until they catch on the angel's wing bone.

We all tumble together in a mass as we fall through the air.

Raffe stabilizes us with great sweeps but he can't fight with his wings and fly too. He untangles their wings as the angel reaches for his sword.

Raffe doesn't have a sword.

And he has me – a hundred pounds of dead weight that can only mess up his balance and fighting technique. His arms are holding me instead of being free to fight. His wings need to work that much harder to keep us in the air.

My only thought is that I am not going to end up truly dead this time in Raffe's arms. I am not going to be one more wound on his soul.

The angel pulls out his sword.

Having trained with the staff, I know there are weapons that need distance to be used effectively. The sword is one of them.

Right now, the angel has enough space to reach back and skewer us or raise his sword and slice us. But if he was hugging us, a feeble cut would be the most he could do.

It's just water. It'll be cold as hell, but it won't kill me if I fall.

Not right away, anyway.

It's amazing how many times we have to go against our survival instincts to survive. I grip my legs even tighter around Raffe's middle and push my upper body away from him.

His arms give way in surprise before they tighten back around me. That's enough time for me to lean out and grab the angel's sword arm in one hand and his high-collared tuxedo shirt in the other.

I lock my elbow and hold his sword arm to keep him from swinging toward us. I sure hope he's not strong enough to crush my shoulder socket. With my other hand, I yank him forward.

It all happens within a second. If the angel had been expecting that move, there's no way he would have let me do it. But what attacker expects his victim to pull him closer?

Without his wings fully in his control to balance him, I manage to pull the exceptionally light angel toward us.

Up close, his sword is less of a threat for skewering, but Raffe is forced to fly awkwardly to avoid shredding his wing on the blade. We teeter in the air, not far above the black waves.

Raffe holds me tight with one arm while using the other to fend off the angel who is trying to punch him.

I lean over and grab the sword's hilt. I don't have a chance of getting it away from him, but I might be able to distract him from his fight with Raffe. And if I'm really lucky, I might even convince the sword that an unauthorized user is trying to lift it.

We grapple in the air, awkwardly dipping, then gaining a little altitude, bobbing and twisting up and down above the water. I manage to grab the sword's hilt with both my hands and although I can't move it from the angel's grip, I can angle it.

As soon as I do, the sword suddenly becomes heavy, so heavy that the angel's arm flags.

'No!' the angel cries. There's real horror in his voice as the sword threatens to drop from our hands.

Raffe slams him with the fist of his free arm. The angel lurches back.

His sword drops. And disappears into the water.

'No!' he cries again, horrified disbelief in his eyes as he looks at the dark water where his sword sank. I guess they don't have scuba-diving angels to retrieve swords and other valuables from the bottom of the ocean.

He roars a war cry at us, bloodlust in his contorted face. Then he charges.

Two more angels appear out of the thick mist.

Not surprising, with all the noise the first angel is making, but my heart jumps anyway when I see them.

All three come at us. Raffe spins around and flies toward the open sea.

There's no way he's going to outfly them with me weighing him down.

'Let go,' I say into his ear.

Raffe holds me tighter like there's no room for discussion.

'We'll both be safer with me in the water than weighing you down during a fight.' Still, he holds on. 'I can swim, Raffe. It's no big deal.'

Something large slams into us from behind.

And Raffe's arms jar loose. I shove away.

That first moment of falling feels like slow-mo, where every sensation is amplified. A sheer knee-jerk survival reaction makes me flail and grab the first thing I can.

One hand grabs air. The other hand grasps the tip of a feathered wing.

Having my entire weight on one wing, the angel twists and goes out of control. I channel all my panic into the grip.

We plunge into the ocean together.

60

Every cell in my body freezes, then explodes into ice shards. The ice needles pierce and collide all through me. At least, that's what it feels like.

It's the most intense when the water engulfs my head, as if the top of my head was the last bastion of warmth in my body. I need to shriek from the shock of it but my lungs are so frozen and contracted that shrieking is beyond me.

Dark turbulence rolls me around as I cannonball down. I lose all sense of body and direction.

I eventually stop tumbling but as soon as I stop, I'm not sure which way is up. My body tries to thrash around as the stopwatch on the air in my lungs ticks away.

I never would have thought that I might not know up

from down but without gravity and light, I can't tell what's what. I'm terrified to pick a direction.

Bubbles brush by me and I have thoughts of horrible things coming at me from the watery depths of hell. All those half-lucid nights with Mom chanting away in the dark, painting images of demons dragging me into hell, come flooding back in the enormous coffin that is the sea. Are those dark shapes moving in the water or—?

Knock it off.

Air. Swim. Think.

No time to get sucked into a swirl of pointless drivel that isn't going to help in any way.

Bubbles.

Something about the bubbles.

Don't bubbles float up?

I put my hand to my mouth to feel the bubbles and let a precious bit of air out of my burning lungs. They tickle as they float across my face and past my ear.

I follow them sideways, or what feels like sideways. Water currents can drift bubbles in any direction but eventually, they go up, right? I certainly hope so.

I let out more bits of air, trying not to let out more than I need to, until the bubbles consistently touch my nose on their way up. I kick as hard as I can, following the bubbles as fast as my burning lungs can drive me.

I begin to despair that I'm going the wrong direction when I notice that the water is becoming more iridescent, lighter. I swim harder.

Finally, my head breaks through the surface and I take a huge gulp. Salty water pours into my mouth as the choppy sea slaps me in the face. My lungs constrict and I desperately try to control my coughs so that I don't breathe in another mouthful of water.

The sea erupts beside me and something bursts up.

Head, arms, wings. The angel I tangoed with has found his way up too.

He thrashes, desperately gulping air and splashing all over the place. His feathers are drenched and he doesn't look like he can swim very well. His arms flounder and his wings flap, slapping the water pointlessly.

He's being kept afloat by his thrashing but that's a very exhausting way to swim. If he was human, he would have spent all his energy by now and drowned.

I turn away and kick the water. I'm so cold I can barely lift my arms.

The angel's wing sweeps forward and blocks me. It corrals me into him as he thrashes.

I fumble for my knife, hoping it's still stuck in my nylon band. My hand is so frozen, I can barely feel it but it's there. It's just a regular knife, not an angel blade, but it'll still cut him. He'll still feel the pain and bleed.

Well, maybe in this cold, he won't feel much but I have to try.

He reaches for me and I slash at his hand.

He pulls back, then reaches for me with his other hand, grabbing my hair. I stab into his forearm. He lets go but grabs me with his slashed hand as he splashes about.

He pulls me in toward him, his arms climbing over me and pulling me down in the classic drowning thrash that water safety instructors warn you about.

I take a deep breath. He shoves my head into the icy water and it engulfs me again.

I don't know if he's trying to drown me in a final I'm-taking-you-with-me gesture or if he's just thrashing on instinct. Either way, I'll end up dead if he has his way.

I slash with all the panic I have of my own, cutting him deep across his torso and arms. Over and over again.

Blood warms the water.

His grip loosens and I manage to bob my head up to gulp a lungful of air. He's not pushing me under any more but he's still holding onto me.

'You're not the only monster in this world,' I gasp. There are great white sharks in northern California. Our surfers and sharks seem to have a truce for the most part, except for the rare shark attack. But no one would ever go into our water while bleeding.

I slash hard across his chest. Ribbons of blood flow out around him.

My eyes meet his. He thinks I'm talking about me being the monster. Maybe he's right.

I'm no great white but all this knife stabbing and slashing is reminding me of Mom and her victims. For once, I'm okay with the similarities. For once, I hold onto her craziness for strength. Sometimes, I just have to let go and let my inner Mom out.

I slash repeatedly like a madwoman.

He finally loosens his grip on me.

I kick away as fast as I can. I wasn't bluffing about the sharks.

The knife makes swimming harder but I keep it in my hand until I'm out of reach of the bleeding angel. Then, I stash it again in my nylon band.

I'm so worked up that it takes a few strokes before I notice the freezing cold again. My breath mists in front of my face and my teeth chatter but I force myself to keep moving.

61

A huge crash rocks the water.

A tangle of wings and limbs rockets across the surface, ripping a channel through the sea.

It's Raffe and two angels entangled in a grappling match. They twist and fight as they plow through the waves.

They soon separate and end up spending their energies splashing and bobbing in a drowning way. Both enemy angels have their swords out which makes swimming even harder. They hang onto them, fighting the water with their drooping, useless wings.

Raffe fares no better. His leathery wings shed liquid better than the angels' feathered ones but they're big and clumsy and he obviously has no idea how to swim with them. Maybe there's no ocean in heaven.

I swim toward him.

One of the angels drops his sword, crying out in pain and frustration. He probably held it as long as possible but it's hard to stay afloat while putting a sword into its scabbard and even harder to swim with a sword in your hand.

The other angel bobs on the surface, trying to stay afloat with one hand clamping his sword. The third time the angel dips under water, the blade tip swings down as though too heavy for him. The angel's head comes back up and he gasps 'No, no, no' with real anguish.

The blade's tip falls into the water and disappears. The angel's sword has made the decision for him.

Aside from their comrades in arms, it wouldn't surprise me if the sword is the only thing most warriors bond to. It brings back memories of Raffe's stunned shock and hurt when his sword rejected him.

I swim faster. Or I try. The cold has made me so numb and shivery, it's hard to feel like I'm in control of my body.

They're all staying afloat but just barely. I wonder how long they can keep it up.

Just outside Raffe's wingspan, I call out. 'Raffe, stop thrashing.' He turns to me. 'Calm down and I'll come get you.'

I've heard that most drowning victims can't calm down. They have to impose their will against every survival instinct to stop flailing and let themselves feel like they're drowning. It takes an infinite amount of trust to count on someone else to save you.

Raffe must have enormous willpower because he immediately stops splashing. He moves his arms and legs gently but it's not enough to keep him afloat.

He starts sinking.

I swim with every bit of turbo I've got.

His head is below water before I can reach him. I tug up on him but his giant wings are a huge drag and I'm pulled down instead.

We both sink below water.

Even as we submerge, he still doesn't thrash. I'm awed by how much iron will it would take to override his instinctive needs. And how much trust.

Underwater, I can't tell him to close his wings all the way to reduce the drag. I frantically reach for his wing and shove at it.

He understands and closes his massive wings tightly along his body. They look as light and thin as air. I'm sure that if he knew how to use them in the water, he could glide like a stingray.

Kicking and pulling as hard as I can, I drag us to the surface. I'm not a super strong swimmer but like most California kids, I've had enough time in the ocean to feel comfortable in it. With Raffe's hollow bones, or whatever it is that makes him light, he's not a heavy burden.

Relief floods through me when his head pops up and he can breathe. I swim with one arm angled across his shoulder and chest, keeping our faces up.

'Scissor your legs, Raffe. Keep kicking them.' His legs are a powerful motor. Once we get going, we get into a steady rhythm and we make good progress away from the splashing angels.

The one I cut up is still bobbing feebly in the bloody water not too far from the others. I don't know what would happen in a fight between a gang of angels and a school of great white sharks but I'm glad I won't be close enough to see it.

Since the angels are squarely in the sharks' territory, my bet is with the sharks. Who says angels can't be killed?

They quickly disappear in the mist and I rely on Raffe's uncanny instinct for direction to get us to shore.

I hear Southern California water is warm but no one ever says that about Northern California water. It's not exactly Alaska, but it's cold enough to give me hypothermia, or at least what feels like hypothermia. I've never seen a surfer go in the water here without a wetsuit. But Raffe's body is warm even in the freezing water, and I suspect that his heat is keeping me alive.

When we get tired, we rest with his wings open. The buoyant wings keep us steady and afloat without any effort on our part.

When we near shore, the waves become whitewater and we tumble awkwardly. We time it so that we dive under the water when a big wave hits and pop back up when it's calmer.

We manage to wash up onto the sand. We crawl just far enough to be above the pounding surf before collapsing in a heap of soaked hair and clothes.

I look over to make sure he's all right.

He's panting for air and staring right at me with a look so intense it makes me squirm.

I grasp for something to say. We haven't really talked since he left for surgery from our hotel room at the old aerie. A lot has happened since then. Until a couple of hours ago, he thought I was dead.

I open my mouth to say something meaningful, memorable. 'I . . .'

Nothing comes.

I reach out, thinking that maybe we could touch hands, wanting to connect. But seaweed is tangled between my fingers, and I reflexively shake it off. It lands on his face with a slimy plop before sliding off.

He sprawls on the sand, quietly laughing.

His laugh is weak and in need of air but it may still be the greatest sound I've ever heard. It's full of warmth and genuine mirth, as only a living, breathing – um – person can have.

He reaches out and grabs my arm. He drags me to him along the sand. My dress bunches up, more sand than fabric, but I don't care.

He pulls me into his arms and holds me tight.

He is the one pocket of warmth in a sea of ice. Being in his arms feels like the home I never had. He's still panting his laugh that rumbles through his chest. My chest moves with his, making me smile.

But somewhere along the way, the mood changes. He keeps going, his chest convulsing in spasms that sound a lot like a weak laugh but isn't. He holds me so tight that if an army of scorpions came and tried to drag me out of his arms, they wouldn't be able to.

I stroke his hair and repeat the words of comfort he whispered to me the last time we were together. 'Shhh,' I say. 'I'm here. I'm right here.'

He's as warm as the afternoon sun on a summer day.

We hold each other in our little pocket of warmth, hidden from the monsters of the night by the mist swirling around us and the bloody surf pounding at our feet.

62

We manage to stagger to a beach house among a row of houses shrouded in the mist. In the World Before, these houses were within walking distance of the water but not beachfront properties. In the World After, they sit in a sea of rubble, and they're the closest houses to the water. Many of them still look undisturbed with their seahorse flags and wooden lounge chairs on the porch, as if waiting for their residents to come home.

I stumble into the living room behind Raffe, so exhausted as to be almost oblivious to my surroundings. Inside, we're protected from the wind, and although the house is not heated, it feels as if it is by comparison to where we've just been. I'm wet and sandy with my flimsy dress clinging to me like wet tissue paper.

Unlike me, Raffe is on full alert. He checks every corner of the house before relaxing his guard.

There's no electricity so the rooms are dark except for the misty glow of the moon coming in through the picture windows. We're in luck, though. There's a fireplace with a box of wood beside it, along with matches and decorative candles on the mantel.

I try lighting a candle. My hand shakes so badly I break three matches before I can finally get one to light. Raffe starts a fire. As soon as the tiny flame lights up, something in me relaxes a little, as if a part of me was seriously worried that my basic functions were on their way to shutting down before the fire started.

Despite his shivering, he gets up and pulls the vertical blinds closed on the windows. I don't know how he manages to do it. It takes everything I've got just to keep myself from crawling into the fireplace to get closer to the heat.

He even takes the time to grab blankets and towels from somewhere in the dark recesses of the house, and he drapes a blanket around me. My skin is so frozen that I can barely feel the soft warmth of his hand brushing against my neck.

'How do you feel?' he asks.

I answer through chattering teeth. 'As well as can be expected after a swim in angel-infested waters.'

Raffe puts his hand on my forehead. 'You humans are so fragile. If time doesn't kill you off, it's germs or sharks or hypothermia.'

'Or blood-crazed angels.'

He shakes his head. 'One minute you're fine, the next minute you're gone forever.' He stares broodily into the flickering fire.

My hair is still dripping icy water down my neck and back, and my dress sticks to me like it's made of wet sand. As if thinking the same thing, he wraps a beach towel around his waist and rolls it along his washboard stomach to keep it in place.

Then he takes his boots off. And peels off his pants.

'What are you doing?' I sound nervous.

He doesn't pause as he strips beneath his towel. 'Trying to warm up. You should do the same if you don't want your precious heat to get sucked out by your wet clothes.' His pants land with a plop on the rug.

I hesitate while he sits close to me in front of the fire.

He opens his demon wings. I suppose he does it to dry them off, but it has the added effect of being a heat trap. The muscles along my back and shoulders relax as soon as I feel the warmth swirling behind me.

I shiver, trying to shake off as much of the cold as I can. He tightens the circle of his wings, keeping the heat of the fire growing between us.

'Good job out there,' he says. He looks at me with quiet approval.

I blink at him in surprise. It's not like no one has ever said that to me. But somehow this is different. Unexpected.

'You too.' I want to say more. I crack open the vault in my head to see if I can peek in and maybe see something worth saying, but it all pushes against the door, wanting to flood out. I slam the door shut, leaning against it to keep it from bursting open. Still, my tongue gets tangled in all the things I want to say. 'Yeah, you too.'

He nods as if he understands, as if I actually *had* said all those things tumbling out of the vault and he accepts them.

We listen to the fire crackle for a while.

I've warmed enough to want to be free of my gritty, wet dress, which is sucking the fledgling heat from my skin. I wrap my blanket around myself and bite into the overlapping edge to keep it in place as a shield.

He grins when he sees me squirming underneath, wrestling with the wet dress. 'I'm sure a respectable modern man would turn his back so he wouldn't see if there was a slip-up.'

I nod, keeping a tight bite on my blanket.

'But we'd lose our heat shelter.' He raises a wing a few inches to demonstrate. Cool air immediately touches my legs. He lowers his wing back into place again. He shrugs. 'I guess you'll just have to not slip up.'

I continue to squirm, getting myself free of the left sleeve.

'Don't laugh or anything,' he says, 'because that could be disastrous.'

I squint at him, giving him a glare that tells him not to try to make me laugh.

'Have you heard that joke about—'

I rip through the flimsy dress under my blanket. It was ruined anyway. I tear it off and toss it out from beneath the blanket.

It lands on top of his pants on the rug.

Raffe bursts out laughing. It's a beautiful thing – rich and carefree. It calls to me to laugh along with him.

'You are so great at creative solutions,' he says still chuckling. 'They usually involve ripping, tearing, kicking or stabbing, but they're creative.'

I let go of the blanket with my teeth now that I can hold it securely around me with my hands. 'I just got tired of the wetness sticking to me, that's all. I think I was pretty safe from the threat of your joke being funny.'

'I'm wounded by your comment,' he says with a smile.

The word 'wounded' echoes in my head, and I see it does in his, too, because his smile fades.

'What happened back there at the old aerie? I saw you get stung by the scorpion. I watched you die. How did you survive?'

I explain about the scorpion sting paralyzing and slowing down the heart and breathing so that the victim seems dead.

'I thought for sure I'd lost you.'

Lost me?

I stare into the fire without seeing it. 'I thought I'd lost you too.' The words barely come out.

The fire crackles and pops, eating away at the wood. It reminds me of the fire at the aerie when Raffe carried me to safety even though he thought I was dead.

'Thank you for returning me to my family. That was a crazy, dangerous thing to do.'

'I was feeling a little crazy and dangerous then.'

'Yeah, I saw that.' I'll never get rid of the image of him smashing the giant scorpion tubes in rage and killing all the monsters after seeing me die.

His lips twitch as if laughing at himself. 'That must have been entertaining.'

'No, it really wasn't. It was kind of . . .' heartbreaking. 'Heartbreaking.' I blink when I realize what just slipped

out of my mouth. 'I mean . . .' Nothing comes to mind
that I can substitute for what I just said.

'Heart.' He looks deeply into the flames. 'Breaking.'
The sounds flow out between his lips like they're new to
him, like he's never said them before. He nods. 'Yeah. I
suppose that's one way to put it.'

The fire crackles. It's surprising how quickly a fire can
warm you up.

'I wasn't saying you were heartbroken.' I sound like
English is a new language for me, the way I stutter out
the words. 'I just meant it was hard for me to . . . to
watch.'

He neither confirms nor denies that he might or
might not have been even a teeny bit heartbroken.

'Well, okay, maybe you did seem just a *little* heartbroken.' So embarrassing. Now, I'm totally fishing. A part
of me is chastising me for being such a dork. The rest of
me is listening carefully for a reaction.

The orange and red flames grow larger and warmer.
The crackling and popping is rhythmic and hypnotic.
The heat is exquisite.

'You're shivering,' he says. He sounds reluctant.
Maybe even sad. 'Take a shower. Maybe we'll be lucky
and there will be hot water.'

He hesitates while I hold my breath.

Then he turns away from me.

He stands and heads into the darkness of the house.

As soon as he moves the shelter of his wings, the cold seeps back in. I watch him fade into the shadows. His dark wings and bowed head disappear first, then the broad shoulders and arms.

Then nothing.

63

I sit there, watching him go, wanting to say something but not knowing what.

I reluctantly get up and move away from the fireplace. The house feels colder now as I head upstairs to find a bathroom.

There are plush towels there, folded in a way that suggests they haven't been used since they were washed. That was probably months ago.

I shower by candlelight. The water is lukewarm, but compared to the ocean, it feels good on my still-frozen skin. I don't linger, though. Just long enough to rinse off the sand, soap up and shampoo as fast as I can. I'm still shivering from the cold seeping into my bones and I can't wait to be dry and warm again.

There's a thick robe hanging on the bathroom door that I wish I could snuggle up in. But those kinds of luxuries are for people in the World Before, not for people who might be chased out of here any minute by monsters or marauders.

I quickly rummage through the closets and drawers for clothes. The best I can find is a sweater dress that's probably meant to be just a sweater. Everything else is about four sizes too big. I cinch the sweater around my waist with a scarf and throw on a pair of stretchy pants. The legs fit comfortably down to my ankles even though they're probably meant to be capris.

I'm sure I could have found something better but I don't want to linger with my candle lighting the upstairs window. The fog should keep the tiny light from traveling far but why invite trouble?

Downstairs, the living room is warmly lit by the glow from the fireplace. Raffe stands on a chair, duct-taping blankets over the picture windows. He must have had the same thought as I did about the candle glow being visible.

There's something about him standing on a chair to reach the top of the windows that puts me at ease. It's such a normal thing to do.

Well, it's normal if you ignore the dark wings gently gliding back and forth behind him. I suppose he's drying them. The hooks and scythes are out and gleaming in the candlelight. No feathers to preen. I wonder if he polishes his scythes?

'You're not Fallen, are you?' The question pops out of my mouth before my head can censor it.

'From everything I've heard, that would just make me more sexy to you Daughters of Men.' He finishes taping the last bit of the blanket. 'What is it that you all see in bad boys?'

'I'm asking the questions here, Raffe. This is serious.'

'Is it a chance for you to provide redemption?' He hops off the chair and finally turns to look at me.

When he sees me, his shoulders shake in a silent laugh that quickly builds into a full chuckle. Raffe's laugh is something I would normally enjoy, except that he's clearly laughing at me.

I look down at my outfit. I admit that I might have rushed a bit too much while getting dressed upstairs.

What looked like a muted patterned sweater by the light of one candle turns out to be leopard-spotted by the light of several candles. And because it's so big on me, it folds and hangs everywhere. What I took to be a dark scarf around my waist turns out to be a red tie and my brown socks are actually a mismatched pair of pink and purple.

'Why is it that everyone else can look like they're part of a zombie hunting party, but I still have to worry about fashion?'

He won't stop snickering. 'You look like a leopard-spotted Shar-Pei.'

I think those are the little pug-like dogs drowning in massive folds of skin. 'You're scarring me, you know. It could haunt me for the rest of my life to be called a wrinkly little dog at the tender age of seventeen.'

'Yup. A sensitive girl. That just defines you, Penryn.' The firelight softens his features and warms his skin. 'But if you must have an ego boost for your tender side, I will admit that you looked great with wings.' Raffe says this last part in a wistful voice.

I suddenly feel awkward. 'Thanks . . . I think.'

'You don't want to look great with wings?'

'I'm just scared this may be a setup for me being the butt of a so-called joke, like, um, how I may look like a wrinkly dog with wings but I have a nice personality or something.' I look up at the ceiling as I think about it. 'Okay, that didn't come out funny at all, so it would have been a really bad joke.'

'Oh, don't worry. You're safe,' he says in a reassuring voice. 'I'd never tell you that you have a nice personality.'

I give him a dirty look and he chuckles at his own teasing comment.

And just like that, he's back to the same Raffe I got to know on the road.

We heat water on the gas stove, which still works as long as you light it with a match. Then we sit by the fireplace, drinking hot water from mugs while I tell him what I've been up to since we last saw each other. The warmth feels so good I want to curl up and fall asleep.

'Where is my sword?'

I take a deep breath. I haven't mentioned the sword dreams. It would feel a little too much like admitting I snooped into his life. 'I had to leave it in a pile of stuff on Pier 39 in San Francisco when I got caught.'

'You left her?'

I nod. 'I had no choice.'

'She wasn't made to be alone.'

'I guess none of us are.'

Our eyes meet and an electric tingle runs through me.

'She missed you,' I say in a whisper.

'Did she?' His voice is a soft caress. His gaze into my eyes is so intense that I swear he sees straight into my soul.

'Yes.' Warmth flushes my cheeks. *I* . . . 'She thought about you all the time.'

The candlelight flickers a soft glow along his jawline, along his lips. 'I hated losing her.' His voice is a low growl. 'I hadn't realized just how attached I'd gotten.' He reaches and moves a strand of wet hair out of my face. 'How dangerously addictive she could be.'

His gaze pins me to my spot and I can't move, can't breathe.

'Maybe a girl needs to hear that. Maybe she wants to be with you, too.' The words come out in a rushed whisper.

He closes his eyes and takes a deep breath. He shakes his head. 'It can't be.'

'Why?'

'Rules. Custom. Danger. It's dangerous to be with me.'

'It's dangerous to be without you.' I nudge closer to the fire.

He reaches out and adjusts my blanket around my shoulders. 'That doesn't change the rules, though.'

I close my eyes and feel the warmth of his fingers brushing my neck. 'Who cares about the rules? It's the end of the world, remember?'

'Rules are important to us. Angels are a warrior race.'

'I noticed. But what does that have to do with it?'

'The only way to keep a society of killers together for eons is to have a strict chain of command and zero tolerance for breach of rules. Otherwise, we all would have slaughtered each other a long time ago.'

'Even if the rules make no sense?'

'Sometimes they make sense.' He grins. 'But that's beside the point. The point is to have warriors follow their orders, not to judge them.'

'What if it keeps you from things and people you care about?'

'Especially then. That's often the most effective punishment. Death is not much of a threat to a true warrior. But take away your Daughter of Man, your children, your friends, your sword – these are true punishments.'

I can't help myself. I lean close to him so that my face is just a kiss away. 'We're really scary, aren't we?'

He looks at my lips almost involuntarily. But he doesn't back off or lean forward one millimeter. He arches his brow at me. 'Daughters of Men are truly dangerous. Not to mention truly annoying.' He shrugs. 'In a yappy, occasionally cute kind of way.'

I lean back. 'I'm beginning to understand why your sword left you.' Ouch. That came out wrong. 'Sorry, I didn't mean—'

'She left because she had standing orders to do so should she ever sense the darkness.'

'Why?'

He looks into his mug. 'Because a Fallen with an angel sword is too dangerous. Their wings change over time and eventually grow their own weapons if they survive enough battles. To have both Fallen wings and an angel sword is too dangerous a combination to allow.'

'But you're not Fallen, are you? Why would your sword leave you?'

'The wings confused her.' He takes a drink, looking like he wishes it was stronger than water. 'She's partially sentient but it's not like she has a brain.' He half-grins.

I sigh and put my mug down. 'Your world is so different from mine. Do you guys have anything in common with humans?'

He looks at me with those killer eyes in that perfect face over his Adonis body. 'Nothing we'll admit to.'

'There's no way around it, is there?' I ask. 'We're mortal enemies and I should be trying to kill you and everyone like you.'

He leans over, touches the tip of his forehead to mine, and closes his eyes. 'Yes.' His gentle breath caresses my lips as he says the word.

I close my eyes too, and try to focus on the warmth of his forehead resting on mine.

64

Raffe comes back from foraging with a box of cereal and a jar of peanut butter. I wanted to get moving but he insisted that soldiers need food to fight properly. Besides, he said he needed time to think about his next step. So he took off into the night with his very handy night vision while I sat in the house beside my candles.

The cereal is raisin bran and the raisins taste like heaven – I mean, nirvana – or whatever wonderful place doesn't remind me of deadly angels.

For once, our hands are clean, so we eat handfuls of cereal and lick the peanut butter straight from our fingers. I suppose this place probably has utensils in the kitchen but why bother? There's something kind of fun about scooping the gooey goodness with our fingers and licking it like ice cream.

Raisin bran and peanut butter. Who knew it could taste so good? If we could just add a bit of chocolate, it would probably make a great, peanutty, crunchy chocolate bar for the high school bake sale. Okay, maybe it wouldn't taste quite so good compared to the foods in the World Before, but right now, it tastes amazing.

'I need to go back to the aerie,' says Raffe as he scoops his fingers into the jar.

My handful of cereal stops midway to my mouth. 'Seriously? The place full of crazed, bloodthirsty Neanderthals where we barely escaped with our lives?'

He arches a brow at me. Sucks the peanut butter off his fingers.

I pop the cereal into my mouth and start crunching. 'Just because your people are pretty, doesn't mean they're not Neanderthals inside.'

'Based on what you've told me, I'm guessing that the riot wasn't what Uri had in mind. Any soldier could have told him that's what was going to happen. You dangle the apocalypse in front of frustrated warriors unclear about their mission and you have a bit of a tussle on your hands.'

'A bit of a tussle?'

'Too old-fashioned?' He scoops up more peanut butter. He seems to prefer not to mix it with cereal.

'People were torn to pieces. Literally. In bloody, little, horrible bits. That's not exactly a tussle.'

'And I'm sorry about that but there was nothing I could do to stop it.' He doesn't sound sorry. He sounds cold and calculating and pragmatic.

'What's with all the cheering over the apocalypse, anyway? Oh, yay, we get to kill poor helpless humans.' I sound cranky. I dip my handful of cereal into the peanut butter, making sure I leave some of the cereal in it. For good measure, I drop a couple of raisins in it too.

'The excitement over the apocalypse has nothing to do with humans.'

'Could have fooled me.'

He peers into the contaminated peanut butter jar. He throws me an arch look and puts it back down without dipping into it. 'Humans are incidental.'

'Killing and destroying an entire species is incidental?' I can't help but sound like I'm accusing him, even though I know he wasn't part of the plan to wipe us out.

Or at least, I think he wasn't personally involved, but I don't really know that, do I?

'Your people have been doing it to all kinds of species.' He grabs the cereal box.

'That's not the same.' I grab the peanut butter jar.

'Why not?'

'Can we please just get back to how your people are partying over killing my people?' I scoop out more peanut butter.

He watches me licking the peanut butter off my fingers. 'They're celebrating the possibility of freeing their friends.'

'Angels have friends?' I pucker my lips around my finger, sucking every bit of the treat off it.

He shifts uncomfortably in his seat and glares at me. 'When you fight side-by-side with other warriors, they become your brothers. Every one of us has a brother who has fallen. The only thing that offers any hope for them is Judgment Day. On that day, they finally get their trial.'

'An eternity of punishment comes before the trial?' I'm about to dip my fingers into the jar again when he dumps cereal into it. I'll have to eat through the cereal before I can lick up more peanut butter.

'The system is purposely harsh to keep everyone in line. It's what keeps our warrior society together.'

I poke my finger in the cereal-peanut butter mix, wondering if he's annoyed. 'And if they're judged guilty?' My finger comes out with a dab of peanut butter on the tip. I lick it off, savoring the last of the sweet taste.

He gets up abruptly and starts pacing the room. 'Then eternity gets longer.'

I know the answer to my next question, but I need to ask anyway. 'And when does Judgment Day happen?'

'At the end of the apocalypse.'

I nod. 'Right. The one that everyone's so eager to have.' Being right never seems to make me feel better these days.

He takes a deep breath and releases it as if needing to blow off steam. 'Let's go find my sword.'

I hate to waste time flying to Pier 39 but both the sword and Mom's tracker are there. That tracker is still my best bet for finding Paige. Besides, I might get a chance to see if Mom, Clara and the others made it off the island. If they didn't, maybe there's something I can do to help them.

Doc had said that the scorpions would be out somewhere tonight and now I know that Beliel must have orchestrated the locusts' flyby over the angel death rally. The Alcatraz escape should have either succeeded or failed by now. I can't even stomach the thought of what might be happening now if it failed.

I quickly find an oversized coat and a pair of tennis shoes that fit me surprisingly well. In the meantime, Raffe picks out a wicked-looking kitchen knife and sticks it in his waistband, sheath and all.

Outside, the fog has lifted, showing a crisp night with the waning moon and stars reflecting off the ocean.

Between us and the sea is a beach blanketed by pieces of wood and glass from pulverized houses.

The broken glass reflects the light from the sky like a carpet of flickering fireflies that stretches out as far as I can see. It's so unexpectedly beautiful that I pause to look at it. How can something so wondrous come out of such devastation?

I glance over at Raffe to see if he's appreciating the same thing. But he's watching me instead.

I walk over to him, feeling self-conscious. Flying in his arms earlier was the business of war, and we didn't have much time to think about anything other than escape.

This time it's by choice, and I can't help but think about his strong arms holding me and his warm skin brushing against mine.

I lift my arms like a child who wants to be picked up.

He hesitates for a second, looking at me. Is he remembering holding me in his arms at the old aerie when he thought I was dead? What must it be like for him to hold someone this many times after being isolated for so long?

He lifts me in his arms, cradling me while I wrap my arms around his neck. My cheek brushes against his as he picks me up. Warmth flows from the touch and I resist the impulse to nuzzle.

He runs two steps and we're in the air, heading toward Alcatraz.

If I hadn't already flown with him, I'd be scared. I'm above the water with nothing but his arms between me and an icy plunge. But his arms are wrapped tightly around me and his chest is warm. I lean my head against his muscular shoulder and close my eyes.

He rubs his cheek against my hair.

I know that soon I'll have to think about Paige, Mom and Clara. My priorities will be all about survival and getting my family together and keeping them safe from monsters and people alike.

But for now, for just for this moment, I let myself be a seventeen-year-old girl in a strong guy's arms. I even let some of the what-ifs seep in, the kind of possibilities that might have blossomed between us in the World Before.

Just for a little while.

Before I carefully fold my dreams away into the vault in my head.

65

Instead of flying up the peninsula, we fly across it until we reach the San Francisco Bay. From there, the plan is to fly up the length of the bay, roughly following the peninsula coastline. It's a longer route to Alcatraz but the fog sits thick over the water, just as we suspected. With all the angels and scorpions in the air tonight, Raffe figured we'd be better off flying over water, and he was right.

The air is damp and the wind is harsh. Despite my coat, Raffe is my true source of warmth, and I can't help but bask in the feel of his body as we whoosh through the fog.

Raffe cocks his head like he hears something.

He veers to investigate. I have no idea how he even knows we're going in the right direction in the middle of this cloud, much less how he can pinpoint some minor noise that I can't even hear, but he does.

We glide out of the thickest fog and skim silently along the bottom tendrils of mist hanging over the bay. The smoky moonlight glows faintly against the oily darkness below.

I hear the muffled sound of engines chugging in the water before I see the boats.

Below us, half-a-dozen boats work their way through the bay. I don't see Captain Jake's ferry. Of course, there's no reason why it should be here, but I can't help but hope that these are the Alcatraz escapees. These boats are smaller and sleeker but still large enough to carry dozens of people each.

Did Dee and Dum manage to bring together a rescue team?

If so, I'm impressed. That would mean they were able to gather enough boats to hopefully get everyone out in one trip. And it looks like they also smartly decided to take advantage of the darkness and fog by traveling over water instead of land.

Raffe glides down, circling silently near the ships, as curious as I am about what's happening.

The decks are covered with people huddling together for warmth. Someone must have caught a glimpse of our darker shape against the sky because the engines shut off and the boats float silently through the night. There are men with rifles pointed at the sky, but most of them are not pointed at us, so we must not be very visible. And the best news is that none of the guns go off.

I'm guessing they have orders to shoot only as a last resort since the noise from a single shot could beckon a horde of monsters to them. The boats seem to be doing okay silently drifting through the fog. If this is the Alcatraz escape, they've probably been on the water for hours, which means they've had their engines off most of the time.

There is no light, motion or sound anywhere except on the roof of the largest boat that's leading the fleet. The reflection from the water's ripples and the moonlit glow of the mist are enough to see that there's something tied to the roof.

It's a thrashing scorpion.

Someone hovers over the writhing monster. As we silently glide past, I get a better look.

The beast's body and tail are securely tied. Its mouth is gagged and making a muffled hiss as it tries frantically to sting the woman who bends over it.

The woman is absorbed in whatever she's doing and doesn't notice us. She's drawing something on its chest. I can't see her face but there's only one person she could be.

My mother is alive and apparently uninjured.

Two men holding rifles stand on either side of her. I'm guessing by the bulging arms of one and the yuppie collar of the other that they're probably Tattoo and Alpha. If so, Mom must have impressed the hell out of them during the escape or they wouldn't be protecting her as she draws on a scorpion.

We sweep over the boat, but it's too dark for me to see what she's writing.

'She's drawn a heart on his chest in lipstick and is writing "Penryn and Paige" inside the heart,' whispers Raffe in my ear. We circle back on our way to the pier. 'Now she's drawing flowers on his stomach.'

I can't help but smile and shake my head.

I feel lighter.

And for a moment, I hold Raffe tighter in what some people might mistake as a hug.

66

Pier 39 is mostly as I remember it. Broken planks sticking out every which way, demolished buildings, a boat on its side.

Captain Jake's ferry has been driven into the pier, plowing the planks in a crown of jagged splinters. The ship sits lower than it should, slowly sinking. A spotlight from the deck remains on and throws a ghostly ray of light across the pier.

So not everyone chose to go down the bay to the peninsula. Some must have wanted to take the shortest crossing to the mainland and then scattered. That would make sense if you thought your chances were better on land than on water, or if you had loved ones in the city. But whoever piloted the ship probably wasn't Captain

Jake. Unless he was seriously drunk, which is a real possibility.

We circle above the pier, scoping out the situation. Looters scatter when they glimpse our moon shadow. A couple of them are just kids. Word must be getting around about the valuables left on the pier. I wonder if they have any idea how dangerous it is for them to be here?

As soon as everyone disappears, we land silently in the shadows.

Raffe holds me a second longer than necessary before he puts me down. And then it takes me a second longer than necessary to slide my arms away from his neck and step back from his warmth. Anyone watching us might assume we were a couple kissing in the dark.

The lights illuminate the beams and planks sticking up on the dock. The moist air of our breaths condenses into mist and swirls together as we watch and listen to make sure no one is around.

Someone is crying.

There's a lone figure sitting in the debris of a half-standing candy shop. She's trying to be quiet but the soft sobs are unmistakable.

There's something about the shriveled figure and the voice that seems familiar. I gesture for Raffe to stay back while I go talk to the person. I skirt around the beam of light to reach her.

It's Clara. She hugs her shriveled body, looking even smaller than usual. The cheeks that look like beef jerky glisten with tears as she sobs alone.

'Hey, Clara. It's me, Penryn.' I call softly to her from a few feet away so I don't scare her to death. She gasps, and it's clear I practically give her a heart attack anyway.

She half-smiles and half-sobs when she realizes it's me. I walk over and sit by her. The broken boards are hard and damp. I can't believe she's been sitting here for hours.

'Why are you still here? You should be running as far away as you can.'

'This place is as close as I can get to my family now.' Her voice breaks. 'We had happy Sundays here.' She shakes her head slowly. 'That, and I have nowhere else to go.'

I'm about to tell her to go to the Resistance camp when I remember how they treated her and the other scorpion victims. People who would rather bury their loved ones alive than risk having them changed like Clara will probably never accept someone like her. No wonder she didn't go down the bay with the Resistance.

I put my arm around her shoulder and give her a squeeze. It's all I can think to do.

She gives me a weak smile but tears streak down her face again and her face crumples.

Something clanks and rolls nearby.

We both tense, proving that Clara is not quite ready to give up.

A grubby little girl with a mass of finely tangled hair runs a couple of steps out of hiding behind a car. An adult arm reaches out and tries to grab her.

'No, it's her,' says the girl. 'I heard her. She's here.'

Someone whispers urgently from behind the car.

The girl shakes her head. She turns and runs toward us.

'Get back here!' whispers the urgent voice from behind the car. A man sprints out, running half-crouched. He snatches the little thing into his arms and runs back. The kid squirms like a sack of puppies. She kicks and twists and tries to scream bloody murder but he has his hand over her mouth.

Her muffled yells sound a lot like, 'Mommy!'

Beside me, Clara sits perfectly still.

A second girl's face peeks out from behind the car. She's a little bigger but just as grubby with hair just as tangled. She looks wide-eyed at us.

'Ella?' Clara whispers so softly that even I have trouble hearing her. She gets up, almost panting. 'Ella?' She lurches, then runs toward them.

Uh-oh. This could be really wonderful or really awful.

It's dark and we're far enough away that I'm pretty sure they can't see the details of what Clara looks like yet. I get up and follow discreetly in case she needs backup. Not that I can really help her if her family rejects her, but at least she'll know she has one person in her corner.

The man freezes on his way to the car. He turns around with the girl in his arms. The kid is going ballistic with her muffled screams of 'Mommy!'

The second girl steps gingerly out from behind the car. 'Mom?' She sounds totally lost and unsure.

'Chloe.' Clara sobs out her name as she runs toward them.

The older girl approaches Clara. I'm about to have a full-blown smile on my face when the girl stumbles to a stop, staring wide-eyed at her mom. She's close enough now to see us better. I see Clara again the way my mother sees her, the way the others see her. She really does look like she crawled out of her grave after being dead for a while.

Please don't scream, Chloe. That would be the end of Clara.

She was strong enough to survive a scorpion attack, strong enough to crawl out of being buried alive and escape from monsters on Alcatraz. But having her little girl scream at the sight of her would shatter her into so many pieces that nothing could glue her back together.

Clara's steps falter and she stops too. Her face shifts from amazed delight to horrible uncertainty.

The younger girl has managed to squirm out of the man's arms and dashes over to us. Unlike her sister, she has no hesitation about jumping into Clara's arms.

'I knew it was you!' The girl looks like she's about to melt with happiness as she hugs her mom. 'Daddy made us wait until we knew for sure. We watched forever. You just cried and cried and we couldn't tell. Then you started talking and I knew! I heard your voice and I knew. See Daddy? I told you.'

But Daddy stands frozen a few steps away, staring at Clara.

Clara strokes Ella's hair with a trembling hand. 'Yes, baby girl, you were right. I missed you so much. So very much.' She looks fearfully at Chloe and her husband, her eyes begging.

Chloe takes a hesitant step toward her. 'Mom? Is it really you? What happened to you?'

'Yes, sweetheart. It's me. I'm all right,' says Clara. 'I'm all right now.' She puts out her arm in an invitation and Chloe gingerly steps into it.

Dad yanks the girl back. 'Is it contagious?'

'What?' Clara looks confused.

'Are you contagious?' Dad enunciates every word like she no longer speaks his language.

'No,' whispers Clara. Her voice cracks and I know she's barely holding it together. 'I swear.'

Chloe slips out of her dad's hold. She pauses, staring at Clara. Then she hesitantly steps into Clara's arm. Once there, though, the older girl clings onto her mom as tightly as her baby sister.

Clara's husband stares at them, looking like he's torn between running to join his family and simply running away. He stands there, watching his kids chatter to their mom about how they came here to scavenge, that they'd heard valuable things were left here on the dock. How they'd begged their dad to come here one last time. How they pretended they were coming here for their Sunday lunch like they used to.

Hearing Clara chat softly with her girls brings up a picture of a mom that every kid deserves to have. The girls look cozy and happy in the shelter of their mother. I'm guessing that feels pretty great.

Eventually, their dad steps over to Clara like a man in a dream. Without a word, he enfolds all of them in a hug and begins to cry.

I can almost see this pier the way it was when Clara and her husband brought the kids here for lunch. The sound of the seagulls, the salty smell of the ocean on the breeze, and the warmth of the California sun. I can see the couple walking hand-in-hand as the girls run ahead. Clara, the way she used to be with fresh skin and a smile, holding flowers from the farmers' market, laughing with her husband on a lazy Sunday afternoon.

I melt back into the shadows.

67

I brace for Raffe to be sarcastic about Clara's little reunion. He's leaning against a shop wall that is mostly intact – a dark, menacing figure against the night. If I didn't know him, I would walk a long way around to avoid him.

When I get close enough to see his face, there's no sarcasm in it. He watches Clara's reunion with her family with far more sympathy than I could have ever predicted for an angel, even Raffe.

But then I remember Beliel's comment about how angels weren't meant to be alone. So maybe he understands better than I give him credit for.

'I'm revoking your warrior status,' he says as he watches Clara and her family.

'I had warrior status?'

'For about thirty seconds.'

'What heinous crime did I commit to lose my exalted status?'

'A true warrior would have retrieved her sword first before doing personal business.'

'I'm all about personal business. Every battle I have is personal.' I lead Raffe toward the pile of broken wood and shingles where I hid the sword.

'Hmm. Good answer. Maybe you'll eventually regain your status.'

'I won't hold my breath.' I shove the wooden debris out of the way until I see the smudged face of the teddy bear. 'There she is.' I carefully pull out the bear and sword. I proudly flip the bridal veil skirt to show him the scabbard.

Raffe stares at the disguised sword for a second before commenting. 'Do you know how many kills this sword has?'

'It's a perfect disguise, Raffe.'

'This sword is not just an angel sword. She's an *arch*-angel sword. *Better* than an angel sword, in case that's not clear. She *intimidates* the other angel swords.'

'What, the other swords quake in their scabbards when they see her?' I walk over to the pile of scattered junk by Captain Jake's boat.

'Yes, if you must know,' he says following me. 'She was made for ultimate respect. How is she supposed to get that disguised as a teddy bear in a bridal gown?'

'It's not a bridal gown, it's a skirt for her scabbard. And it's cute.'

'She hates cute. She wants to maim and scar cute.'

'Nobody hates cute.'

'Angel swords do.' He arches his brow and stares down at me.

I guess I won't tell him how many cutesy angel figurines and pictures we used to have in the World Before.

Mom's tracker should be here but I don't see it in the scattered debris. I do spot a detachable strap hanging out of a purse with keys tethered to it, though. I've been meaning to tether the bear to the scabbard and this looks perfect. I clip one end around the ribbon sewn to the bear's neck and the other end to the scabbard's strap.

'Have you named her yet?' he asks. 'She likes powerful names so maybe you could appease her by giving her a good one.'

I bite my lip as I remember telling Dee-Dum what I named my sword. 'Um, I could rename her anything she likes.' I give him a cheesy smile.

He looks like he's bracing himself for the worst. 'She gets named once by each carrier. If you've named her, she's stuck with it for as long as she's with you.'

Damn.

He glares at me as if he already hates it. 'What is it?'

I consider lying but what's the point? I clear my throat. 'Pooky Bear.'

He's silent for so long I'm beginning to think he didn't hear me when he finally says, 'Pooky. Bear.'

'It was just a little joke. I didn't know.'

'I've mentioned that names have power, right? Do you realize that when she fights battles, she's going to have to announce herself to the opposing sword? She'll be forced to say something ridiculous like, "I am Pooky Bear, from an ancient line of archangel swords." Or, "Bow down to me, Pooky Bear, who has only two other equals in all the worlds."' He shakes his head. 'How is she going to get any respect?'

'Oh, come on, seriously? No one's going to respect that kind of pompous announcement anyway, regardless of the name.' I sling the sword strap around my shoulder, and the bear sword settles on my hip where it belongs.

I spot Mom's tracker sitting by a purse. I rush to it and turn it on.

'You'd be surprised at how many would-be opponents I've dispatched just by announcing that I am Raphael, the Great Archangel, the Wrath of God.' He gives me an intimidating look.

It occurs to me that because of the demon wings, he's lost the power of using his name and title too. I see by the sadness in his eyes that he's thinking the same thing.

On the tracker, a yellow arrow pops up at Half Moon Bay near the aerie. I sigh heavily. Just for once, couldn't I find my sister somewhere safe and easy?

'Paige is at the aerie.'

Raffe gives me a don't-you-dare look. 'You mean the place where I barely got you out alive because they were killing every human they could get their hands on?'

'Thank you, by the way.'

He rakes his fingers through his hair, looking agitated. 'Look, I'm sure I could find you a nice little bomb shelter somewhere with two years worth of supplies.'

'I'm guessing those are all taken.'

'And I'm guessing someone would happily give one up for you, especially if I asked nicely.' He gives me a dry smile. 'You could take a little vacation from all this and come out after things settle down. Hole up, wait it out, be safe.'

'You'd better be careful. You might be mistaken for someone who's worried about me.'

He shakes his head. 'I'm just worried someone might recognize my sword in your hands. If I squirrel you away for a couple of years, then maybe I can save myself the embarrassment.'

I bite my lip to keep from asking but it comes out anyway. 'And what would you do while I was hidden away?'

'Get my wings back. Find out what's happening with my people and set things right.' He takes a deep breath. 'And once I get my business settled, I'd return home with them.'

I nod, digging my nails into my palm to help me focus. 'I can't say I'm not tempted, Raffe. Being safe sounds wonderful.' I give him a sad smile. 'Maybe I can take you up on your offer just as soon as I get my family back together. I mean, if you're still around and are willing to help.'

He sighs. 'I miss the days when females could be ordered around and they'd have no choice.'

'Sure that wasn't just a myth? I'm pretty sure nobody ever ordered my mom around – ever.'

'You're probably right. The unruliness of the women in your family must go back for generations. You're like a plague upon the land.'

'So long as we're also a plague upon angels, I'm sure everyone else will forgive us.'

'Oh, you're definitely a plague upon at least one angel. Is there anything I can say that will stop you from going to the aerie?'

I pause to think about that. 'I wish there was. My life would be a whole lot easier.'

'What if I refuse to help you get there?'

'Then I'll walk or drive.'

'What if I drag you into a prison and lock you up?'

'Then I'll use my nifty little sword to cut my way out.'

'What if I leave my sword outside the prison?'

'You won't. If you can't have it, you want me to have it, right? We're better off together than apart.'

Our eyes meet.

'Besides, who'd let me out if something happens to you?'

He throws me a sideways glance, like the thought of something happening to him is ridiculous.

'Beliel is probably still at the aerie,' I say.

'And why would you think that?'

'The doctor who operated on Paige thinks that she's drawn to Beliel. Who knows what strange animal sense they put into her? She might have a sense of where he is.' I lift Mom's tracker. 'I'm tracking Paige. She's tracking Beliel. You can't stop me from following Paige so why not take advantage of the situation and just fly me there?'

He glares at me. 'I've had to watch you die once, isn't that enough?'

'All you have to do is make sure it doesn't happen again.' I give him a sunny smile. 'Simple.'

'The only thing simple is you. Stubborn little . . .' His grumbles fade to the point where I can't hear them, but I suspect they're not compliments.

Eventually, he puts out his arms.

It's unnerving to be so close to him that I feel his heart beat against my breasts. I hold him tightly as he opens his wings and we take off into the night.

68

We skim so close to the water that we might as well be swimming. I keep expecting us to fly right through a large swell. As it is, the spray feels like an icy shower. I bury my face in Raffe's neck, seeking his endless warmth.

It's so cold that my arms want to crack and fall off in protest. It's no consolation that this is the only way we can get near the aerie without being seen. If we had flown over land, they would have spotted us.

Raffe is stoic and calm this close to the water despite having swum probably only once in his entire existence. I'm a little less calm. I can't help but think that this might be the last thing I do. I can't get the images of the crazed warriors sprayed in blood out of my head.

Raffe holds me tighter. 'It's about time you showed some sense. You should be afraid.'

'I'm shivering because I'm freezing.'

'You're cute when you're afraid.'

I give him a dirty look. 'Yeah, you're cute when you're afraid too.'

He actually bursts out laughing. 'You mean I'm devastatingly handsome when I'm *not* afraid. Because you've never seen me afraid.'

'I said you were cute, not "devastatingly handsome".'

We're nearing the shore. So far, the sound of waves crashing onto the sand and rocks should have disguised our banter. But we're getting close enough that we both instinctively shut up.

We, of course, don't have a plan. We'll simply have to see what's going on and take it from there. We drift a little to the side of the new aerie so that we can go on shore unnoticed. We land on the beach below the bluff at the edge of the hotel grounds.

Hiding behind rocks, fences and bushes, we sneak up as close as we dare near the circle of light by the edge of the hotel's lawn. New torches have been set up to replace the old ones that got knocked down during the brawl. But they're placed randomly and at drunken angles as if whoever put them up couldn't be bothered with them.

I try to match Raffe's stealth and smooth coordination, but my frozen limbs are clumsy, and I have to grab him several times to keep myself from tipping over. He throws me a look with a clear message that I should deal with my issues.

We dart to a row of low bushes and follow them closer to the lawn. The edges of the grounds are crammed with the remains of the party like debris washed up on shore. Fallen party tables, upside-down lounge chairs, torn costumes and other broken things.

The lawn also has a motley carpet of trampled wing coverings, masks and shattered things that are now hard to identify. There are dark patches on the grass that probably look red in daylight. If there are any servants left, they're not inclined to come out and clean up.

The angels scattered on the lawn seem too hung over to notice much. One group is singing in the middle of the grass, still wearing their masks. Their voices blend beautifully but with all their swaying and kicking of debris, they look more like drunken pirates after a raid.

Another group is putting something together near the mansion-like hotel. They're setting up a table with wooden boxes. Beside it are poles of different heights.

An angel hovers at the top of the poles, tying triangular flags that wave colorfully in the ocean breeze like castle flags. Two angels fly up with a banner in their hands. They tie it to the top of the two highest poles. It has several symbols that run across the banner like script.

Raffe's eyes become cold and hostile as he looks at the banner.

I give him a questioning look, asking him what it says.

He leans over, his words barely slipping into my ear. 'Vote for Uriel today, start the apocalypse by tomorrow.'

I don't understand all the implications of angel politics but I know this isn't good. They're setting up an election booth for the Messenger.

Another banner goes up, this one angled up so it can be seen from above. One of the angels unfurling the banner is a giant with snow-white wings. Beliel.

Raffe and I exchange a look and we head his way.

As we sneak closer, Raffe finds wing coverings draped over a bush. A ripped layer of sequins hangs over the dark feathers but he easily discards them, leaving only the feather coverings. He swings them over his wings and I help the feathers lie flat.

He also grabs one of the discarded masks as it tumbles off the lawn in the ocean breeze. I tie it on for him. The mask is deep red shot through with silver around the eyes and cheeks. It covers his entire face except his mouth.

He gets up and without a word pulls me up beside him, placing himself between me and the hotel lawn. I have to peek around him to see the angels, which means they can't see me either. Raffe is big enough to hide me. From a distance, we must look like a warrior walking to the other side of what was once the party.

I worry that angels might fly directly overhead and see me. Luckily, they must be hung-over or something because none of them are energetic enough to fly beyond what's necessary. We walk briskly near the edge of the lawn, getting ever closer to Beliel. I keep up with Raffe, which is not too difficult since he's walking at a casual pace.

Beliel stands behind Uriel. He's at the edge of Uriel's entourage as Uriel gives them orders.

Raffe glances up at the sky and I wonder if he hears something. Beliel also looks up toward the same place. He leans over to Uriel and they have a quick exchange.

One by one, the angels pause in their tasks and all look up. The dull roar that blended so well with the crashing waves is becoming thunderous and hard to ignore.

A cloud darker than the night sky swarms toward us. It twists, expands, then contracts, swinging this way and that.

The angry sound of a thousand scorpion wings is unmistakable as they fly over our heads.

69

Shadows swoop down beyond the reach of the torches at the edge of the lawn. Raffe watches a scene that's too dark for me to see. I catch a glimpse of shadows flying back up into the air, though, giving me an impression of iridescent insect wings.

Out of the darkness walks little Paige.

She moves stiffly and carefully as if she was part machine, part girl. In the torchlight, the stitches that run across her face are red-black and her razor-edged teeth reflect the flames as she passes by the torches.

Now that I'm looking for it, she does move like someone in pain but her expression doesn't show it. She's toughing it out, maybe because it probably hurts to wince or make any expression. I never knew she had such steel in her.

Beliel tilts his head, watching her as she walks toward him.

'Little Worm,' he says. 'Is that you?' His mouth stretches into a smile that's part surprise and part pride. 'You're no longer crawling in the dirt.'

He puts out his hand. 'You're coming into your own, aren't you?'

It kills me to see my baby sister slip her small hand into his.

Doc was right. Somewhere in me, I clung to the hope that he was off his rocker. But seeing her turn to a demon like Beliel only reminds me how horrible it must have been for her to be with the rest of us.

Paige looks up at him. Her neck strains as she meets his eyes. Holding hands like that, they could almost be father and daughter.

Beliel partially opens his stolen wings and holds up Paige's hand as he turns to smile at Uriel. His smile says, *See? Look at my trophies*.

Paige tugs his arm so that Beliel ends up leaning down toward her. For a second, I think she might give him a kiss. The thought makes my stomach roil.

Instead, she leaps and bites into his neck.

She shakes her head like a rabid dog as a chunk of his neck comes ripping off in her mouth.

Beliel shrieks.

Blood flows everywhere.

Uriel and his entourage jump back from the attack. Everyone else just stops in the middle of whatever they're doing and stares.

The buzzing above gets more frantic as the swarm of scorpions twists in the distance and heads back for another flyby. Hadn't the scorpions been following Beliel's commands all this time? Will they be angry?

Paige spits out the still attached piece of flesh and grabs Beliel's head before he can pull out of her reach. She rips into his face.

Three scorpions dive toward them from the sky.

I gasp, thinking they are attacking Paige.

But instead, they grab Beliel.

Their stingers zap in and out, pumping him full of paralysis venom.

Instead of finishing him off, Paige begins kicking him. Screams at him. Rips out clumps of his hair and skin. She tears out chunks of his flesh and spits them into his face.

And all the while, she is crying.

I am mesmerized by the sight of my little sister raging against Beliel. He's no small opponent, but she caught him utterly by surprise.

I have never seen a seven-year-old with this much fury. I've certainly never seen Paige with anything like this much anger. She pummels him with her tiny fists in a way that I know is more about dealing with her internal demons than about the demon that is Beliel.

It feels like my heart chars and turns to crumbling ash as I watch the remnants of my sister. Salty wetness touches my lips before I even realize I'm crying.

The ocean wind blows against me, making me shiver like a frail petal in a storm.

70

Raffe runs along the cliff toward Beliel and dives toward a scorpion. He grabs it just before it's about to plunge its talon-like fingers into Beliel's back.

At first, I'm confused. Why is Raffe protecting Beliel?

But as the blood trickles from Beliel's neck onto his snowy wings, I understand. Raffe deflects Paige's hands from ripping out a fistful of feathers.

Instead, she grabs Beliel's hair and tears it out. White feathers puff out as the group wrestles.

While Raffe, Beliel, Paige and three scorpions fight, the angels on the lawn watch curiously. They don't seem inclined to jump in to save Beliel. My guess is that those who've met him don't like him, and those who haven't might sense that he doesn't belong with them.

Raffe's mask is still on his face but he's not the only one still in costume. No one takes notice of me, as if the humans they were so focused on just a few hours ago don't really matter now.

I glance around to see if there's anything I can slink back behind. There is nothing unless I'm willing to hide behind a bush that's too far away for me to see anything. Nearby, there's only the ocean, cliff, grass and torchlights.

The trickle of angels quickly turns into a flood. The oddity of it must be fueling their curiosity. They crowd in and jostle me. Late-coming angel spectators have to take to the air to see the action.

Above us, a cloud of scorpions dips and dives, approaching, then receding like a hive of bees agitating around their nest.

I end up on the inner edge of the wall of bodies. So much for not bringing attention to ourselves. I stroke the soft fur of my teddy bear sword, trying to stay calm.

Beliel's tortured screams fill the night.

Everyone watches as he gets mercilessly torn and stung. Aside from Raffe, who is only protecting his wings, not a single living thing comes to his aid. No one even cringes sympathetically for him.

Beliel was right. He is unloved and unwanted.

Paige, who has been panting and crying over Beliel finally looks up and seems to notice the angels for the first time. Even in this light, I can see the fear and uncertainty dawning on her face as her eyes move from cold-hearted warrior to warrior.

The angels are partially lit by torches, looking savage with red-tinged shadows flickering along their faces.

Her eyes pause when she sees me. She blinks several times as if unsure that it's me. Her face scrunches up, giving the eerie illusion that the stitched-up monster melts away from her face, leaving a terribly upset Paige in its wake.

She looks the way she did in the video in Beliel's cell – tiny, alone, lost. A little kid trying to hang onto the belief that her big sister will come and save her.

I extend my arms out toward her, realizing how long it's been since I've touched her. She's not the same Paige that I knew but I can't write her off as a monster, either. If we're all going down, at least I'll be able to comfort my baby sister in the last few moments of our lives.

Paige drops her gaze and looks unsure of herself. Tears leave track marks in the blood on her face.

I step into the center circle and walk over to her. Her crying intensifies as I get nearer. When I reach her, she wraps her arms around my waist as tight as can be.

My little sister looks up at me.

Mom was right. Her eyes are the same as they've always been. Brown eyes fringed with long lashes and steeped with the memory of sweetness and light, laughter and joy – trapped in this mangled, corpse-like face.

'It's all right, baby girl,' I whisper into her hair as I hug her. 'I'm here. I came for you.'

Her face crumples and her eyes shine. 'You came for me.'

I stroke her hair. It's as silky as ever.

71

At Raffe's feet, Beliel lies on the dirt. He bleeds through gashes, bites and missing chunks. The three scorpions latch their mouths onto his open wounds and begin to suck him dry like enormous leeches with stingers.

Beliel yells, clumsily batting away the scorpions with the last of his energy.

Beliel's skin becomes parched and begins to crinkle. Soon, I know he'll shrivel and his flesh will look like beef jerky.

Raffe glances at the angels watching them, then back at Beliel's shriveling skin. Even with his mask, I can tell he doesn't want to do anything drastic in front of the angels. But he can't let his wings be sucked dry and shrivel. And even if he could get these scorpions off Beliel, more could come down from the sky.

He spreads one of Beliel's stolen wings and holds it firmly in one hand. From his waistband, he pulls out the kitchen knife he took from the beach house. It reflects the torch flames as he raises it, just before he swings down with the blade.

Beliel, still not entirely paralyzed, shrieks as Raffe cuts through his wing joint.

The wing falls on the ground.

The angels watch, stunned.

Raffe lifts his knife again.

A few warriors leap toward Raffe with their wings spread back and their fists ready. They think he's cutting off an angel's wings and that they're defending their own. I guess it's one thing to let an angel fend for himself against a little girl and her pets but not against another angel amputating his wings.

But they can't reach him fast enough. Raffe slices through Beliel's second wing.

The snowy wing falls to the ground, still glorious and full of life.

Raffe kicks at the first angel to reach him.

He fights hand-to-hand with the first two angels who come at him. He yells at them, probably trying to explain what's really going on but his words get lost among the roar of the scorpions above, the angry clamor of the angels and the crashing of the waves.

He can hold his own with the first two but a third one pulls out his sword.

The only effective weapon Raffe has is his demon wings which are still hidden beneath the feathered disguise. He backs up, hesitating to show them to so many angels even though it's unlikely that anyone will recognize him with his mask. But his attacker gives him no choice as he winds up to slice with his sword.

Raffe's demon wings burst open.

The crowd becomes silent. The scorpion buzzing fades as they finish their flyby. And Raffe's wing scythes slide out with a snick.

His scythes clang and deflect against his opponent's sword. The sword flies into the air and lands on the lawn.

Raffe lowers his chin and glares at the angels with a menacing look. With his giant bat wings behind him and the scythes glinting red by the torchlight, he's the perfect picture of the devil.

The two severed wings lie on either side of Beliel. The white feathers blowing in the breeze look surreally out of place on the blood-soaked ground. Raffe's festive mask only adds to the horror of it as he looms over Beliel.

As everyone stares, the only sound is the buzz of the locusts flying away and the waves smashing against the cliffs below.

Then the sound of a hundred angel swords being pulled from their scabbards fills the night.

72

My breath comes out shaky and I don't think I can feel my fingers. I can't see a way out of this.

Raffe stands over Beliel, watching the warriors all around him. His eyes are fierce but it's obvious that our situation looks pretty bad. Even if Raffe was in his best form, he couldn't fight off an entire legion of his own people, even assuming that he wanted to.

Paige and I are just as surrounded as Raffe. My sister seems to have some new tricks up her sleeve but the odds aren't exactly in our favor. I look around to see if there's a gap in the wall of angels that I could sneak Paige through to safety but there is none.

We're trapped.

They've fanned out around us, cut off every direction – land, water and air. I guess this isn't the first time they've trapped their quarry. They know how to move in for the kill, I'll give them that.

Several angels step toward Raffe with their swords. He assesses them, then glances at his wings on the ground as if memorizing their location. He steps over Beliel's head to get in front of his wings for the fight.

The scorpions watch Raffe with a wary eye but continue their life-sucking of Beliel as he shrivels. When the angel swords clash with Raffe's wing scythes, the scorpions startle and fly away.

Beliel's eyes stare blankly while the rest of him bleeds through gashes, bites and missing chunks. If I didn't know better, I'd assume he was dead.

Raffe tries to keep the angels from treading on his wings but there's only so much you can do when you're fighting for your life.

I get down on the ground and snatch a snowy wing before anyone tramples it. I quickly fold it and hand it to Paige.

'Hold this. Don't let anything happen to it.'

I duck to the other side of Raffe and crawl on the ground to grab the other wing just as an angel is about to step on it. Above me, Raffe slices and blocks in a frenzy of motion with his demon wings.

I crawl backwards with the wing to get out of the way. I fold the wing and give it to Paige. The wings are light but they practically cover her whole body as she holds them in her arms.

I guide Paige back away from the fight. But our way is blocked by a warrior who glares down at us.

In the torchlight, his wings look more like flames but I know that they would be burnt orange under a street-light. It's Burnt, the one who kidnapped Paige out of spite.

He looks the same as he did in Doc's surveillance video – bitter and mean. He takes a step toward us.

'There you are,' says Burnt as he reaches for Paige. 'You finally came in handy for something, didn't you? It's about time someone took that reject down.'

I push Paige behind me and yank the bear from my sword. I'm almost glad that I get a chance to fight him. I have a special hatred for Burnt, the Kidnapper of Helpless Little Girls.

73

Burnt looks at me like I'm a mosquito. 'What are you going to do? Pummel me with your teddy bear?'

I pull my sword out and get in my combat position.

He actually bursts out laughing. 'You're going to fight me with your tin sword, little girl?'

I can almost feel the rage pulsing from Raffe who is fighting several warriors.

Burnt casually swipes at me with his sword.

I automatically meet his steely blow with my own. The dream training must have worked, at least to some degree.

Burnt looks surprised. But that doesn't stop him from immediately winding up for his next blow. I can tell he takes this one more seriously.

His sword comes down like a sledgehammer.

I swing my own sword to meet his.

The shock of the impact rattles my bones all the way down to my ankles. My teeth clack so hard I'm surprised they don't fall out.

Amazingly, I'm still standing.

But just barely.

It's clear I can't take too many direct blows. Now I know why none of my dream training involved an opponent with a sword.

Burnt expected me to go down with a single blow. He lifts his sword again, looking annoyed.

I duck and scramble under his sword arm. Probably not a recommended move but there's a reason why you have to wind up for a hit. With me up close, he can cut but can't do a lot of impact damage.

I try to kick out his knee but he's ready for me and spins out of the way. Unlike the other opponents I've been fighting lately, Burnt is neither drunk nor an amateur.

He swings for another blow.

I duck. I feel the wind of his blade along the top of my head.

I'm off balance and don't have enough time to set myself up for a good defensive stance.

I have just enough time to raise my blade to block.

He hits me again with bone-smashing force.

When the impact hits, my skull rattles so much, it feels as if it's vibrating off my spine. I almost lose the sword but miraculously manage to hang onto it.

I stagger and fall to my knee.

I vaguely register Paige screaming behind me. Paige may have a killer bite but she's no match for a warrior angel with a sword and I'm glad she knows it.

A part of me sees Raffe wading through blades and blows, trying to make his way to me. But there are too many opponents ganging up on him.

Waves of fury swamp me. What I thought was rage pulsing from Raffe is actually coming from me.

No, not me.

The sword.

Burnt was part of the gang that cut off Raffe's wings. Because of that, the sword had to leave Raffe. Now, she's stuck with me, a weakling little human. She's had to suffer insult upon insult since then, including being laughed at. And now, the final humiliation – Burnt's about to beat us into the ground with no more than two or three blows.

Boy, is she pissed.

Fine. I'm pissed too. This bastard took my sister and look what happened.

We might as well go down in flames together. At least

we can vent some of our anger in a final push. I hope I can hit him somewhere where it really hurts.

Burnt has the nerve to impatiently motion for me to get up. He'd probably never live it down if he swung his killing blow while his scrawny-girl opponent was down.

I wind up all that anger as I take my stance and get ready.

Burnt and I both draw back our swords.

With all my might, I yell and swing at the same time he does.

Paige cries my name. Raffe shouts as he shoves warriors aside, trying to reach me.

When the two swords crash, the impact neither rattles my bones nor has me tasting blood. It's as if all the force stopped at the blade before it vibrated down to me. As if all that tremendous killing power got redirected.

Burnt's blade shatters.

It sounds simultaneously like glass smashing and someone screaming. A jagged piece hits Burnt's wing, slicing right through it.

I keep swinging and my blade cuts through Burnt's chest.

It's a clean stroke that leaves no mark until the blood seeps out in a line from one arm to the other.

He crumples.

Burnt lies on the trampled grass, bleeding. His eyes are wide open in shocked disbelief. His body trembles. His breathing is ragged and strained.

He struggles to breathe.

One . . . Two . . .

His eyes lose focus and gaze at nothing.

There's no life in them.

I stare at him for a second longer to make sure he's dead, reassuring myself that angel swords really can kill angels.

I look up. Raffe and the others are frozen in the middle of their fight. Everyone is staring at us.

A human girl. Killing a warrior angel. In a sword fight.

Impossible.

I'm frozen too. My arms are still up, holding the blade, poised to strike again.

I glance back at the dead body of Burnt, trying to wrap my mind around the fact that I killed an angel warrior.

Then, another incredible thing happens.

One second, we are surrounded by angels holding their swords. The next second, one of their arms drops and his sword thunks to the grass like a lead weight. The angel stares at his blade uncomprehendingly.

Another sword drops.

Then another.

Then a whole bunch, until all the other unsheathed swords fall, thudding on the grass like subjects bowing down to their queen.

The angels stare at the swords at their feet in utter shock.

Then everyone looks at me. Actually, it's probably more accurate to say they're looking at my sword.

'Whoa.' That's about the most intelligent thing I can say right now. Did Raffe say something about an archangel sword intimidating other angel swords if she could gain their respect?

I swivel my eyes to look at the blade in my hands. Was that you, Pooky Bear?

74

Paige runs over to me, still holding the wings. She tentatively buries her face in my ribs again like she used to when she had a nightmare and needed a hug.

I put my arm around her. I swear her shoulders are skinnier than they've ever been. But that thought leads me to all the dark places I don't want to go so I ignore it. Judging by the wall of warriors around us, her hunger won't be a problem much longer.

I pull her with me as I gingerly step over to Raffe. Everyone is still in shock so no one stops me even though I'm now an angel killer. I stand back-to-back with Raffe, putting Paige and the severed wings between us.

I know Paige is deadly now. But that doesn't change the fact that she won't survive this any better than the rest of us. And if there's one thing I know that a kid her age shouldn't be doing, it's having to fight for her life while her big sister is around.

I hope her last few moments are filled with the knowledge that she was surrounded by those who tried to protect her.

We must be quite the sight. Raffe in his red mask with his demon wings spread out in all their scythe-edged glory. A scrawny teenage Daughter of Man brandishing an archangel sword. And a little girl stitched-up to look and behave like a nightmare who is clutching a pair of angel wings.

My hair blows all over the place, and I realize that the scorpion buzz has been steadily growing into a roar again. They must have looped and are coming back our way. It feels like a storm is building up as they near.

The warriors get over their shock and begin moving toward us, barehanded. Only now, there are as many coming for me as for Raffe. I guess they've got a thing against human girls killing one of their own. Either that or they want to try to claim my sword.

I swipe my blade at an angel coming too close to me. He ducks and tries to grab my hair. I kick him in the stomach.

As far as I can tell, there's an endless supply of warriors. The outcome is obvious. It won't be long before we wear out.

We know it. They know it.

But we keep on fighting.

I'm swiping my blade at a buffed-out warrior, trying to catch him in the throat when something knocks him down.

It's a scorpion.

For a moment, it's a jumble of wings and a stinger rolling on the trampled grass. The scorpion isn't really fighting the angel. I think it's just trying to get up and fly. But the angel isn't going to let that happen.

Another scorpion crashes into Raffe's opponent. They roll in the dirt, tumbling in a jumble of limbs and wings. Three more scorpions clumsily crash into angels.

It takes me a moment to figure out what's really going on.

The swarm above us has flown down, dipping and twisting like a cloud of wasps. As it dips lower, the scorpions at the bottom of the swarm crash into the angels. The collisions knock down the warriors like grass being mowed.

I have no doubt that an angel can take on a scorpion and not break out in a sweat. But there are far more scorpions than angels, and the scorpions behave like mindless beasts crashing into bodies. Even as some of them swerve at the last second to try to avoid fatal colli-

sions, they can't seem to stop their own group momentum as they slam into the angels.

The sheer force of the bodies repeatedly ramming
into the crowd brings them all down flat onto the lawn.

Everyone but me, Raffe, and Paige, that is.

The swarm splits around us, knocking everything in
its path but leaving us untouched.

The wind caused by their wings makes me stumble
backwards into Paige until she's squeezed between Raffe
and me. I reach back to hold her hand. Her little hand
clings tightly to me.

Raffe spreads his wings to shelter us so that he's at our
backs with his wings protecting us on either side.

Doc may have been wrong about Paige's feelings for
Beliel, but I'm becoming convinced that he was right
about Paige having something special about her. Whatever
it is that Doc secretly did to her, it gave her some kind of
connection with the scorpions. They're swarming around
her and protecting her with their own bodies.

They keep coming. Some sting, some don't, as if the
scorpions are confused about what they're supposed to
do. But even the ones who sting don't linger. It's more of
a hit-and-run as if they sense that they'd be in big trouble if they stayed.

The swarm lifts, leaving the lawn littered with angels
on their knees and bellies. Everyone stares up at the

sky to see what's next. We're the only ones still on our feet.

The swarm twists and turns around to make another pass. The angels who are on their knees dive down on their stomachs, and everyone covers their heads.

Maybe if they could use their swords, the dynamics would change. But no one seems to want to risk having their sword refuse them even if it's just for one battle.

I look around to try to see what we should do. Since they haven't aimed for us, ducking for cover doesn't make a lot of sense.

The swarm keeps coming. A huge gust of wind makes my eyes sting and almost knocks me off my feet.

But they split around us as before, letting us stay upright while everyone else flattens on the ground.

Still holding the folded wings, Paige slips out from between us and lies on top of Beliel. The wings are sandwiched between them with the downy feathers fluttering in the wind.

Beliel has shrunken and is almost unrecognizable lying like the dead on his stomach. The wings covering his back, though, look contrastingly full of life as they droop over him like a white blanket.

A scorpion hovers over Paige, trying to lift her but she won't let go of Beliel.

My skin turns cold at the sight of that curved tail with the stinger so close to my sister. I'm tempted to slice it off. But Raffe puts out his hand to stop me as if he knows what I want to do.

'Put her away,' he whispers as he nods to my sword.

I hesitate, thinking of all the reasons why I should keep my blade out. But I wipe the blood on my pants and slide the sword back into the scabbard at my hip. This is not the time to argue.

More scorpions slow down and hover over Paige. Four of them grab Beliel around the armpits and legs while two others pull on his belt. They lift him with Paige clinging on top like a princess on a demon palanquin.

I reach for her, wanting to pull her off.

Raffe grabs my hand and begins running after them as the last of the swarm passes by. He swings me up and pulls me into his arms.

I hold him as tightly as my trembling muscles will let me.

A few steps of running and we're leaping over the cliff into the air.

75

Angels immediately pop up from their prone positions and begin chasing us. Some look stung and sluggish but too many of them manage to shake it off. Raffe's wings sweep powerfully as we fly above the crashing waves.

Behind us, a horde of angels takes off from the cliff.

The thunderous sound of the scorpion wings gets louder as the swarm twists and doubles back. The scorpions fly so close to us that their insect wings almost brush my head as they dive toward the angels.

My eyes squint against the rush of insectile bodies. Watching over Raffe's shoulder, my field of vision narrows and widens rhythmically as Raffe beats his wings.

The swarm dips down, colliding with the angels just behind us.

The titanic clash knocks out the angels and all I can see are stingers and insect wings. No angel can penetrate the mass. I imagine this isn't exactly what Uriel had in mind when he created the scorpions.

The scorpions dive and double back toward us without a single angel in sight.

We are in the swarm.

Bodies fly above, ahead and below us. Behind us, the mass of stingers and wings is so dense that it's a wall of giant insects.

We look around nervously until enough time goes by that we stop worrying about whether they're going to attack us.

Beside me, my little sister rides on what's left of Beliel. Her legs wrap around his waist and she presses Raffe's severed wings onto him with her body. The tips of the snowy wings hang off him, fluttering in the wind.

Beliel is a gruesome picture with his head hanging down. Chunks of him are missing and he's still bleeding. His skin and muscles are shriveled and sucked dry, making him look frail and long dead.

They're carried by six scorpion monsters fluttering their iridescent wings, and they are a freakishly bizarre sight. Paige turns to me and gives me a shy smile that stops when the crisscross stitches on her cheeks move too much.

My dad once told me life would get complicated when I grew up. I'm guessing this isn't what he meant. My mom, on the other hand, agreed with him, and I'm guessing this kind of thing is exactly what she meant.

I curl up in Raffe's arms. Our flight is in sync with the swarm, as if his instincts are perfectly honed to synchronize with his flight mates. It's clear that he was meant to be an integral part of something larger than himself.

Raffe is warm and strong and he feels like home. Our faces inch closer as the swarm shifts. For a moment, I can feel his breath feathering my cheek.

We'll fly wherever the swarm takes us, and we'll land wherever they do. And when we arrive, I have no doubt that I'll have to be fully alert and ready for anything. Until then, I can bask in the knowledge that my family is safe for the moment and I'm with Raffe again.

The sun is rising, giving the dark ocean below a glow that shimmers with blue, gold, and green.

It's a new day in the World After.

Acknowledgements

Much thanks to my fabulous beta readers who helped take the book to the next level: Nyla Adams, Aaron Emigh, Jessica Lynch Alfaro, John Turner, Adrian Khactu, Eric Shible and David L. M. Preston. Additional thanks goes out to Aaron Emigh for being my fight advisor, and Steaphen Fick for the sword fighting lesson and knife fighting tips. And of course, a huge thanks goes out to the readers of *Angelfall* for their wild enthusiasm and support.

Enjoyed this book?
Want more?

Head over to

CHAPteR 5

for extra author content,
exclusives, competitions – and lots
and lots of book talk!

Our motto is
'Proud to be bookish',

because, well, we are ☺

See you there . . .

Chapter5Books @Chapter5Books

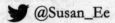